International Praise for *CARIBOU ISLAND*

"*Caribou Island* gets to places other novels can't touch. . . . Though it wears the clothes of realism—the beautiful exactness of the language, the unerring eye for detail—it takes us someplace darker, older, more powerful than the daylit world. This Alaska with its salmon boats and trash dumps becomes a stage for ancient stories of survival and will and connection and love, and also, in the end, the failure of love." —Kevin Canty, *New York Times Book Review*

"Greatness has arrived: *Caribou Island* is a powerful first novel of love, lust, and regret set on an island near Soldotna, a fishing town on Alaska's Kenai Peninsula. . . . Vann slowly and quietly builds the drama toward an emotional gut punch of an ending—think Cormac McCarthy on ice."
—*Outside*

"Abounding in language that heightens our senses for the next evocative metaphor, *Caribou Island* gives us a climax as haunting and realized as any in recent fiction." —*San Francisco Chronicle*

"[Vann uses the] American landscape as a metaphor to tremendous effect. . . . Vann's brilliance as a writer lies in his willingness to expose everything. . . . A writer to read and reread; a man to watch carefully."
—*The Economist*

"*Caribou Island* is a beautiful, richly atmospheric if unsettling novel, and deserves to consolidate Vann's position among America's literary highfliers." —Melanie McGrath, *London Evening Standard*

"Transfixing and unflinching. . . . Full of finely realized moments. . . . Comparison with Cormac McCarthy is fully justified."
—*The Times Literary Supplement* (London)

"Vann, who was born in Alaska, handles conflicted feelings of love and resentment, and the raw, existential cries of ordinary people, extraordinarily well. And although he's a graceful writer, he never spins the kind of poetic prose that infects too many literary novels with distracting prettiness. . . . As the final pages rise into the piercing registry of Cormac McCarthy—or Euripides—some readers may spot Vann's thumb on the scale, making sure every drop of agony is paid. But just wait: For a few moments after this perfectly choreographed horror, it's impossible to say anything at all."

—Ron Charles, *Washington Post*

"Arguably the first literary masterpiece to take place on the Kenai Peninsula. . . . Like a macabre machine, the narrative ratchets ever tighter until the closing image of one final, forlorn hope that will be smashed as soon as the storytelling stops and the reader closes the book."

—Mike Dunham, *Anchorage Daily News*

"Compared to *Caribou Island, The Road* is grim-lit lite. . . . Welcome to Vann's demon land."

—Ian Sansom, *London Review of Books*

"When writing about landscapes, David Vann writes with a poetry born of connectedness, of deep observation."

—Max Winter, *Boston Globe*

"[David Vann] has come fully into his own voice, from the striking opening scene to the fateful final sentence. . . . An oddly exhilarating horror story in which human demons spring from the smoke of their own disappointment and regret. *Caribou Island* earns Vann a seat beside the masters. A+"

—Sheerly Avni, *San Francisco Magazine*

"*Caribou Island* builds to a horrific climax and stands as an engrossing and disturbing work of art."

—Alan Cheuse, NPR

"Compelling. As the plot moves toward a gruesome finale, the reader is submerged in 'slow waves of pressure, water compacting but no edge to it.'"

—*The New Yorker*

"Explodes in a tremendously disturbing conclusion. The ending of *Caribou Island* is amply foreshadowed, but the minor incidents that build to it are so believably presented that it still has the capacity to shock."
—Sam Sacks, *Wall Street Journal*

"A novel as precise and unflinching as this makes other recently celebrated books seem melodramatic. *Caribou Island* proves that art wrought from personal pain and obsessed with negative emotion can still be profoundly positive."
—*The Canberra Times*

"An existential page-turner and literary breakthrough."
—*Kirkus Reviews* (profile)

"A work of art."
—*El País* (Spain)

"Vann forces us to watch, to pay attention. He refuses to provide his characters—or us—with an easy, happy resolution. Instead, he gives us something much more valuable: an unflinching portrait of what can happen to lives when hopes and ambitions wander off, get lost, and surrender to the merciless cold."
—Kevin Grauke, *Philadelphia Inquirer*

"Vann's brilliance lies in his willingness to expose all. . . . A striking novel filled with the violence born of a bitter life."
—*Kirkus Reviews* (starred review)

"This tortured dissolution of dreams is simply exquisite. . . . If Jack London and Raymond Carver could time travel, move to Iowa, get married, and raise an adopted son, this is the story *he* would write—sparse, unforgiving, man against nature, and man against his own nature. . . . It will stick with you for a very, very long time."
—*Publishers Weekly*

"Reaffirms Vann as a talented conjurer of the natural world, and of our nakedness in the face of its power and cruel impassivity."
—*The New Republic*

"Vann, an Alaska native, nails his locale—the small towns and wilderness."
—*Sunday Oregonian*

"Like Melville, Faulkner, and McCarthy, Vann already is a great one of American literature."
—*ABC* (Spain)

"It's rare when a fiction writer of extraordinary literary merit is equally brilliant in both the short story and novel forms. David Vann is a dazzling exception. *Caribou Island* is deeply in touch with the same dark truths of the human condition as his remarkable story collection, *Legend of a Suicide,* and in the longer form he gives the reader sustained, rich joy. Yes, joy. Vann knows the darkness, but he writes from the compassionate light of art. This is an essential book."
—Robert Olen Butler, Pulitzer Prize–winning author of *A Good Scent from a Strange Mountain*

"This is how David Vann's language is: so precise, so cold, so beautiful. . . . Displaying wonderful mastery, David Vann demonstrates once again his immense talent. . . . A real accomplishment."
—*Le Monde*

"The reader's awareness of real deaths, real griefs, gives his work something of the lethal intensity of handling an unsheathed knife: at times the power is exhilarating, and at other times it cuts bloodily and to the quick."
—*New Statesman*

"In this exceptional first novel by the celebrated author of *Legend of a Suicide,* an oncoming Alaska winter becomes metaphor as a troubled marriage moves implacably toward a bleak reckoning. *Caribou Island* is an unflinching portrait of bad faith and bad dreams."
—Ron Rash, author of *Burning Bright*

CARIBOU ISLAND

ALSO BY DAVID VANN

FICTION

Legend of a Suicide

NONFICTION

A Mile Down: The True Story of a Disastrous Career at Sea

CARIBOU ISLAND

a novel

David Vann

NEW YORK • LONDON • TORONTO • SYDNEY • NEW DELHI • AUCKLAND

HARPER PERENNIAL

This novel is a work of fiction. Any references to real people, events, organizations, or locales are intended only to give the fiction a sense of reality and authenticity, and are used fictitiously. All other names, characters, and places, and all dialogue and incidents portrayed in this book are the product of the author's imagination.

A hardcover edition of this book was published in 2011 by HarperCollins Publishers.

FIRST HARPER PERENNIAL EDITION PUBLISHED 2012.

Designed by Eric Butler

Interior art by Linda Rae
http://midnightstouch.deviantart.com

The Library of Congress has catalogued the hardcover edition as follows:
Vann, David.
Caribou Island : a novel / David Vann.—1st ed.
293 p. ; 24 cm.
ISBN 978-0-06-187572-4
1. Marriage—Fiction. 2. Loneliness—Fiction. 3. Alaska—Fiction. I. Title.
PS3622.A667 C37 2011
813'.6 2010015703

ISBN 978-0-06-187573-1 (pbk.)

12 13 14 15 16 OV/RRD 10 9 8 7 6 5 4 3 2 1

CARIBOU ISLAND

My mother was not real. She was an early dream, a hope. She was a place. Snowy, like here, and cold. A wooden house on a hill above a river. An overcast day, the old white paint of the buildings made brighter somehow by the trapped light, and I was coming home from school. Ten years old, walking by myself, walking through dirty patches of snow in the yard, walking up to the narrow porch. I can't remember how my thoughts went then, can't remember who I was or what I felt like. All of that is gone, erased. I opened our front door and found my mother hanging from the rafters. I'm sorry, I said, and I stepped back and closed the door. I was outside on the porch again.

You said that? Rhoda asked. You said you were sorry?

Yes.

Oh, Mom.

It was long ago, Irene said. And it was something I couldn't see even at the time, so I can't see it now. I don't know what she looked like hanging there. I don't remember any of it, only that it was.

Rhoda scooted closer on the couch and put her arm around her mother, pulled her close. They both looked at the fire. A metal screen in front, small hexagons, and the longer Rhoda looked, the more these hexagons seemed like the back wall of the fireplace, made golden by flame. As if the back wall, black with soot, could be revealed or transmuted by fire. Then her eyes would shift and it would be only a screen again. I wish I had known her, Rhoda said.

Me too, Irene said. She patted Rhoda's knee. I need to get to sleep. Busy day tomorrow.

I'll miss this place.

It was a good home. But your father wants to leave me, and the first step is to make us move out to that island. To make it seem he gave it a try.

That's not true, Mom.

We all have rules, Rhoda. And your father's main rule is that he can never seem like the bad guy.

He loves you, Mom.

Irene stood and hugged her daughter. Goodnight, Rhoda.

In the morning, Irene carried her end of log after log, from the truck to the boat. These are never going to fit together, she said to her husband, Gary.

I'll have to plane them down a bit, he said, tight-lipped.

Irene laughed.

Thanks, Gary said. He already had that grim, worried look that accompanied all his impossible projects.

Why not build a cabin with boards? Irene asked. Why does it have to be a log cabin?

But Gary wasn't answering.

Suit yourself, she said. But these aren't even logs. None of them is bigger than six inches. It's going to look like a hovel made out of sticks.

They were at the upper campground on Skilak Lake, the water a pale jade green from glacial runoff. Flaky from silt, and because of its depth, never warmed much, even in late summer. The wind across it chill and constant, and the mountains rising from its eastern shore still had pockets of snow. From their tops, Irene had often seen, on clear days, the white volcanic peaks of Mount Redoubt and Mount Iliamna across the Cook Inlet and, in the foreground, the broad pan of the Kenai Peninsula: spongy green and red-purple moss, the stunted trees rimming wetlands and smaller lakes, and the one highway snaking silver in sunlight as a river. Mostly public land. Their house and their son Mark's house the only buildings along the shore of Skilak, and even they were tucked back into trees so the lake still could seem prehistoric, wild. But it wasn't enough to be on the shore. They were moving out, now, to Caribou Island.

Gary had backed his pickup close to where the boat sat on the beach with an open bow, a ramp for loading cargo. With each log, he stepped onto the boat and walked its length. A wobbly walk, because the stern was in the water and bobbing.

Lincoln logs, Irene said.

I've heard about enough, Gary said.

Fine.

Gary pulled another small log. Irene took her end. The sky darkened a bit, and the water went from light jade to a blue-gray. Irene looked up toward the mountain and could see one flank whited. Rain, she said. Coming this way.

We'll just keep loading, Gary said. Put on your jacket if you want.

Gary wearing a flannel work shirt, long-sleeved, over his T-shirt. Jeans and boots. His uniform. He looked like a younger man, still fit for his mid-fifties. Irene still liked how he looked. Unshaven, unshowered at the moment, but real.

Shouldn't take much longer, Gary said.

They were going to build their cabin from scratch. No foundation, even. And no plans, no experience, no permits, no advice welcome. Gary wanted to just do it, as if the two of them were the first to come upon this wilderness.

So they kept loading, and the rain came toward them a white shadow over the water. A kind of curtain, the squall line, but the first drops and wind always hit just before, invisible, working ahead of what she could see, and this always came as a surprise to Irene. Those last moments taken away. And then the wind kicked up, the squall line hit, and the drops came down large and heavy, insistent.

Irene grabbed her end of another log, walked toward the boat with her face turned away from the wind. The rain blowing sideways now, hitting hard. She wore no hat, no gloves. Her hair matting, drips off her nose, and she felt that first chill as the rain soaked through her shirt to her arms, one shoulder, her upper back and neck. She hunched away from it as she walked, placed her log, and then walked back hunched the other way, her other side soaking through now, and she shivered.

Gary walking ahead of her, hunched also, his upper body turned away from the rain as if it wanted to disobey his legs, take off in its own direction. He grabbed the end of another log, pulled it out, stepping backward, and then the rain hit harder. The wind gusted, and the air was filled with water, white even in close. The lake disappeared, the waves gone, the transition to shore become speculative. Irene grabbed the log and followed Gary into oblivion.

The wind and rain formed a roar, against which Irene could

hear no other sound. She walked mute, found the bow, placed her log, turned and walked back, no longer hunched. There was no dry part left to save. She was soaked through.

Gary walked past her a kind of bird man, his arms curved out like wings first opening. Trying to keep his wet shirt away from his skin? Or some instinctive first response to battle, readying his arms? When he stopped at the truck bed, water streamed off the end of his nose. His eyes hard and small, focused.

Irene moved in close. Should we stop? she yelled over the roar.

We have to get this load out to the island, he yelled back, and then he pulled another log, so Irene followed, though she knew she was being punished. Gary could never do this directly. He relied on the rain, the wind, the apparent necessity of the project. It would be a day of punishment. He would follow it, extend it for hours, drive them on, a grim determination, like fate. A form of pleasure to him.

Irene followed because once she had endured she could punish. Her turn would come. And this is what they had done to each other for decades now, irresistibly. Fine, she would think. Fine. And that meant, just wait.

Another half an hour of loading logs in the rain. Irene was going to get sick from this, chilled through. They should have been wearing rain gear, which they had in the cab of the truck, but their stubbornness toward each other had prevented that. If she had gone for her jacket when Gary suggested it, that would have interrupted the work, slowed them down, and it would have been noted, held against her, a small shake of the head, perhaps even a sigh, but removed by long enough he could pretend it wasn't about that. Above all else, Gary was an impatient man: impatient with the larger shape of his life, with who he was and what he'd done and become, impatient with his wife and children, and then, of course, impatient with all the little things, any action not done correctly, any moment of weather that was uncooperative. A general and abiding impatience she had lived in for over thirty years, an element she had breathed.

The last log loaded, finally, and Gary and Irene swung the bow ramp into place. It was not heavy, not reassuring. Black rubber where it met the side plates of the boat, forming a seal. This would be their only way back and forth from the island.

I'll park the truck, Gary said, and stomped off through the rocks. The rain still coming down, though not as blown now. Enough visibility to know direction, though not enough to see the island from here, a couple miles out. Irene wondered what would happen when they were in the middle. Would they see any of the shore, or only white all around them? No GPS on the boat, no radar, no depth finder. It's a lake, Gary had said at the dealership. It's only a lake.

There's water in the boat, Irene said when Gary returned. It was pooling under the logs, gathered especially in the stern, almost a foot deep from all the rain.

We'll take care of it once we're out, Gary said. I don't want to use the battery for the bilge pump without the engine on.

So what's the plan? Irene asked. She didn't know how they would push the boat off the beach, weighed down with the logs.

You know, I'm not the only one who wanted this, Gary said. It's not just my plan. It's our plan.

This was a lie, but too big a lie to address right here, right now, in the rain. Fine, Irene said. How do we get the boat off the beach?

Gary looked at the boat for a few moments. Then he bent down and gave the bow a push. It didn't budge.

The front half of the boat was on land, and Irene was guessing that meant hundreds of pounds at this point, fully loaded. Gary hadn't thought of this, obviously. He was making it up as he went along.

Gary walked around to one side and then the other. He climbed over logs to the stern, to the outboard engine, leaned against this and pushed hard, trying to rock the boat, but it might as well have been made of lead. No movement whatsoever.

So Gary crawled forward, hopped ashore, looked at the boat for a while. Help me push, he finally said. Irene lined up beside him, he counted one, two, three, and they both pushed at the bow. Their feet slipped in the black pebbles, but no other movement.

It can never be easy, Gary said. Not a single thing. It can never just work out.

As if to prove what he was saying, the rain came down heavier again, the wind increasing, cold off the glacier. If you wanted to be a fool and test the limits of how bad things could get, this was a good place for it. Irene knew Gary wouldn't appreciate any comments, though. She tried to be supportive. Maybe we could come back tomorrow, she said. The weather's supposed to improve a bit. We could unload and push it out, then load again.

No, Gary said. I don't feel like doing it tomorrow. I'm taking this load out today.

Irene held her tongue.

Gary stomped off to the truck. Irene stood in the rain, soaked and wanting to be warm and dry. Their house very close, a few minutes away. Hot bath, start a fire.

Gary drove the truck onto the beach, curving up toward the trees, then down to the boat until he had the bumper close to the bow. Let me know how close, he yelled out the window.

So Irene walked over and told him, and he eased forward until the bumper was touching.

Okay, Irene said.

Gary gave it a little gas, and pebbles flew out behind his rear wheels. The boat didn't budge. He shifted to low four-wheel drive, gave it more gas, all four tires digging in, pebbles slamming the underside of the truck body. The boat started to slip, then went back fast into the water, drifting away in a curve.

Grab the bow line! Gary yelled out his window. Irene rushed forward to grab the line that was loose on the beach. She caught it and dug in her heels, lay back on the beach pulling hard until the pressure eased. Then she just lay there, looking up into the dark white sky. She could see the rain as streaks before it hit her face. No gloves, her hands cold and the nylon line rough. The pebbles and larger stones hard against the back of her head. Her clothing a wet and cold outer shell.

She heard Gary drive the truck up to the parking area, and then heard his boots on the way back, large determined strides.

Okay, he said, standing over her. Let's go.

What she wished was that he would just lie down beside her. The two of them on this beach. They would give up, let the rope go, let the boat drift away, forget about the cabin, forget about all that hadn't gone right over the years and just go back to their house and warm up and start over. It didn't seem impossible. If they both decided to do it, they could.

But instead, they walked into the cold water, the waves breaking over their boots up to their knees, and climbed into the boat. Irene grabbed on to the logs and swung her legs in, wondering why she was doing this. The momentum of who she had become with Gary, the momentum of who she had become in Alaska, the momentum that made it somehow impossible to just stop right now and go back to the house. How had that happened?

Gary at the motor squeezed the bulb for the gas line, pulled the choke out, pulled back hard on the starter cord. And the engine caught right away, ran smooth, spit out its stream of cooling water and not as much smoke as Irene was used to. A four-stroke, a nice engine, ridiculously expensive, but at least it was reliable. The last thing she wanted was to be adrift in a storm in the middle of the lake.

Gary had the bilge pump running, a thick stream of water over the side, and all seemed briefly manageable. Then Irene saw the bend in the bow. From where Gary had pushed with the truck, the front of the boat had a bend to it. Not extreme, but Irene shifted forward to examine the seal where the gate met side plate, and she could see a trickle of water coming in. They were loaded down so heavy, part of the ramp was underwater.

Gary, she said, but he was already backing away in a half-circle, then shifting the engine into forward. He was focused, not paying any attention to her. Gary! she yelled out, and waved an arm.

He shifted into neutral and came forward to look. He made a growling sound, his teeth clamped tight. But then he returned to the engine and put it in gear. Not a word, no discussion of whether they should go on or have it repaired first.

Gary didn't go fast, no more than five or ten miles per hour, but this was straight into wind waves with a flat front, and every wave was a hard blast of spray that drenched them entirely.

Irene turned away from the waves, facing back toward Gary, but he was looking backward, also, steering by reference to the shore they had left, slowly receding into the distance. The truck still visible through patchy trees. No one else parked in the campground. Usually a few boats and campers were here, but today, if anything happened, it was just them, the thud and blast of water every few seconds, the logs humped up dark and soaked, the gunwales low, the steady stream from the bilge pump. A new kind of covered wagon, almost, heading to a new land, the making of a new home.

Rhoda's beaten-up Datsun B210 didn't belong off pavement. She was careful to keep momentum up hills but could feel her tires slipping in the mud. And she couldn't see a thing, just the rain hitting her windshield hard, blur of green trees beyond, the brown dirt and gravel road curving away. She'd been in dealerships for years now looking for the right new truck but never seemed to have enough money when they sat down to make it all final. What she wanted, anyway, was an SUV, not a truck. And since she was expecting a raise, and expecting also to marry a dentist, she didn't think she'd have to wait very long.

Which put Rhoda in mind of Jim, who probably was eating pancakes right now for dinner, his usual, wondering where she was. Pulling peach halves from a can to put on these pancakes, and clicking the sides of the can unnecessarily with his fork. But Rhoda was feeling a good mood come over her and didn't want to wreck it by thinking of Jim.

By the time she pulled up to her parents' house, she could see the truck was gone. She was late to help them move logs. She got out anyway and ran past the flower beds to the door.

Rhoda's parents lived in a small, one-story wooden house that had been added on to in several places over the years so that it bulged oddly now and the parts did not all match. Rhoda's father had been dreaming of frontier life and mountain men when he moved up from California in his mid-twenties, and by now he had all the Alaskan accoutrements. Antlers of elk, moose, caribou, deer, mountain goats, and Dall's rams hung from nails along the edge of the roof and along the outside walls. The raised flower bed to the right of the door featured an old hand pump, a small sluice, and various other rusted pans, picks, pails, old boards and such from the mining days, dragged down mostly from the Hatcher Pass Mine northeast of Anchorage but purchased also from other collectors and the odd garage sale. Farther down the wall to the left of the door, he had stacked wood for the fireplace and the antique cast-iron and nickel stove, and between the wood stack and the door, an old dogsled, its hide straps and wood rotting away a little more each year in all the rain, snow, wind, and occasional sun. The place had always seemed a junkyard and an embarrassment to Rhoda. What she did like were the flowers and the moss garden. Twelve kinds of moss and all the varieties of Alaskan wildflowers, even the rare ones. Whole beds of chocolate lilies and every color of fireweed and lupine, from white and pink to the deepest purple-blues, though only the fireweed was in bloom now.

Rhoda banged on the door again, but they were gone. She drove on toward the campground and launch ramp. Maybe she'd catch them there, though she had no idea why they'd persist on a day like this. Why not stay home?

Her tires slid a bit coming down the hill to the campground.

She saw their truck parked, drove to the ramp at the water's edge. No boat. No one around. Her parents were nuts to go out in this. Why not wait for a better day? Even if it was the cabin to end all cabins, the dream of a lifetime and all that crap. What Rhoda didn't understand at all was why her mother would allow this.

Whatever, she said, and headed back to town.

Rhoda and Jim lived in a large peaked house overlooking the mouth of the Kenai River. One of the pluses about being with Jim. The steeply pitched A-frame roof reminded her of Wienerschnitzel franchises but shed snow easily and created a twenty-foot vaulted ceiling in the living room out front and the master bedroom in back. The double-paned windows, nearly fifteen feet high, caught sunsets over the Cook Inlet, and the exposed beams were stained dark as a mead hall's, the furniture all Scandinavian wood and leather. It was the kind of house Rhoda had once dreamed of.

And now I just live here, she was thinking as she stood at the kitchen counter and squeezed small samples of beagle poop into glass vials for testing.

I wish you wouldn't do that while I'm eating, Jim said. He was having his pancakes and canned peaches on the other side of the counter.

Get over it, Rhoda said. It's just dog shit.

Jim laughed. You're the best.

No, you, Rhoda said. They had only been living together a year, so what the hell. Rhoda's former boyfriend had been a different story, a fisherman who whined and complained daily about the forces of nature, industry, and government, all equally inscrutable and heartless. The price for halibut was too low one year, licensing fees too high to enter another fishery the next year, the sea out to get him personally every year. Boring to listen to, and the payoff had been a small trailer home with a few free halibut steaks. Whereas with Jim she had unlimited canned peaches and all the Krusteaz pancake mix anyone could ever want.

Rhoda smiled. She was happy, she realized. Or happy enough, anyway. She put down the plastic syringe, circled behind Jim, and breathed a little in his ear.

On the shore of Skilak Lake, less than a mile from where his parents were slamming into waves with their load of logs, Mark was just taking off his clothes with his partner Karen and a couple friends from the Coffee Bus. He stoked the fire and they all hopped into the sauna, then banged the door shut behind them. The sauna was right at the edge of the lake with a narrow pier straight out the door, and it was hot and dark, windowless, insulated with tar paper behind the wood, the sitting bench and foot bench so high his head brushed the ceiling and taller people had to duck. Mark always brought along a branch or two of hemlock with the leaves still on for whipping, and as soon as they had broken a good sweat and the steam was so thick that in the red light they could see each other only faintly, Karen bent over with her head between her knees and her arms locked around her calves and Mark started whipping her. This was to bring the blood to the surface and get the circulation going. It woke a person up, too, and seemed faintly medicinal and purifying. It made a loud rustling slapping sound and left Mark in a deep sweat, Karen in pain, both of them gasping.

Then it was Mark's turn to bend over. His skin so slick and salty now he couldn't grab his calves or grip his hands together, so he held on to the boards beneath his feet as Karen began whipping. She got a rhythm going, swinging as hard as she could, and incorporated her voice, too, after a while, until she was yelling deep from her gut with every whip. She grabbed the back of his neck with her other hand and whipped him hard until most the leaves and side branches had been ripped off and she collapsed on him and he was whimpering.

Then Carl and Monique wanted to try. Mark stumbled out for some new branches and offered to whip Monique when he returned, but she grabbed one of the branches and said, in her low, sexy voice, No, I want to do Carl. So Carl bent over, perhaps a little hesitantly, and Monique whipped him once hard and he yelped.

Hey, he said. That really fucking hurts.

Bend over, Monique said. Grab your ankles. Then she started with a few soft slaps and worked up gradually to the harder ones. In the end, Mark assisted at Monique's request by holding Carl's head down until Monique said, God, I can't breathe, and dropped the tattered whip and stumbled out the door and down the pier, where she dove headfirst into the lake.

The others piled out after. Again, Carl was a bummer. He dove in last, then got a stricken look on his face, the silent scream thing, and dog-paddled in a panic back to the pier. He lay on the wood gasping and swearing, saying how he couldn't believe this and how cold it was, how it was ice and glaciers and such, which was true in a way, since a glacier did in fact feed into the lake.

The others ignored him and swam out a few hundred feet, remarking on the beauty of the heavy rain, the constant wind, and the mountain towering invisibly above them.

I'm alive, Monique said. Even the most stupid things are true. I don't want to be dead ever again.

But then they all had to get out of the water or they would in fact die. They had already gone numb. They piled back into the sauna and decided to get high before the second round.

Best weed in the world, Mark said, exhaling finally. Highest THC content.

Karen went semi-catatonic, her usual. She had been raised on much weaker pot, and the Alaskan stuff hit her hard. So Mark felt free to check out Monique as much as he liked. She was tall and had short dark hair in a kind of European-looking bob, like the woman who modeled for Clinique. This got Mark hard, the fact that this woman beside him, her nipples hard and skin deserving of comparisons to alabaster and marble and such, looked like a model. He reached out to touch her neck.

Yeah, she said, pushing his hand away. You're a prince.

Hey, Carl said.

Shut up, Monique said. We don't need a male thing now. I'm enjoying this.

I'm so high, Karen said, raising her arms and falling back against the wall, her head thumping.

So Mark helped her sit up again, threw water on the hot rocks, and in an explosion of steam, they began the second of three rounds of Scandinavian custom.

Irene shivered, her teeth chattering, her wet clothing a kind of wick, something to chill and guide the wind, nothing more. And the water was very nearly freezing, a new shock every time it hit.

Their property came into view, three-quarters of an acre of waterfront looking toward the mountain and head of the lake, where the Kenai River fed from the glacier. Forest at the back of the property but also smaller growth in front, blueberry and alder thickets, wildflowers and grasses.

Gary aimed for the rocky shore. No beach, no sand or small pebbles. Big rounded rocks. Snags of wood on either side, waves breaking, and Gary didn't slow at all, came in at full speed. Irene yelled out for him to slow down, but then she just held on, braced a foot against the ramp, and they hit. The logs on top slid forward and Irene moved her foot just in time. Jesus, Gary, she said.

But Gary wasn't paying her any attention. He tilted the engine up, climbed forward over logs, and hopped into shallow water, about ten feet from shore. Help me lower the gate, he said. The rain and wind dying down, so at least she could hear. She climbed over the front, sank to her knees, over the tops of her boots, cold water, the rocks very slick beneath, and helped him undo the latches.

As she released the final one, the gate sprung at them, under pressure from the logs. Whoa, Gary said, but neither of them was hurt and they caught the ramp and lowered it, the waves breaking against their thighs and flooding the boat now from the open bow. They weren't far enough onto the shore.

We have to unload fast, Gary said, and I need to get the engine running for the bilge pump. So he climbed over logs to the stern, tilted the motor down, pulled the cord, switched on the pump. Time to hustle, he said, as he rushed to the bow. He grabbed a log and walked backward. Just grab your own log and drag it ashore.

So Irene grabbed a log and pulled hard. Her feet cold in the water and her entire body chilled, her stomach starting to hurt from being cold and then going to work.

The boat's already sinking, she yelled to Gary. The bilge pump wasn't keeping up. The boat was flooding too quickly from the bow, slogging back and forth in the waves.

Shit, Gary said. Let's put the gate up.

They latched the gate in a hurry, then he hopped aboard, the back end sitting very low, every third or fourth breaking wave dumping in some water from its crest, and he gunned the motor full throttle to jam the boat closer to shore. Irene could hear the bow scrape over rocks. It moved about a foot and then stopped. The stern tipped lower, though, too, because of the angle, and more water came in. Damn it, Gary yelled, and he grabbed the bailing bucket, throwing fast to get ahead of the waves, bending and springing up and bending again, throwing gallons at a time. Irene didn't know what to do except watch. No second bucket or room enough back there. But she climbed onto the bow, in case her weight in front might help tip the boat forward.

Gary dark and drenched, breathing hard and yelling out on the full buckets from the strain. The smoke from the outboard blowing over him, bilge pump spitting, waves breaking over the back. Irene knew he was frightened now, and she wanted to help him, but she could see, also, that he was making it, that the stern was rising higher, the waves dumping less water each time. You're doing it, Gary, she yelled. The stern's coming up. You're going to make it.

He was exhausted, she knew. The bucketfuls slowing, and sometimes his throw was short and some would land in the boat. I can take a turn, she yelled, but he just shook his head and kept dipping the bucket and throwing until finally the waves were slapping against the transom but not breaking over. He stopped then, dropped the bucket and bent over the outboard to vomit into the lake.

Gary, Irene said, and she wanted to comfort him but didn't want to add weight to the stern. The bilge pump clearing out the remaining water but taking some time. Gary, she said again, are you all right, honey?

I'm okay, he finally said. I'm okay. I'm sorry. This was a stupid idea.

It's okay, she said. We'll be okay. We'll just unload the rest of these and then go home.

Gary slumped over the motor a while, then turned the engine and pump off, climbed forward slowly, and kneeled on logs next to her in the bow. She gave him a hug and they stayed like that a few minutes, holding each other as the wind picked up and rain came down heavier again. They had not held each other like this for a very long time.

I love you, Gary said.

I love you too.

Well, Gary said, meaning time to move on. Irene had hoped the moment might extend. She didn't know how everything had changed. In the beginning, she had slept with an arm and a leg over him, every night. They had spent Sundays in bed. They had hunted together, footsteps in sync, bows held ready, listening for moose, watching for movement. The forest a living presence then, and they a part of it, never alone. But Gary had stopped bowhunting. Too worried about money, using the weekends to work, no more Sundays in bed. In the beginning, Irene thought. There is no such thing as in the beginning.

They left the gate latched and each grabbed another log, pulled it over the bow. The wind accelerating, coming in blasts, the rain spiking into their eyes if they looked toward the lake. Irene sneezed, then blew her nose by holding a finger to one nostril, wiped off with the back of her hand. Getting sick already.

A long time to finish the logs, moving slowly now, both tired. Gary dragged some of Irene's logs a bit farther from the water. But finally the boat was unloaded and light enough they could pull it ashore. They leaned against the bow, their backs to the wind and lake, and looked at their land.

We should have done this thirty years ago, Gary said. Should have moved out here.

We were on the shore, Irene said. On the lake, and easier to get to town, easier for the kids and school. It wouldn't be possible to have kids out here.

It would have been possible, Gary said. But whatever.

Gary was a champion at regret. Every day there was something, and this was perhaps what Irene liked least. Their entire lives second-guessed. The regret a living thing, a pool inside him.

Well, we're out here now, Irene said. We've brought the logs, and we'll be building the cabin.

My point is that we could have been here thirty years ago.

I get your point, Irene said.

Well, Gary said. His lips tight, and he was staring ahead into an alder thicket, stuck in there, unable to work his way out of the sense that his life could have been something else, and Irene knew she was a part of this great regret.

Irene tried to rise above, tried not to get caught in this. She looked at the property, and it really was beautiful. Slender white birch along the back portion, bigger Sitka spruce, a cottonwood and several aspen. The land had some contour, several rises, and she could see where the cabin would go. They'd put a deck out front, and on nice evenings, they'd watch the sun set on the mountain, golden light. This could all work out.

We can do this, Irene said. We can build a nice cabin here.

Yeah, Gary finally said. Then he turned away from the property, looked into the wind and rain. Let's push off.

So they pushed the boat free and climbed over the bow. Gary at the engine and Irene in the bottom of the boat, hugging her knees, trying to get warm. The way back not as bad, the waves behind them, the square gate in the bow above the waterline now, the boat no longer a barge. They rolled a bit on each wave, but no slamming, no spray. Irene's teeth chattering again.

A long way from the island to the campground. Gary going slow, the bilge pump working. The campground and truck came into view finally and he cut the motor, landed on the beach beside the ramp. The waves pushing the stern up and down and slewing it to the side.

We could skip the trailer, Gary said. The waves are too big here. It'll be a nightmare. We could just pull the boat onto the beach a ways and tie it to a tree.

So they did that and were home in minutes. So close, and they'd been freezing for so long. Pointless, Irene thought.

Gary took a quick hot shower, and then Irene ran a hot bath. Painful to sit down into it, her fingers and toes, especially, gone partially numb. The heat delicious, though, surrounding her. She sank into it and closed her eyes, found herself crying carefully, without sound, her mouth underwater. Stupid, she told herself. You can't have what no longer exists.

On his way back to the office after lunch, Jim swung by the Coffee Bus for a sticky bun. Brown sugar, honey, and nuts, and it meant supporting Rhoda's brother, too, who might be in need of that kind of thing. Loiterers out front, as usual, but this time, one of them was so beautiful he didn't realize he was staring until too late, which made him feel like an ass, of course, which then pissed him off. Probably little more than half his age, but her gaze made him feel like his willie was standing out in the breeze for everyone to look at.

Jim gave his customary grunt and half-smile in her direction. This was rarely loud enough for anyone to hear, and many in Soldotna who didn't know him well considered him a misanthrope because of it, he knew, but this amazed him. To him, this muffled greeting sounded like a full and cheery, if soft-spoken and not overly aggressive, hello.

The woman, leaning against the side of the bus, nodded to him in return, pulled her old down coat tighter, and Jim walked stiff-legged and awkward up the wooden steps to the window, trying not to look at her. She was only a few feet away now, and he was embarrassed. Desperate, also. Desperation reached like a cold hand through his genitals into his lower back.

Hey Jim, said Karen. Sticky bun?

That would be the item.

Mark came to the window and stuck his hand out.

Jim shook it. How are you?

Meet a friend of mine, Mark said. Jim, this is Monique. Monique, this is Jim. Jim's a dentist, fastest drill in the west. Monique's a visitor to our fair state, come to see the wild lands.

Monique put a hand out, and Jim reached down to shake it.

Hi, Jim said. Having a good trip?

I am, she said. Mark and Karen are taking good care of me. Then she waited as he stared. She seemed, to Jim, not just to have time but to be the one behind it. Like the Wizard of Oz, maybe, in his little booth.

Maybe you could tell me, Monique said. You're a dentist. I have a tooth that feels cold sometimes and hurts a little if I've been in the cold. It hurts today, for instance. She rocked her jaw a bit, feeling it. Is that a cavity, or just something else?

Could be, Jim said. I'd have to take a look to know for sure. Jim checked his watch. One thirty-five. Actually, I could take a quick look now before two if you're free.

Huh, Monique said. Then she shrugged. Okay.

So Jim drove her to the office. No one else back from lunch yet. He flipped on the lights and took her to one of the chairs in the back. Oh, maybe I should have given you a tour first.

That's all right, Monique said, sitting back in the chair. Lovely ducks on your ceiling. Jim had glued the undersides of rubber ducks up there, webbed orange feet paddling around midair as if the office were underwater.

For the kids, Jim said.

For the hunters.

Yeah, maybe so, Jim said, trying to chuckle lightly, not sure whether or not she was throwing him in with the hunters here.

Jim turned the light on then, asked her to open her mouth wide, and probed around her teeth and gums for a while.

Just the small beginnings of one, he said. We should take a couple films, and if we need to, we can do a quick job on it, preventative mostly.

Uh, she said, and he pulled his fingers out so she could talk.

I'm concerned about cost.

It's on me, Jim said. And he waited until the others arrived, had the X rays done, and put a small filling in right then, though it shot his afternoon schedule all to hell.

Don't tell anyone, he said after he had finished and was bringing up the chair. She was taking off her bib. He leaned in close over her and smiled a little as he said this, trying to imply, and feel, all kinds of secrets between them. He had heard a man say once, Now she's a breeder, and as ugly and psycho as this line was, and distasteful to him, it occurred to him now that this was nonetheless true. Here was the woman he wanted to make babies with. He couldn't imagine her changing diapers or even being pregnant, but he could see his strong, tall, beautiful children in a portrait some day, all devoid of any type of insecurity or struggle. She managed to eliminate the possibility of any other woman and seemed to imply wealth, also, though she was dressed like a hippie and probably couldn't have afforded this filling if he had asked her to pay.

I won't, she said.

He looked at her blankly. He had no idea what she was saying.

I won't tell anyone, she said.

Oh, he said. Hey, could I make you dinner sometime? I have

a view of the sunset over the Cook Inlet. I could fix salmon or halibut or whatever you like, just to give you a taste of Alaska while you're here. This had come out surprisingly well, with a nice little tag at the end, even. He hadn't stiffened or looked suddenly frightened.

She looked at him, considering. He felt his spine collapsing, his shoulder blades folding down into his stomach.

Okay, she said.

Monique spent the rest of the afternoon and evening reading at the confluence of two rivers, looking up occasionally to watch Carl not catch any red salmon. He was lined up with hundreds of other tourist fishermen, men and women, from all over the world. The river not that large, fifty yards across, but these fishermen stood at five-foot intervals along both its banks for half a mile. The best fishing was reputedly on the far side of this particular bend, where the water ran deeper and faster along a steep gravel bank.

Carl was on the shallow, near side, however, out twenty feet or so from shore in hip waders, using a fly, yanking it along the bottom, where red salmon were swimming peacefully in place against the current. Monique could see them as shadows in the dappled light, imagined their mouths opening and closing, taking in water, contemplating with a wary eye the rows of evenly spaced green boots growing in pairs and the large red flies cruising around everywhere.

The fishermen were all so earnest. To Monique, the best part about this place was the scenery: the high, lush mountains close along either side of the river, the short valleys dotted with wildflowers, the swampy areas dense with skunk cabbage, ferns, mosquitoes, and moose. But not one of the fishermen looked up from the water, ever, even for a moment. The mood along the riverbanks was like the mood in a casino.

Monique was reading a book of short stories by T. Coraghessan Boyle. They were funny, and she often laughed out loud. In one, Lassie goes after a coyote, forbidden love. This appealed to her especially. She had always hated Lassie.

Monique was lucky enough to look up in time to see Carl huck his pole into the river. This stopped a few fishermen. Their lines stalled for a moment along the bottom, so then several were whipping their poles back and forth trying to free snags.

Carl came splashing through the water in his waders, slipping a bit on the smooth stones and fish entrails and whatever else was down there. He came right up to Monique, who closed her book.

Fishing not good? she asked.

Carl grabbed her by the shoulders and kissed her hard. God, I feel better, he said.

Monique smiled and grabbed him for another kiss. This was one of the things she liked about Carl. Given enough time, he could recognize shit. And unlike most men, he didn't persist in stupidity just because someone was watching.

Rhoda came home to find Jim with a drink on the coffee table beside him. Facing the windows, drinking and looking out to sea. Very strange, since Jim almost never drank at all, and certainly never alone. Rhoda began noticing the random things she noticed during tragedies: the refrigerator clicked on only briefly then clicked back off; sunlight reflected off the dark wood of the coffee table but wasn't hitting his drink; the house seemed unusually warm, also, almost humid, claustrophobic. She set down the grocery bags and walked over to him.

What's wrong? she asked in a voice that sounded to her like fear. She touched his shoulder lightly as she said this.

Hey, he said, perhaps a bit flushed as he turned to her, but not drunk, his speech fine. How was your day?

What is this? Why are you sitting here drinking?

Just having a little sherry, Jim said, and he picked up his glass and swirled the ice around. Enjoying the view.

Something's up. I thought someone had died or something. Why the sudden change in behavior?

Can't a man have a drink? Jesus, you'd think I was burning down the house or writing on the walls with crayons or something. But I'm forty-one years old, a dentist, I'm in my own house, and I'm having a glass of Harveys after work.

Okay, okay.

Lighten up.

Okay, Rhoda said. I'm sorry, all right? I picked up some chicken. I was thinking maybe we'd have lemon chicken.

Sounds good. Which reminds me, by the way. I may have found a new partner for the practice. A dentist out of Juneau, named Jacobsen, and I was thinking I'd have him over for dinner tomorrow to talk about specifics. So I'm wondering whether you'd be willing to make other plans for just a few hours in the evening. Would that be okay?

Sure. That's fine. I'll have dinner with my parents. I'll call Mark tonight to let Mom know.

Great, Jim said. Thanks. Then he looked out to the inlet again and the mountains beyond, the snow on Mount Redoubt, and he thought how clever he was, and how deserving.

Irene was sick and miserable the day after the storm, but the following morning she woke with something much worse, an awful headache that started at her eye socket and spiraled across her forehead. If she closed her eyes, she could see red tracery of the pain. A new pattern with each blink or pulse, a dark limitless sky. Coming from behind her right brow, so she pressed all around the eye, and if she pressed with her thumb at the top inside corner of the socket, this helped briefly.

She couldn't breathe through her nose. Her throat sore, perhaps from breathing all night with her mouth open. She swallowed, and that felt raw and painful.

Gary, she managed to croak out, but no answer. She curled on her side, not wanting to leave the warmth of the comforter and blanket, but now she could feel the draining from her sinuses into the back of her throat, drowning. She sat up and grabbed a tissue, blew her nose, but it was all locked in, rock solid. Blowing only pressurized her ears. It didn't relieve anything.

Gary, she called again, more desperate this time, but still no answer. She looked at the clock and saw she had slept late, after 9:00 a.m. She lay back down and moaned. The pain in her head unlike any she'd experienced before, so focused, so insistent.

She got out of bed and walked to the bathroom. Needed to pee, and then needed painkiller. Took two Advil, and then two more, and walked back to bed. It hurt to walk. She could feel the impact of her footsteps in her head. The back of her eye a new zone she had never even noticed before.

She slipped under the covers, moving carefully, and tried to blow her nose again, then tried to just fall asleep. She didn't want to be awake for this.

Gary was at the boat, working on the bent bow ramp. A solid break in the rain, finally, and he was taking advantage of it, though he felt like hell, some kind of flu and fever, his stomach weak. He'd spent much of the day before in bed. Irene even worse off.

With several big clamps and a rubber mallet, he was making progress, swinging hard with both hands, the mallet bouncing but also gradually bending the plate back into place.

You'd think they would have made this bow a bit stronger. It was a ramp, after all. It should have been strong enough to drive on, the boat big enough to carry a small car. But whoever had designed it hadn't put enough reinforcement across the center. Gary was an aluminum welder and boat builder himself and had thought about just building a boat with a ramp, but Irene hadn't wanted that. Too many problems with his cost estimates for earlier boats. A lack of faith. So they wasted a lot of money on this one.

No other boats two days ago in the storm, but today there was constant traffic on the ramp beside him, five or ten small boats launched. The fishermen looked him over, and several came by to inspect.

Got a bend there, a man said. He was wearing hip waders with straps over his shoulders, a great way to drown.

You go in with those, Gary said, the waders become an enormous bucket.

The man looked down at the bib of his waders. You could be right.

Yeah, Gary said, and went back to hammering. The man left, which was good.

Maybe it was just that he'd been feeling sick for two days, his stomach weak, but Gary was feeling self-critical as well. Thinking he didn't have a good friend up here, after so many years. No one offering to help on the cabin. A few friends, but no one he could call up, no real friendship. And he wondered why that was. He'd always had good friends before, in California, still had a couple of them, though he saw them only every few years. Irene hadn't helped things, not very social—she was shy, somehow, and rarely wanted to leave home—but still he didn't know why he didn't have better friends here.

The bow plate wasn't going to get any straighter. He loosened the clamps and could see the fit at the latches still wasn't a perfect seal. He'd have some water intrusion. But this was good enough.

Gary picked up his tools and looked at the lake. Small waves, some wind, not like two days ago. No rain. He'd get Irene and they'd take another load out. It was almost eleven, a late start, but they could accomplish something.

Back at the house, Irene was still in bed.

The weather's better, he said. We could take a load out.

Turn off the light, she said, and rolled over to face the other way.

What's wrong? Not feeling well?

I have a terrible headache. Worst I've ever felt.

Irene, he said, Reney-Rene. And he switched off the light and sat on the bed, put an arm over her. Fairly dark in here, the thick curtains closed, light coming in from the door only. His eyes weren't adjusted yet, so he couldn't see her well. Want some aspirin or Advil?

I tried that. It doesn't work. It doesn't do anything. She sounded exhausted.

I'm sorry, Irene. Maybe I should take you in to a doctor.

Just let me sleep.

So he kissed her forehead, which didn't feel hot, and went out, closing the door. Then he opened the door again. Do you want some lunch?

No. Just sleep.

Okay, and he closed it again.

Gary walked into the small kitchen, crammed with too much stuff, and grabbed smoked salmon from the fridge, capers and cornichons, crackers, sat at their dark wooden table. Like a mead hall, the dark table and benches near the hearth. A big stone fireplace, something he'd always wanted. But the space was too small, too cramped, the ceilings too low. It felt cheap, not real. Carpet on the floor, not wood. He'd always hated carpet. Irene wanted the carpet, said it was warmer. He wanted wood or even stone. Slabs of slate. He didn't know yet what the cabin would have. Maybe just dirt. Dirt or wood.

They usually played two-handed pinochle together at lunch, so Gary didn't know what to do. He leaned over to the bookshelf and grabbed his copy of *Beowulf*, set it on the table but didn't open it.

Hwaet. We Gar-Dena, he recited, and he went through the opening lines. A circus trick. He still knew the opening lines to *Beowulf* and "The Seafarer" in Old English, and Chaucer's

Canterbury Tales in Middle English, and the *Aeneid* in Latin, but he couldn't actually read the languages anymore. He could translate a few lines, struggling through with a dictionary and his notes from thirty years ago, but he couldn't just read. He had lost that, and though he kept trying to get it back, every few years, his attempts never lasted more than a week or two, and then something always happened, something else needed his attention.

The salmon so good he closed his eyes. White king, the meat richer, a bit more fat, rare but he had caught one last summer, soft-smoked it and still had a couple vacuum-sealed bags left. He'd need to get out fishing again before the season ended, get a smoker going at the cabin.

Gary looked out the window at the lake through the trees, ate the salmon, knew he should feel lucky, but felt nothing except a mild, background terror of how he'd get through the day, how he'd fill the hours. He'd felt this all his adult life, especially in the evenings, especially when he was single. After the sun went down, the stretch of time until when he could sleep seemed an impossible expanse, something looming, a void that couldn't be crossed. He'd never told anyone about it, not even Irene. It would sound like he was defective in some way. He doubted anyone would really understand.

Well, Gary said, and stood up. He needed to get moving. Irene wasn't going to help him today, but he needed to be doing something. He'd have to get Mark or Rhoda to help him. So he washed his plate and fork, stepped outside, and walked the path to Mark's house.

Well traveled by now, a winding route around alder thickets into spruce forest. He should have come in years ago with a machete, cleared a more direct path. But there was something he liked about the character of the twistings and turnings, saplings he'd seen grow into trees, the changing look of seasons, green now, lush, closed in, the trail ahead blocked from sight.

Hey bear, he called out. Hey bear, hey bear, as he came around a bend. Mosquitoes buzzing at his ears, going for his neck. The forest damp and rotting, smell of wood. Wind in the treetops, a reassuring sound, the rise of it, the way it always seemed far away, even in close.

New deadfall from the storm. He cleared branches as he went, tossed them aside. Twigs snapping underfoot.

He was curious to see the creek, and when he came upon it, finally, the water was high on the banks, but not discolored. The boards he'd set in for the footbridge remained above water, moss-covered edges a bright green. He stood there, the water rushing at him. Ferns all through here, devil's club rising in horizontal planes, wide flat leaves.

He moved on, up a rise through spruce and cottonwood, onto Mark's land, and could already see Mark's house below in the trees, at the edge of the lake. A large garden to the side, and marijuana plants in the weeds farther back, in plastic tubs. Nearly everyone in town knew about them. Mark had bought the house and land two years before for $18,000, all of which came from cash advances on credit cards. That first winter, he struggled to meet the minimum payments and waited for summer, when he, along with the rest of Alaska, made his entire yearly income. And he did get lucky. The price for salmon was unusually high, the run good, and he made nearly $35,000 in less than two months, a new record for him, because he was getting an unheard-of 30 percent cut on a drift-netter. The woman who owned this boat had acquired it from a divorce settlement and had very little experience, so she needed someone good and was willing to pay. He was known by everyone, had been fishing out of Kenai since thirteen, with only a four-year break when he went to Brown.

After he paid off the cards, Mark made a mobile out of them that he called Floating Credit and hung from the light over the kitchen table. The house was unfinished, though, lacking much of its drywall and insulation, cold in winter, and still without a toilet or running water. The bed of his pickup always filled now with large plastic barrels to haul water. The yard littered with several other vehicles as well. A Dodge van, rusted out, a dead VW bug, and a multicolored VW van that ran marginally.

Gary couldn't say he approved of Mark's life, but he also knew it didn't matter whether he approved or not. And he could see Mark wasn't home at the moment. Neither was his partner, Karen. Mark out fishing, no doubt, and Karen at the Coffee Bus. Gary had figured this would be the case, but he liked the walk, and he could use the phone here, too, to call Rhoda. He opened the front door, which was always unlocked, and went to the phone in the kitchen. A plate of chocolate-chip cookies on the counter, so he had one of those.

I'm working today, Dad, Rhoda said when he called. She was at Dr. Turin's office, helping to sew up a black Lab. I can't talk on my cell phone.

Sorry, honey. Lost track of the days. Come out and see us when you get a chance. Your mother's sick.

What's wrong? Rhoda sounded worried.

Her head hurts. A bad cold.

I'll get someone to come out, Rhoda said, and I'll bring some meds. That's awful she's feeling so bad.

No need to come out. I think she just needs to sleep.

I'm coming out anyway, Dad, for dinner tonight, remember?

Oh yeah. Sorry.

So that left Gary on his own for now, and he had a limited

amount of time before dinner to get everything done. He returned on the path, backed his pickup to the pile of logs, and started loading. Not as easy with one person, but not all that difficult, either. Just drag a log to the tailgate, prop one end up, then grab the other end to walk it forward.

He drove the logs down to the boat, and this time he knew to push the boat out farther first. Everything went much more smoothly. Irene had seen the worst of it. Hardly any wind today, the waves very small, so unloading at the island wouldn't be a problem, either.

It did occur to Gary that he could have waited. Instead of going out in that storm, both of them getting sick, they could have just waited, as Irene had wanted. That would have been better. But somehow it had not been possible.

Irene woke disoriented. She raised her head to see the time, after 2:00 p.m., and this movement somehow put pressure on her forehead, the pain a pulse.

Gary, she called, her throat raw. She was hungry, and thirsty, and wanted Gary to help her, to take care of her. This was not a time to be alone. The pain behind her eye so intense she had to get away from it, starting to feel panicked.

Gary, she called again, but no answer, no other sound in the house. He had left her here, gone out in the boat, no doubt, sticking to the project, the plan.

Gary, she yelled, enraged. Damn you.

She pressed at both eyes, at the sockets, pressed at her forehead, her neck. An animate pain, burrowed inside her head.

She pulled the blankets aside slowly, not wanting to move too abruptly, sat at the edge of the bed, feeling dizzy. Waited until she felt she wouldn't fall, then walked slowly along the bed, down the hallway into the bathroom, grabbed the open bottle of Advil, took four more, then four aspirin, then NyQuil. She wanted to be knocked out. Wanted to feel nothing. She didn't care what this would do to her in the long run. All that mattered was now.

She walked back to bed, curled on her side under the covers, and whimpered. Like a dog, she said aloud.

The medications kicked in, and though they couldn't do anything to the pain, they did make her drowsy, and finally she slept.

Irene woke again after dreams of pressure and panic and called out again for Gary, but still no answer. The clock showed almost five thirty.

So she got up and walked slowly to the kitchen. Could breathe only through her mouth, and it hurt to swallow. But she was starving.

She went for the yogurt. That was fast and would be easy on the throat. Swallowed carefully, worked her way through a bowl of it, a smooth and cooling vanilla, then heard Rhoda's clunker pulling up. Thank god, she said. She was ready to be cared for.

Rhoda came in fast, still wearing light blue scrubs from Dr. Turin's. Oh, Mom, she said. You look awful. She straddled the bench seat and scooted closer to Irene, put her lips to Irene's forehead. You don't have a fever.

No. The pain is behind my eyes, especially my right eye.

I don't know what that is, Rhoda said.

Your father has left me alone all day.

What?

Checked on me once and then disappeared.

But he knows you're sick.

He knows.

Did he try to help? Did he ask if you needed anything?

Irene thought for a moment. I guess he did. He asked if he could take me to a doctor, and asked if I wanted lunch.

So he tried, Mom.

That was about six hours ago. More than six hours.

Well I'm here now, and Frank Bishop is coming out. He'll be here any minute. I've brought some painkillers, too, in case he doesn't have anything with him.

I'll take them now, Irene said.

Sorry, Mom. We have to wait.

Irene sighed. Sickness and health, she said. In sickness and health. And if anything ever happens to me, your father goes running.

He loves you, Mom. You're not feeling well, so you're not being fair to him.

It's who he is. He can't take care of anyone except himself.

Why don't you lie down again, Mom?

So they walked back to the bedroom, and Rhoda tucked Irene in, then a car pulled up.

Must be Bishop, Rhoda said.

Irene waited in bed absorbed in pain, wanting it just to go away.

Frank Bishop came in with a cheery hello. Howdy, Irene. What did you do now?

You're only thirty years old, Frank. Don't condescend to me.

Okay, he said, with a roll of his eyes at Rhoda.

Don't do that, Irene said.

So he stopped talking. Rummaged around in his bag, sitting in a chair Rhoda had brought to the edge of the bed, and pulled out a thermometer, stuck it in Irene's mouth. Then he took her pulse.

All three of them waited a minute in silence for the thermometer, and finally he pulled it out. No fever, he said.

Yep, Rhoda said. She doesn't feel hot.

So what are your symptoms, Irene? he asked.

Terrible pain behind my right eye, in a spiral. My whole head and neck hurt, but the pain behind my eye is unbelievable.

Aspirin and Advil don't do anything to it. I need something stronger. And my throat is raw, my nose completely stuffed. I feel like hell.

Okay, he said. Sounds like a sinus infection.

Yeah, Rhoda said.

I need to bring you in for X rays. I need to see how bad it is.

Can you give me painkillers now?

Tomorrow, he said.

That doesn't help me much.

Sorry, Irene, that's all I can do. I have to know what I'm treating. He stood up, gave her a pat on the shoulder, and left.

Rhoda walked him out to his car, a Lexus, muddy all along the bottom. Sorry, she told him. She's just not feeling well.

Yeah, he said. Bring her in tomorrow morning. Then he got in his car and drove away. Rhoda had gone to high school with him, everything since grade school. And now he was rich and got to play God, while she sewed up dogs and sampled poop.

When Rhoda returned bedside, her mom wanted the painkillers.

Okay, Mom, she said. I have Vicodin. Only one every four hours, though. No more than that or you could have problems. And it may make you feel nauseated. It can have other side effects, too.

Just end this, Irene said. I don't care if all my skin falls off and I grow a third tit. I just want to sleep and not feel anything.

At the turnoff to the Lower Salmon River Campground, Monique was standing by one of the blue concrete igloos that used to be gift shops, looking like a hitchhiker, or maybe a biker chick. Guilt and fear already riding Jim hard. He considered just driving on by, but she was watching him.

Nice rig, she said as she hopped up onto the seat. Room for twelve.

Yeah, it's pretty spacious, Jim said. It was just a Chevy Suburban, and he wasn't sure whether she was making fun of him. How come you're staying all the way down here? It's over twenty minutes to Soldotna.

Carl likes to move around and see different places. He has this idea that if he sees everything, it will amount to something.

Carl?

Yeah, Carl.

Who's Carl?

He's my boyfriend. We came up here together.

Oh, Jim said, as if the world had just collapsed.

It doesn't matter, Monique said. It's not as if I'm married.

No. No, Jim said. That's true. It's not as if you're married. Hey, it's not as if I'm married, either.

Are you seeing someone?

No, not really.

Hmm, said Monique, and Jim wondered whether she already knew about Rhoda. Then he remembered he had met Monique through Rhoda's brother, Mark. Monique had certainly heard about Rhoda, then, and may even have met her. They could become good friends soon, for all he knew.

Fuck, Jim said aloud.

What?

Oh, sorry. I just forgot something important today.

I hate that.

Yeah. Jim wondered how he'd get through the next twenty minutes. Somehow he had imagined they'd just flirt a little and then fall into each other's arms when they got to his place.

So where are you from? he asked.

D.C., Monique said. Where it is not beautiful and there are no mountains.

What do your parents do there? He was hoping to get some idea of her age.

My mother's a bigwig with the AID.

Ah, Jim said. He couldn't just admit he didn't know what the AID was. Probably an organization of some sort, or a government thing. He didn't keep up with the papers all that well.

What kind of things does she do with them? he asked.

Mostly health programs, Monique said. She was trained as a medical anthropologist. She's always flying off to places she won't take me, and coming back with shoes or something. We do travel together sometimes.

And your father?

He's dead.

Oh, I'm sorry to hear that.

It's all right, really. It's not a big deal. We're happier without him.

Huh, Jim said.

So what about you, darling? And she asked it in some famous actress's voice, someone he should know. Tell me about yourself.

My father was a dentist also.

A grand old tradition. And your mother?

She didn't work.

You mean she did child care, home engineering, and billing?

How old are you? Jim asked.

Old enough to be your grandma.

Jim laughed. That's good, he said.

Yeah, she said.

Carl, meanwhile, was back at the campsite huddled in his tent against the rain, writing postcards. Saying hi to his friends in D.C., telling them how he was and how Monique was, too, since Monique didn't write postcards. Monique also didn't sleep in tents, apparently. She had found higher ground somewhere. The note said only, I'll see you tomorrow. This pissed him off. He would have run out into the rain and torn his clothes and raged like Lear, but no one was around to watch. Monique couldn't have heard or cared. In the end, he would only have been wet, with torn clothing. The whole thing sucked.

It was the kind of thing that had been happening since the first day they arrived in Soldotna. Carl and Monique heard that first day about treble-hook snagging at the gravel spit in Homer and rushed down in a rental car. This was when Carl still had some money.

Monique thought Homer was beautiful. While Carl got his

gear together, she walked around the harbor. The mountains on the far side of the bay rose straight out of the water in jagged rows and still held snow at their summits. Flocks of cormorants skimmed along the black-sanded beach, the water was jeweled in late evening sun, and looking out into the bay, shielding her eyes, Monique saw the spray of a humpbacked whale rise up golden and glittering then sweep along the surface in the wind. This is a place I could live, she thought. Then she walked on the docks, looking at the boats, and met a fisherman who had dark hair and blue eyes and spoke to her of king crab and halibut and the softness of the sea at night.

Carl knew all this because Monique had told him afterward, in detail. She was like that. It didn't occur to her that she might be stepping on something.

Unaware of the dark handsome man with blue eyes and this shit about the softness of the sea, Carl had tromped down to the edge of a gravel pit partially filled with unclear water. A hundred feet across and three times as long, it looked like a stagnant pond. He could see small, iridescent rings on the water's surface from gasoline. But the king salmon came here anyway, apparently, with the high tide.

The tide was dramatic along the Cook Inlet, a current like a river, and when it came in at about eight o'clock, it did come in fast. Carl was impressed. The salmon poured in, and a hundred fishermen, Carl among them, ripped huge, weighted, baitless treble hooks through the water from all directions trying to snag the salmon as they darted past. A hook often came free of the water and shot through a row of fishermen to bury itself in the gravel bank behind. It was stupid and dangerous. Getting snagged and ripped wasn't all that uncommon, Carl heard with a chuckle from one of the regulars. There were ten-year-old kids out there whipping their lines around not looking behind them and old men tottering on alcohol and medications, their vests and hats already a jumble of hooks. It was ridiculous and demeaning. The salmon caught were tattered and frayed, ripped up from all the previous snags that had pulled free.

Carl wrote on a postcard to Monique's mother, It's gorgeous here. Monique and I are really enjoying Alaska, the scenery and the people, the fishing. We met a fisherman who told us about king crab and halibut, and this was after we saw cormorants, whole flocks of them. Carl ripped up the postcard. Monique's mother didn't think he was quick enough. Slow Carl, she called him behind his back. Monique had told him this. Carl curled up into the drier part of his sleeping bag and tried to sleep.

Monique and Jim were having their own problems with sleeping arrangements. They had just finished a lovely salmon dinner, with wild rice and white wine and a somewhat battered-looking but, in Jim's opinion, delicious Baked Alaska he had read up on and prepared himself. Yo-Yo Ma was playing on the stereo, and Jim was imagining great sex. Then Monique asked where she would be sleeping.

What? Jim asked.

I'm a little worn out, she said. Stayed up too late last night, so I was thinking I might turn in early after such a wonderful dinner. It really was superb. You're quite a chef. And she raised her glass to toast him.

Uh, he said. Hmm. I was kind of thinking I'd be taking you back at some point tonight. Jim was panicking. Rhoda sometimes stayed over with her parents when she had dinner there, but not always, not even frequently.

You can't be thinking of taking me back to that campsite in the middle of the night.

No, no, of course not. I don't know what I was thinking.

Is it Rhoda? Is she coming here tonight?

Yes.

You're not the only one who lives here, are you?

No.

And Rhoda's planning on marrying you, isn't she?

Jim's erection had died. He closed his eyes and massaged his temples.

Jim, Monique said. This is poor planning, don't you think?

Jim moaned a little and tried to think without thinking.

Look, Monique said. A nice hotel would be fine. I don't want to get you in trouble with Rhoda.

Really? Jim asked, perking up. You're the best.

I don't mind.

So Jim took her to the King Salmon Hotel, where he hoped he wouldn't know whomever was on duty. But after they had waited at the desk and rung the bell, one of his patients came out and smiled and said, Hello, Dr. Fenn.

Jim had to look quick at her name tag.

Hi, Sarah, he said.

How can I help you? She smiled at Monique, too.

This is my niece, Monique, Jim said. She's up visiting for a while, but we're having some work done on the house, so we thought we'd put her up here temporarily until we can clear out the drop cloths and the paint smell and all that, you know. He crinkled his nose for the paint smell and Sarah crinkled hers back.

Monique laughed when they were inside the room. Thank you, Uncle.

Don't call me Uncle, Jim said.

Then she gave him one long kiss and pushed him out the door.

While her mom tried to sleep, Rhoda looked around the kitchen for dinner ideas. Canned baked beans, canned corn, instant mashed potatoes from a packet. That would be easy enough. She put a kettle on for the potatoes, nuked the corn, opened the can of beans into a pot, and by the time the kettle went off, her father drove up in his battered old F-150. No one in the family drove anything worth looking at.

Her father walked partway to the house, then stopped and looked around. The trees, the mountain, antlers along the roof, the flower beds. He always did this. All her life, from her earliest memories. She didn't know what it was about.

Hey Dad, she said when he finally stepped inside. Looking at the trees?

What?

You always stop and look around before you come in the house, or into any building, or even into a boat or truck. What is that?

What? he asked. I don't know.

You're in trouble with Mom.

What?

Leaving her alone all day. She's ready to kill.

I asked if I could take her to a doctor, he said.

I know, Rhoda said.

You know?

She told me. I was sticking up for you. And I brought a doctor, Bishop. He said she has a sinus infection and needs to go in for X rays tomorrow morning.

Okay, her father said.

Okay? I'm worried about her, Dad. She seems really sick. The pain is making her crazy.

Huh, he said. Then he walked down the hallway and eased the door open into the bedroom. He could hear Irene's ragged breathing, her throat clogged up. He eased the door shut and walked around the bed in the dark, lay down behind Irene, and put an arm around her.

Mm, she said, and pushed back into him, something so natural and easy. He closed his eyes, not wanting to lose this, a moment increasingly rare between them. Basic comfort, the two of them needing each other. Why wasn't this enough?

His first attraction to Irene had been instinct. He was in grad school at Berkeley, becoming a medievalist, but he was outclassed and he knew it. Couldn't keep up with the others. He was fine on the primary texts but couldn't keep up on the secondary documents, long histories and registers, almanacs, journals, all in Middle English. Religious documents in Middle English, Old English, and Latin. Then all the criticism, keeping up with current books and articles. It was just too much. And he didn't have French or Old French, which was a big problem.

A friend in the program introduced him to Irene, at a group dinner in a cheap restaurant. She had long blond hair then, blue eyes. She looked like something from an Icelandic saga. She didn't talk in jargon. A preschool teacher, still in education, but not intimidating. He felt he could breathe, finally. She was safe.

Gary held Irene and tried to remember back to who they had been at twenty-four years old, tried to feel what he had felt then, but it was a long way back. Irene moaned again, moved away from him and tried to clear her throat, threw back the covers suddenly.

I can't swallow, she said. I can't breathe, and now I can't swallow. How am I supposed to get any air?

She walked into the bathroom and Gary sat up. Is there anything I can do?

Make it stop, she said. I can't breathe. I can't sleep. The pain won't go away. And now I'm dizzy. The Vicodin. She gargled, tried to clear her throat.

Come back to bed.

I'm drowning, she said. Maybe food will help. And some tea.

So she dressed and they went to the kitchen. Rhoda had food on the table, a cup of hot tea ready.

Thank you, Irene said, and she gave Rhoda a kiss on her forehead. Gary wadded up newspaper at the fireplace, stacked small sticks in a tepee, a few thicker pieces and a log, lit the edges and fanned it until a good fire was going.

Irene started crying. She was trying to eat some mashed potatoes and beans, but then she was just crying.

Mom, Rhoda said.

Irene, Gary said, and they sat on either side of her, put their arms around her.

It really hurts, she said. It just won't stop. But she wasn't crying only about the pain, she knew. She had an excuse, finally, to cry without hiding, and it was impossible to stop. It had a volume and depth, a physical space inside her, vaulted, a carving out of everything. Gary leaving her, after thirty years spent in this cold, unforgiving place. She didn't know how to stop that, how to slow the momentum of years, how to make him see.

By the time Jim returned from dropping Monique at the hotel, Rhoda was already home. At the sink, doing his dinner dishes.

Hey, she said. This was a hell of a spread. How come I don't get Baked Alaska? She was smiling. Making up. And she looked pretty good to Jim. He kissed her and pulled her close.

Hey, wait. Let me get the soap off my hands first.

Jim was taking off Rhoda's jeans right there at the sink.

I take it the meeting went well? Rhoda asked, but her voice was getting lower.

Jim kneeled before her on the kitchen floor.

Never mind, she murmured.

Afterward, they played Yahtzee at the kitchen table. Rhoda got a Yahtzee with ones. She gloated and he groaned. Then, her next turn, she got another Yahtzee with ones, on only two rolls.

Whoa, Jim said. The gods are out there.

He got a crap roll, everything but a three, went for twos, got one more but that was it.

Okay, he said. And then Rhoda rolled a third Yahtzee, again with ones.

Aah! They both yelled. Rhoda put her hands to her teeth and began bouncing in her seat. Jim was screaming, seriously freaked. They both got up and ran around the room, brushing themselves off instinctively and shivering, as if luck, with its little batlike hands, were still clinging to them.

Irene could feel every bump in the road on the way to town. Every rut and ridge, washboard and pothole, all of it sending arcs of red spinning into the world behind her right eye. A sunny day, a summer's day, but even the light hurt, so her eyes were closed.

We'll be there soon, Gary said. Just hold on a little longer.

The Vicodin's making me nauseated.

Only a few minutes, Gary said.

At the office, they took the X rays and Frank read them on a lit whiteboard. Here's a frontal view, he said, and it was Irene's skull, eye hollows and fleshless jaw, rows of grinning teeth, just like in a skull and crossbones. A vision ahead to her own death.

Creepy, she said.

And here's a side view, he said. And the other side.

Where's the infection? Irene asked. What does it look like?

Well, that's the problem, Irene. There's nothing here.

What do you mean, there's nothing?

You don't have any locked-in infection according to the X rays.

But I do have one.

You certainly have a cold, with maybe a bit of an infection. If you really want, I can give you an antibiotic for seven days.

I don't understand.

The X rays just don't show anything.

Irene started crying, rocked forward in her seat, her head in her hands.

Irene, Frank said, and he patted her shoulder awkwardly.

I have something, she said. Something's wrong.

I'm sorry. I'll give you the prescriptions. But there's just nothing there.

So Irene waited until she could pull herself together, tried unsuccessfully to blow her nose, then took her prescriptions, paid, and had to tell Gary in the waiting room. Nothing showed up on the X rays, she said.

What?

I know there's something, she said. It just didn't show up.

Irene, he said, and pulled her into his arms. I'm sorry, Irene. But maybe this is good news. Maybe you'll get better soon.

No. I have something.

I'll take you home, he said. We'll set you up by the fire.

So they did that. Filled the prescriptions, drove home, all the ruts and bumps, Irene in agony, and Gary brought blankets out to the couch by the fireplace, laid Irene down, built a good fire.

A stone fireplace, a good home, her husband making her comfortable. Maybe this awful pain will turn out to be a good thing, Irene thought. Maybe it will bring us closer together. Maybe Gary will remember me. A strange time in life, her children gone, her work taken away, only Gary left, and not the Gary she began with. She didn't like retirement. Until only a few months ago, she had danced and sung every day with the children at school. Three- to five-year-olds, learning through play, following their interests from worm gardens to dinosaurs to building trains that could cross to Russia and continue on to Africa. They would come sit on her lap, make themselves at home.

Gary made her tea, and she sipped at it, held the hot mug in her hands. She had taken the new medications in the truck on the way home, and she was still waiting for an effect.

The pain's not going away, she told Gary. I don't feel anything from the medications. What painkiller did he give me?

Gary opened the bag from the pharmacy. Looks like Amoxicillin for antibiotic, some decongestant I can't pronounce, and Aleve for painkiller.

Aleve?

Yeah.

That little shit. Aleve is just Advil. Call Rhoda. I need more Vicodin.

Irene. You should take what he prescribed. He said nothing showed up on the X ray.

The X ray is wrong.

How can an X ray be wrong?

I don't know. It just is.

Rhoda stayed at work late, until Dr. Turin and everyone else had left. Just finishing up some paperwork, she'd told them. In the cabinet of prescription samples, she took the rest of the Vicodin, which had been sent mistakenly. Only a week's supply, and they would never be getting more. She would need something else.

She found Tramadol, another painkiller, and looked it up online. It seemed to be okay for humans. She could lose her job for this, maybe even face some sort of criminal charges. Frank should have prescribed something. She could ask Jim for a prescription, but she didn't want to put any pressure on things with Jim.

Driving to her parents' house, she thought about her wedding.

Jim hadn't proposed yet, but they had talked about it, indirectly. She wanted the wedding in Hawaii, and he had agreed to this, basically. She didn't want cold, or mosquitoes, or any sign of salmon. No moose antlers in the next room, no hip waders. She wanted Kauai, either Waimea Canyon or Hanalei Bay. A ceremony on the beach, or overlooking the ocean or the canyon, something beautiful. Coconut palms, big bowls of fresh fruit, guava nectar, macadamia nuts. Some old plantation house, maybe, white with a covered porch, all the curlicues of wood and banisters. Bird-of-paradise on the tables, long slim stems and multicolored ruffles. Maybe some actual birds, too, parrots or something.

And maybe I'll wear an eyepatch, Rhoda said aloud and grinned. Poor Jim. You have no idea what you're in for.

She turned off toward the lake, rattling and bouncing now on the crap road. What she wanted, really, was something classy. She didn't want anything cheap. She wanted dignified, and this would be tough, given her family. Mark would be high, no doubt, and her dad would want to take off his tuxedo at the first opportunity. Her mom would be all right. She tried to see the place, but all she had were parts of weddings floating around unconnected. Maybe she and Jim would have to take a scouting trip to Hawaii. She needed to see the actual places.

When she pulled up, her father was gardening, working on the flowerpots.

Howdy, Dad.

Hey, Rhoda. Have the painkillers? He got up off his knees, brushed his jeans.

I could get busted for this. We have to get her a prescription.

Yeah, he said. I think another day or two and it'll blow over. There's nothing wrong, really, just a cold.

Hm, Rhoda said, and walked into the house. Her mother was on the couch in front of the fireplace, a blanket over her.

I feel like hell, Irene said.

I have about two weeks of painkillers, Rhoda said. Vicodin and Tramadol, which is what we use for big dogs. It should work about the same. Maybe take two if one isn't enough. But you can't tell anyone where you got these. Rhoda filled a glass of water and gave it to her mother along with a Vicodin.

Thank you, sweetie. Help me back to the bedroom. I need to sleep.

Okay, Rhoda said, but can't you walk?

I feel a little dizzy. Just help me out. Why does everyone have to question it?

Sorry, Mom.

They walked to the bedroom and her mother lay down under the covers, didn't say anything more.

Rhoda did some dishes and then went outside to talk with her father. What's wrong with her? she asked.

Just punishing me, he said. For making us go out in the rain. Which I probably shouldn't have done. But still, she'll draw out this cold as long as she can to let me know how she feels.

Dad, Rhoda said.

It's true. That's what's happening. It's my fault, but that doesn't mean I have to like it.

I don't think she'd do that, Dad.

Well, you don't know her the way I do. You have a different relationship. And that's good.

I think something's really wrong. I don't think she's making it up.

Whatever. I need to get back to the flowers here, and tomorrow I need to get back to work on the cabin. Your mother is supposed to be helping me with that.

I have work tomorrow, or I'd help.

Thanks, he said, tight-lipped, meaning the conversation was

over. He'd always been like this, all Rhoda's life. Any real conversation closed off. Any moment when she might actually see who he was, he disappeared.

Mark returned from another long day of fishing to find his sister sitting with Karen at the kitchen table.

How did you do? Karen asked.

We're freed from poverty another few days, Mark said. Enough grublings out there to keep us off the street.

I made fiddleheads, Karen said.

Oh, cool. Mark went to the counter to grab some, little green spirals marinated in balsamic and olive oil. I love these.

Howdy, Mark, Rhoda said.

Hello my sister. How goes the chase for wealth and happiness?

Thanks, Mark.

He circled behind her and then lunged forward quickly to put his fishy hands over her face.

Rhoda yelled and pushed back into him, fell backward onto the floor as he hopped out of the way. Nice, Mark, she said. You've really changed.

No need for change, he said, when you got something good. Karen laughed. Mark swooped over for a kiss and a quick grab.

Rhoda picked up her chair and sat again. I hate to interrupt the love fest, and I'm sure you're both fine with just doing it on the floor right in front of me, but I actually came here for a reason.

Speak your pain, Sister Rhoda, Mark said, and Karen giggled.

Rhoda ignored this. Mom is in a lot of pain, and Dad doesn't believe there's anything wrong, because the X ray didn't show anything.

Hm, Mark said.

What I'm asking is that you go by a few times a day and check on Mom. You live practically next door. I'm forty minutes away.

I'd love to, but I'm working. Out again tomorrow and the next day. And Karen's working, too.

Okay, Rhoda said. Forget it, then.

I want to help, but I have to work.

Okay, okay, Rhoda said. I understand. You've been an unreliable fuck all your life.

Feel the love, Mark said.

Wanna get high? Karen asked.

Jim canceled his appointments for the day, which pissed off his secretary and the hygienist. Then he tore over to the King Salmon Hotel. Coming in on two wheels, he said to himself. I'm a man on a mission, a boy with a gun. He tried to sing the old Devo song, couldn't quite remember the tune.

This got him thinking of another Devo song: little girl with the four red lips, never knew it could be like this, I'm going under, I'm going under. He was grinning now. Please fuck me today, Monique. Please, please, please.

He slid the Suburban to a fast stop in the gravel, hopped out, and practically ran to her door.

There was kind of a long pause before she answered his knock. But she was dressed and looked ready to go. Wearing a man's shirt. Dark green plaid, untucked, top buttons undone. Jeans.

Wow, he said.

Hey, she said, and stepped forward to clear the door, so he

had to step back. No invite in, no kiss. She locked the door, then turned around to face him. What are we doing today?

Um, he said. Whatever you want.

How about a helicopter ride? I'd like to see this place.

Okay, he said, and they got in the Suburban and drove toward where he had seen a few helicopters. This turned out to be an abandoned gravel lot. So he called information for helicopter tours, found something, and they drove past strip malls and pickups, boats on trailers by the side of the road.

Alaska is a dump, Monique said. But I like it.

We should go out on the water, Jim said. Go fishing. You might like that.

Maybe, Monique said. Helicopter first. Get my bearings, Roger.

Jim was feeling used, and a little pissed off, but he tried to keep the mood light. They'd fly around for a while, and then they'd go back to the hotel and fuck or he'd quit the whole stupid thing.

Whoa, Monique said. You just passed it, cowboy. I saw helicopters.

Sorry, Jim said, and found a place to turn around. He was getting distracted, thinking maybe Rhoda wasn't such a bad deal. She was nice to him, and that had to count for something.

Jim paid half his left nut at the office, because Monique didn't want the quick tour. She wanted the full five-hour tour with glaciers, Prince William Sound, a lunch stop in Seward, on to Homer, the entire peninsula. They climbed into a sleek black helicopter and donned helmets.

Monique leaned close and grabbed his arm. Thanks, Jim, she said in the headset. This is going to be fun. And as the motor whirred up, he felt his spirits rising, too. Maybe this would work out.

The pilot eased them into the air and started saying dumb

things about Alaska. We're almost the size of the Alaska State Bird, and do you know what that is, folks?

The mosquito, Jim said in an unenthusiastic voice.

The pilot paused a minute, thrown off. That's right, he said. Are you from here?

Yeah.

Okay. I'll just point out a few of the sights when we get out farther. Enjoy the ride, folks. Let me know if you have any questions.

They rose up quick and banked off to the east. Forest and then Skilak Lake, which the pilot announced. Jim peered out the window and tried to find Rhoda's parents' house, or Mark's house, but they were buried somewhere in the trees. The lake a deep jade green today in sunlight, ripples on the surface visible even from high up. A river zigging northeast from the head of the lake.

Beginning of Skilak Glacier, folks, the pilot said. This feeds into Skilak Lake. We'll follow it up into the mountains.

The pilot skimmed lower over the ice, the helicopter a tiny thing in a vast expanse of white, the glacier a wide chute with steep rock on both sides.

Wow, Monique said.

The glacier a thing of pressure, crevassed and bent. It looked alive to Jim, and he wondered why he'd never come up in a helicopter before. This was gorgeous. Rhoda should see this, too. She'd grown up basically at the foot of the glacier, but it was around the corner a bit, not quite visible from the lake, and even if she'd seen it on hikes, he was sure she hadn't seen it like this.

I want to land on it, Monique said.

The pilot had a headset, too, but he didn't respond.

Is that okay? Jim asked. Can we land on it?

Well, the pilot said. Yeah. I guess we could. You'll have to stay close, though. No wandering off.

That's fine, Jim said.

The pilot continued toward the head of the glacier, then slowed his airspeed, came in lower, looked around for a safe spot. The crevasses up close were much bigger than Jim had imagined. Everything immense, the distances farther, the rock walls higher. And no sign of other humans.

They came down slowly onto a smooth area of snow, away from any crevasse. Snow whipped up in a cloud around them, the rails touched down in a jolt, and the pilot eased off on the rotors, finally cut the engine. The air cleared again. Bright sunshine.

Monique was the first to step out. She had always wanted to walk on a glacier. A brand-new world, she said over her shoulder. She could hear Jim hop down behind her. She would have preferred the moment alone.

Pretty amazing, Jim said.

So quiet, she said. Let's not talk. Let's just experience this.

Okay, he said.

Monique set off toward a crevasse, a ridge of blue light. It was like a beacon, translucent. Most were hollows, cuts, but this one had been raised up under pressure, and as she walked toward it, she realized the distances here were deceiving. Much farther away and larger than she had thought.

I love this, she said. An expanding universe, right here.

I thought we weren't talking, Jim said.

That rule's only for you. So you don't spoil my moment.

She walked on, her boots sinking through the soft top layer of snow and hitting hard ice. She knew there could be falls here, covered, invisible crevasses, but it all felt so safe anyway. She sat down backward into the snow, did a snow angel, looked up into the bright blue. This rocks, she said.

Hm, Jim said.

Poor Jim. You can talk now.

That's all right, he said. It's a nice spot. I can't believe I've never come out here before.

Mm, Monique said. I love this. She closed her eyes and felt the cold seeping in through her jeans and even through her jacket. Refreshing and clear. I could almost take a nap, she said.

But after a few more minutes, her head was getting cold, so she got up and they walked back to the helicopter.

They buckled in, put on their headsets. Take us to the heavens, sir, Monique told the pilot.

Aye-aye, ma'am, he said, and the rotors whirred up and they rose into an even greater expanse of white, the Harding Icefield, extending maybe a hundred miles. Cushiony, pillowy, with dark peaks protruding. They crossed the range and could see ocean extending outward before them.

Gulf of Alaska, the pilot said. We'll be passing over Mount Marathon up ahead, dropping down over Seward. Resurrection Bay. We'll continue on to Prince William Sound and come back this way to Seward for lunch, if that works for you folks.

Sounds great, Jim said. Thanks.

They dropped below the snow line, green mountains falling into Resurrection Bay. A deep, deep blue. Monique kept looking out her side window, but she also put her hand on Jim's leg and moved it up to his crotch. Not much at first, but then she could feel him getting hard. She rubbed lightly, and could feel he was getting bunched up, bent over in a U shape in his underwear. This was kind of funny, so she kept her hand on it, helped keep it in that shape. She could feel him shifting around, uncomfortable. Then she laughed.

Sorry, she said. He looked a bit hurt, but she couldn't stop laughing. Sorry about that. And she pulled him closer for a kiss, but it was impossible with the helmets. She couldn't reach his lips, and this made her laugh harder. Sorry, she said. Later, I promise. Then she looked out her side window again.

They skimmed low over the coast now, waves crashing white against black rock, evergreen forest grown thick down to the edge. A few wide gray pebbly beaches, driftwood. Spectacular, all of it. And no houses along the shore. This was what most amazed Monique, coming from D.C. It really was a frontier.

I don't want to go back to Soldotna, Monique said. I want to stay out here. Let's get a hotel in Seward, something with a hot tub.

Jim wasn't sure what to make of this. He looked over at Monique, but she was gazing out her side window, turned away from him. He didn't know how he'd explain to Rhoda, but maybe he could say he had to take a trip to meet that potential partner for the practice. That would probably work. And a hotel, the two of them, spending the night, didn't sound bad. Monique might still just yank him around, but there was a chance.

Is that all right? he asked the pilot, finally. Could we stop in Seward and get picked up tomorrow?

Yeah, I don't see why not, the pilot said. There'll be an extra fee, of course.

Gary worked alone through the morning, loading more logs. For a small cabin, it seemed like a hell of a lot of wood. But he had done the math himself.

Underway, finally, crossing the lake on a sunny afternoon, light breeze, perfect weather. Bits of spray from hitting the small waves head-on. He stood at the stern, the throttle arm up, and he liked being here, liked doing this. The air crisp and clear.

As the island came close, he swerved in an arc and drove toward shore. Fell forward onto the logs when the boat hit submerged rocks but caught himself with his hands.

He turned off the engine, climbed forward, and began unloading from over the gate, dragging one log at a time, sloshing through the water. It was not difficult, the work a pleasure.

Gary had always liked physical work, building something, a contrast to the academic life. He liked Vonnegut's idea—really Max Frisch's idea—that we should be called *Homo faber* rather than *Homo sapiens*. We live to build. It's what defines us. This was true, he thought. Imagining something, turning it around in your head, walking through it over and over in dreams, then making it happen in the real world. Nothing more satisfying than that.

Gary dragged the logs ashore until all were lying in rows and small stacks. He tromped through low thickets to the building site, carrying a shovel. He was keeping this simple. He'd just clear some ground here in a rectangle, even it out, and bury the first logs partway into the dirt. No other foundation, because it wasn't necessary. The point was to build a cabin the way it used to be done. No cement pad, no permits. The cabin itself an expression of a man, a form of his own mind.

He looked at the lake, checking the view, checking perspective, shifting a few feet this way and that to make sure he had it right, then he dove the shovel into what would be the center. Breaking ground, he said. Finally. After about thirty years. How the hell does that happen?

Then he walked three paces to the side, made another mark, and walked three paces to the other side. A cabin six paces wide, and he'd make it four paces deep. No measuring tape. Just walk it out. With the sides marked, he made corners.

Okay, he said, standing in the middle again. His left shoulder ached, bursitis from years ago that acted up whenever he worked. He hiked over to a spruce tree and braced his hand against that to give his shoulder a good stretch. Then he stretched the other arm and shoulder, and stretched his legs a bit, too. He was starting this project so late in the season, he didn't have time for injuries. All had to go smoothly. It was mid-August already. He had meant to start in late May.

He hiked back to the cabin site and cleared all the dead wood, throwing branches and also a few stones. Then he dug in with the shovel. Dark earth, rich and airy, but so many runners and roots he could never get a shovelful. A rake might have been more helpful. Something to rip all this stuff out. He had good gloves, so he kneeled down and raked with his fingers, pulled and yanked and found all of it far more resilient than expected. Tough little buggers, he said.

He stood and tried the shovel again, used it to chop. That seemed to work. So he chopped along the outside of his cabin, the entire boundary, the mosquitoes hounding him now, all over his face and neck, slowing the work with all the swatting he had to do.

He dropped to his knees and pulled at the growth he had chopped free, but some of it was still anchored, so he was chopping and digging again with the shovel, the entire area a thick mat of growth, really, and he began to wonder whether he should have just used this as the floor and built on top. Why was dirt better? This entire area was going to become a mud pit when it rained.

Gary lay back in the dirt and closed his eyes. The smell of the earth, wood rot, skunk cabbage. Buzzing of mosquitoes in his ears. He was wearing repellent, but they were undeterred as usual. He opened his eyes, and the sky was spinning. His pulse going in his temples, his head feeling a little dizzy.

Thirty years ago, this place had been new. And he'd been younger, the dream still fresh, still reachable. The air clearer, mountains cut more sharply against the sky, the forest more alive. Something like that. Some animated sense of the world that dissipates over time. We're given a gift but it's a fragile one, impermanent. Now this place was closer to an idea, hollowed out, lacking substance. Reduced to mosquitoes and a tired old body and ordinary air. He was supposed to live out here, but he was supposed to have done it back then.

Irene thought he was just being bitter, some character flaw. She couldn't see the shape of the world, the shape of a life. She didn't understand the enormous differences. He should have gone for someone smarter, but instead he went for someone safe. And his life made smaller because of that.

But he needed to focus. I need to think this out, he said aloud, and he tried to think clearly. He was making a mud pit. The logs set into it would form dams, a kind of pool for gathering water. He was making a cistern, not a cabin. But then his thoughts were wandering to his lunch, to Irene and her headache, to Rhoda and whether she or Mark might ever come out here to help. Meandering, slipping, unable to focus. A once-clear mind reduced.

Okay, he said. A platform, I need a platform. And he could see this was true. A wooden platform, a floor, raised up about six inches off the ground, leveled out. Then he'd build his walls around this.

So he stood up and decided to go for a hike. It was too late today to get materials for the platform, so he might as well explore the island a little.

He tromped up to the birch trees at the back of his property and continued on until he found a path. Much easier to follow this, a game trail, the ground more level. Birch and spruce all through here, no view of the water, and he came upon an empty cabin. A log cabin, like what he had imagined, their logs much bigger than his, about a foot thick. He wondered where they had found those. He came up close to examine, tried to figure out how they got the logs to fit so well. Something in the gaps, but he couldn't tell what it was. Covered in moss now and cobwebs. He peered in a small window and could see a white basin, a dark wood-burning stove. He walked around back, a big cabin, two other rooms, and peered in more windows, tried to see the floor. Looked like boards. Then he knelt down all around the edges, tried to find a clue for how the walls met the floor, but there were no gaps in the walls, nothing to see.

Well, he said, and stood back up. This will be good for a reference. And he wondered why anyone would build here. No water view, just an outpost in the trees. No wonder it was empty. He could do better than this.

Irene waited alone all day, lying in bed, looking at the boards of the ceiling. Her husband out on that island, her children working, the Vicodin making her nauseated and weak, clammy. The room too bright in the sun, but she didn't have the energy to get up and close the curtains. No one cared what happened to her here. She might as well die.

Self-pity, she said aloud. Not a pretty thing. And this felt too close to the years after her mother was gone, after her father was gone. Moving from one distant family member to the next, shuffled around in Canada and then California, unwanted, too often alone.

She popped another Vicodin, the pain mounting to a breaking point again, and she didn't feel anything at first, but after fifteen or twenty minutes, she could feel the cold, prickly slide into nausea and oblivion, a welcome relief. Her head went away, or her awareness of it, and she was left pooling in the rest of her body. She'd gone heavy, sinking deep into the mattress.

Almost like diving when she closed her eyes, the surface far away above. An ocean with a heartbeat, slow waves of pressure, water compacting but no edge to it. No contact with the surface. The world of air a world of myth only, storms and lightning and sun. The only reality the density of the water, the coolness of it, the pressure and weight of it.

Irene awoke hours later. The pain returned, sharp and jagged, slicing through her head.

Gary, she called out, and this time she heard a response. A rustling in the kitchen, and he opened the bedroom door.

How are you feeling? he asked.

I need another Vicodin. I'm really scared. The pain is something else.

I think you should wait a while if you can. You're not supposed to have more than four of those per day, according to Rhoda. And the doctor didn't think you needed them.

The pain is too much, Gary.

Maybe some hot food. Maybe some food and water and that will help a bit. What would you like?

Irene couldn't breathe. She turned on her side, and that only made the pain and breathing worse. I can try, she said. I just want this to end.

I've been thawing out some venison. I'll cook that up with mashed potatoes. You need to eat more.

Okay, she said, closing her eyes again, and heard him close the door. She tried to breathe away the pain, let it go away on each exhale. Tried not to panic for air. But her ears were ringing, a high buzz, the frequency of the pain, and it would not be ignored. She could think of nothing else. She took another Vicodin. It didn't matter what Gary or anyone else thought.

The wait for relief was longer than before, fifteen minutes an extraordinary length of time, and then she faded away for some easier length and Gary opened the door again.

Ready, he said. How you doing?

I had to take another pill.

Irene.

You don't know. You have no idea what this is like. If someone had told me, I wouldn't have believed them.

Well I have dinner ready.

Irene sat up slowly at the edge of the bed, feeling dizzy. My slippers and robe. Can you help me with those?

Do you really need help?

Yes I do.

Okay. He helped her and they were sitting soon enough at the table, a fire going. Breaded venison steaks, from a kill last fall in Kodiak. High up on the flank of a mountain, and her arrow had punctured both lungs. Irene hunched over her food, cut a small piece of meat, and it tasted delicious. She was starving. But she also felt on the verge of throwing up. The meal would be an odd walk of that line.

Thanks, Gary, she said.

I'm sorry, he said. I'm really sorry for taking us out in that storm. And I'll do whatever I can to help you get better. But I'm worried about the painkillers. You could get hooked on those. You may already be hooked.

That's not what I'm worried about. What I'm worried about is that the painkillers may not be enough. Even now, they're not cutting all the way through the pain. And what if that gets worse? What do I do then?

I think you're panicking.

Damn right.

* * *

Jim and Monique checked into a suite in the nicest hotel in Seward. Fake carved ivory on side tables, bad watercolors of fishing boats. A giant and inviting bed, though, which was where Jim's gaze went. Jacuzzi tub, also, big enough for two.

Let's have lunch, Monique said. And then a boat tour.

Okay, Jim said, trying to keep the sadness and longing out of his voice. They were out the door and walking along the wharf.

Other tourists here today also, the sidewalks full. An Alaskan ferry had pulled up. So Jim waited in line at one of the tour companies while Monique went into the shops. A nice day, and Monique, gorgeous and long and thin, was turning every head, and Jim thought he should have felt happy. But he felt used, pissed off, and guilty. Get over it, he mumbled to himself. You're in this far already. He certainly didn't want to miss the payoff.

He had never taken Rhoda on a vacation like this, even for a day or two. They hadn't gone anywhere.

Jim made it to the front of the line, finally, two tickets for a three-hour tour of Resurrection Bay and Kenai Fjords National Park. A three-hour tour, he sang quietly, from the *Gilligan's Island* theme, but the woman had heard this about a million times, so no response.

Jim found Monique marveling at black velvet posters of bears and bald eagles. These are amazing, she said. This has to be as low as art goes. I have to have one.

Okay, Jim said, and bought a four-foot velvet poster of a brown bear catching a salmon.

This is a cultural archive you're preserving, Monique said. Nothing less. She took his arm, laughing at Alaska and tourists, and they walked toward lunch.

Just the touch of her on his arm got Jim hard. He realized he wanted her more than he had ever wanted anyone else. Even high school and junior high crushes hadn't felt this urgent, and he was forty-one. He hadn't thought he was capable of feeling this anymore. Sex with Rhoda every few days was as much as he could usually muster. He wondered again at Monique's age. He was guessing early twenties, but he didn't know. She seemed a lot younger than Rhoda, who was thirty.

They found a table on the wharf, ordered oysters and halibut and champagne. Jim didn't eat oysters usually, because of the stomach sacks. He tried not to eat anything with a stomach sack. But Monique made him try one, and really it wasn't so bad. He tasted the butter, mostly, and the Tabasco burned his lips. He didn't chew much. More of a swallow.

Delight me with tales of Alaska, Monique said. Maybe start with your closest call with a bear.

What about you? Jim asked. I know almost nothing about you.

I'm boring, Monique said. D.C., impressive parents, good schools, no vision or sense of purpose.

How old are you? he asked.

Old enough, she said, and if you want to fuck me, you have to quit asking that question.

Sorry, he said.

Now tell me about the bear.

It was on a river. The same river where I caught my first king salmon, when I was about ten or maybe even younger. I just remember that the fish was taller than me. I was forty-eight inches, and the fish was forty-nine and a half. I played that thing for almost an hour, getting pulled down the river, trying to stay in the shallower water along the bank. I was wearing hip waders, afraid of going under, but my dad was holding on to me.

Ah, Monique said. I bet you were a cute little boy.

Blond hair, blue eyes, full of charm, Jim said.

Monique smiled.

So it was on this same river years later, Jim said. I was in my early twenties, going back for nostalgia, fishing the same spot, but I was by myself, which is a no-no, and it was late in the season, when the bears are a bit more desperate, and when I caught a salmon, I gutted it and then hung it off my backpack as I kept fishing.

No, Monique said.

Yeah, I had it hanging there on my back, about three feet of shiny, smelly, gutted salmon, swinging around on my back while I fished. I was like a lure for bears.

Monique was shaking her head.

So I heard something behind me, heavy splashing, and I turn to see this huge brown bear. A grizzly. The kind that eat people. Crashing through the water at me, and then it stopped. And I realized the salmon was on my back hidden from the bear now, like I was trying to keep food away from it.

What did you do?

I'll tell you the rest later, Jim said.

Monique punched his arm. She had good reach from across the table. Fucker, she said quietly, so no one would hear.

In Alaska, you have to earn your stories, he said and grinned.

We'll see about that.

We have an hour before the cruise, he said, checking his watch.

Let's go shopping. I'd like a pair of heels, and maybe a tie. She had a wicked smile when she said this, and Jim thought he might faint.

He paid and they left, walked along the waterfront looking for a shop, and Monique found a pair of black pumps she was happy with. You like? she asked.

Sure, he said. Kind of sexy with jeans. Unexpected.

I won't be wearing them with jeans.

Then it was time to look for a tie. They had only twenty minutes until the cruise, but they found a place that had ties with salmon and halibut and king crab and fishing boats and also a few more conservative ties. Monique went for a simple dark blue silk.

We'll have to run for the cruise, Jim said.

Do they have a cruise later today? Monique asked.

So they rebooked for four o'clock, which gave them two hours. Walking back to the room, Monique took Jim's hand. They didn't say anything. Jim afraid to speak, afraid he'd somehow ruin this.

Take a quick shower first, Monique said, so Jim did as he was told. When he emerged in a towel, she looked him over. You have a muffin top, she said.

A muffin top?

Just the beginnings of one. She smiled. Don't feel hurt.

But what's a muffin top?

That little pouch on your belly, for hanging over your belt. It comes down at that weird angle.

Hm, he said.

It's all right, she said. I've never been with a muffin top, but I'll adjust.

Then Monique went into the shower, and Jim lay back on the bed feeling old and disgusting. A muffin top. If you had any self-respect at all, he told himself out loud, you'd walk out of here right now. He opened his towel, and his limp little penis lying there just seemed like another target for mockery. She was going to tease him and laugh at him. That was all.

Jim groaned and decided to get under the covers. He'd hide himself. He threw the towel over a chair and settled in, used both of the pillows.

Monique turned the water off, and there was a long wait. Jim thinking of Rhoda, feeling guilty, because here he was, about to cheat. It was inevitable now. Everything until this moment could be passed off, perhaps, but not after this moment.

And then Monique appeared, walking toward him slowly in her tie and heels, nothing else.

She was very tall, especially in the heels, and she had that slim definition only youth can have, the soft lines of her ribs and collar bone, belly and thighs. Her hair still wet, her face angular.

I shaved for you, she said.

She was entirely smooth. She came to the side of the bed, turned around slowly, bent over in her heels, her tie hanging down, her young breasts, and looked at him from between her legs.

No more teasing, she said. Now you can have whatever you want.

Mark invited Carl on the boat. This was out of pity, since Carl was moping around without Monique. She had taken off somewhere.

So Carl, plastic bag of bagels and veggie-burger patties in hand, shivering in his raingear, waited at 3:30 a.m. under a dull yellow light at the end of the Pacific Salmon Fisheries pier. He looked at boats anchored in pairs in the channel of the Kenai River. The boats and water were twenty feet below him, the river lined by mud banks. He was supposed to get to Mark's boat and climb aboard. Mark and the owner had come the evening before and slept out there. But Mark had omitted the part about how Carl would get to the boat or even find the right one. The boat was the *Slippery Jay*, but Carl didn't know where it was parked.

So he stood under the pier light another twenty minutes until some of the boats in the channel switched on their cabin lights and several started their diesel engines and idled. An aluminum skiff, some kind of tender for unloading salmon, it looked like, since it carried three large aluminum bins, came from upriver.

About twenty feet long, with a huge outboard, 200 horsepower, it really ripped along, leaving a wake that glowed white and slapped at the sides of the anchored boats and set them rocking. The sky just beginning to lighten at the horizon under drizzling clouds, and Carl clueless what he should do. He couldn't just jump in and swim around. He was going to be left behind. He would spend his day here on the pier in the drizzle and eat his veggie burgers around noon, then walk or hitchhike back to the campsite.

Then a young Indian-American woman, as in parents from India, wearing fish boots and dark green rain gear, tromped past and went over the side of the pier down a long narrow ladder toward the skiffs bobbing below.

Excuse me, Carl said when she was about ten feet down.

No answer, so he said it again, louder this time, and cleared his throat.

Yes? she asked, looking up.

I'm supposed to get out to the *Slippery Jay* somehow. Do you know where it is or how I can get there?

That's one of our boats, she said. I can take you.

She smiled as she said this, smiled only briefly, but Carl was encouraged and thinking Monique was not such a great find anyway. She was a bit inconsiderate, was the truth.

Carl was grinning, therefore, as he stepped into the skiff. And he made a comic little fuss about getting his last foot over the gunwale. Thanks, he said heartily, standing up straight before her.

Hold on, she said. She fired up the outboard, gunned it, and they shot into the river. Carl, seated just in time, nearly fell into the bottom of the boat, but she remained standing.

Wow, he said, but even he could hardly hear this amid the roar. The young woman kept her eyes ahead on the water. She made a tight turn upriver, zigzagged between several boats, and came to rest suddenly, the motor cut to neutral, inches from the *Slippery Jay*.

Carl climbed out awkwardly, having to straddle the side of the taller boat and getting rocked in opposite directions. But he did make it without falling in or dropping his lunch.

Thanks, he said.

Sure, she said, then gunned it and was gone.

Why was he here? He stood on the back deck and looked vaguely at the horizon. The question seemed larger somehow than just this boat or this sunrise or Monique or even Alaska. Something about his life, something impossible and dimly urgent, but this effect was probably only from lack of sleep.

Carl yawned hugely at the horizon, then turned around and crept into the cabin area. He put his lunch on the bench in the upper cockpit or steering area or whatever they called it. Bridge? But on a boat this small? Down a few steps was a cooking and eating area, with a small table, some cubbyhole shelves, and an old iron stove with metal rails. In front of this, through another small door, was the sleeping area. He could hear breathing in there.

So Carl sat at the galley table next to his lunch, his booted feet dangling, looked through scratched Plexiglas windows at the sky turning lighter blue then yellowish white, and waited until a watch alarm went off.

Mark said a gruff hello, then Carl said hello also to Dora, the owner, who waved her hand and fixed coffee and had a doughnut. The doughnuts looked suddenly very good to Carl, and he wondered whether he'd get through the day without sneaking one on the side. Other people's food had always looked better to him than his own.

Soon they were under way, churning out through the channel.

Mud flats and eroding cliff banks. The air through here cool and the low clouds in the distance turning orange at their edges.

Carl rode on the upper deck, above the cabin. A steering wheel and controls up here, too. Dora shared the bench seat with Carl and drove in a resigned and preoccupied way that didn't invite conversation. She called down occasionally to Mark through a hole in the floor and asked for the depth.

Once they cleared the channel and made the inlet, they turned southwest toward open ocean, and several aluminum boats, drift-netters with one large net reel on the back, sped past. Their engines powerful, throaty over the sound of the *Slippery Jay*. One swooped in close, the pilot waved, Dora waved back, and then it shot ahead.

Gasoline, Dora said. They can do over twenty knots. But if one of their sniffers goes, they blow up.

Sniffers? Carl asked.

Sensors for the buildup of gas fumes in their engine housing. They can pump that air out before they start, flush it with fresh air, but still, if any fumes remain, the whole boat turns into a grenade.

And we have diesel? Carl was only trying to continue the conversation, trying to learn more, but he realized this question sounded pretty obvious and dumb.

Yep. That's about what we have.

Carl nodded. An entire fleet of drift-netters all around them, at least fifty boats he could see heading mostly in a similar direction but some going north into other parts of the inlet.

How many boats are out here? he asked.

On the Cook Inlet? Almost six hundred, probably, and most of them are out today. Have you steered a boat before?

Little outboards, canoes and stuff.

Well take the wheel, Dora said, getting up. See this compass?

Keep us going between this mark and this mark, she said, pointing. The steering's a little slow, so don't overcompensate. I'm going down for a while.

Okay, Carl said. Thanks.

So Dora went below and Carl watched the compass and the horizon. He never went straight exactly. He'd drift a little too far one way, turn the wheel and drift too far the other way, then overcorrect again. Turning constantly. The waves only slow, small rolls, the surface smooth, and the only wind of their own creation, and he was high up, with good visibility, the bow below him, so it should have been easy, but there was some kind of current, it seemed, underneath. It did feel like a river, the entire inlet. He tried to watch for logs, also, figuring he was not supposed to run over those.

How you doing up there? Mark called after a while through the hole.

Fine, Carl said.

Good. Just let it have a little play. Then Carl was on his own again, for a long time. He wondered whether he was still going the right direction, and he wondered whether the two of them were taking naps. There didn't seem to be anything else to do. They could be playing cards.

Almost two hours passed before Mark appeared wearing the bottom half of his rain gear, held up by suspenders. The gear dark green, same as the woman's had been, and he was wearing the same dark rubber fish boots.

Mark pointed off to the right and slightly ahead. Pukers, he said.

What? Carl asked.

Pukers. Sport fishermen. The cabin cruiser drifting up there, though they probably think they've stopped. Going for halibut.

Nice name, Carl said. Does everyone call them that? If I lived here, and I went out sport fishing, would I be a puker?

Mark grinned. Do you cook?

Sure.

Mind fixing breakfast?

So as they reached the fishing grounds, finally, Carl was down in the kitchen cracking eggs. They stopped for some reason, started up and stopped again, then called back and forth, and Carl caught a glimpse of Mark on the back deck letting out the net. The boat rocked tremendously from side to side, far more than the low waves seemed to warrant, so Carl couldn't afford more than a glimpse.

Mark had wanted all twelve eggs scrambled, and the only bowl was small. As Carl braced himself against one of the counters and avoided falling onto the stove, he tried to keep the bowl full of eggs level in midair, and he scrambled these eggs when he could with his other hand.

Then he realized he had to fry the bacon first, so he held this bowl and kept it rocking level with one hand while he bent down to get the bacon out of the small fridge.

Carl ripped the package open with his teeth then flopped it down onto the counter, where it slid back and forth as he went for a pan. The boat rocked suddenly much harder, and he banged his head against a cabinet. Some of the scrambled egg sloshed over yellow and goopy onto his jeans, where it oozed slowly downward and sank in.

Very nice, Carl said over the roar of the diesel. He held the back of his head with his free hand while he watched the remaining eggs, a little lower now, and kept them rocking.

When Carl had finally gotten a pan on the stovetop, the burner lit, and a few pieces of bacon in the pan, Mark ducked his head into the cabin and yelled, Get up here. I need you to throw fish. Then he was gone.

Carl stood rocking in place for a moment, trying to figure out what to do. Then he dumped the eggs into the pan with the raw bacon, turned off the gas, and hauled out onto the deck.

Jesus, he said. There were salmon everywhere, all over the deck and a few even getting wrapped up with the net in the reel.

Get over here! Mark yelled. He was between the reel and the stern, picking the salmon. This didn't look easy. As the net came up over the edge, he untangled a salmon until it hung only by its gills, then yanked down hard until it fell out and hit the deck. Salmon all around his feet, silvery and gasping, flopping and sliding in their own froth of slime, blood, and sea water.

Throw these into the side bins! Mark yelled. The engine and the hydraulic reel combined made a lot of noise.

So Carl grabbed fish and threw. But he kept dropping or threw too low, the salmon thudding against the side of the bins and sliding back, and then he slipped and fell onto them.

Mark grabbed him by his collar and yanked him to his feet. Grab 'em by the gills! he yelled. And get out of my way!

Carl moved a few steps and scooped by the gills, which was easier unless they were clamped closed. But most were gasping, their dark red gills exposed and crenellated like seaweed. Their backs darker, greenish blue, like the ocean itself, then silver on their sides becoming white on their bellies. Their eyes large and roving, bewildered-looking. Carl threw as fast as he could. They were cutting his fingers, something sharp in there.

Irene and Gary loaded sheets of treated plywood into the boat. First time she'd been outside since the storm, except going to the doctor's office. Overcast today, cold with a bit of wind.

You're the storm bringer, Gary said. Darkest day we've had in the last week. It's been calm and sunny.

If I were bringing the storms, they'd be a lot worse, Irene said. All of Soldotna wiped off the map.

Yikes, Gary said as he grabbed the bucket of tools and some nails. Save that for the hammer. We need to put all these sheets down today. He was in a good mood, Irene could tell. He had won. She was coming out to help on his idiot project.

They swung the bow plate up, latched it, and were off. Irene bundled in a coat and hat, ducking her head into her collar, turned away from the wind. The wind and cold making her headache worse. She blew her nose, the end of it sore and raw. The antibiotics and decongestant didn't seem to be doing anything. But she was fine, according to the doctor and everyone else. Nothing wrong at all. Just a little cold. She popped two Tramadols when Gary wasn't looking.

They landed almost on the shore, the boat light enough to get in close, grabbed the big sheets of ply and carried them through all the growth. Wind catching the sheets if they went broadside, Irene trying not to fall. Mosquitoes biting her neck and face, her hands not free. She would have expressed a little frustration, but what was the point? She'd only get a lecture from Gary. The tough get going lecture, or the I need help lecture, or, worse, the big lie about this cabin being for both of us lecture. After a while, the cabin might turn into her idea entirely.

Gary had built the frame of a floor. Slim posts pounded into the earth, joists linking, everything braced. Not entirely level or even, but it looked more stable than she had expected.

This looks pretty good, she said. You've been working.

Thanks. I realized the dirt floor wasn't going to cut it. And I was careful to square the corners, so the ply should fit, hopefully.

How do the walls attach?

I don't think they do. Just attached to each other at the corners, and we'll try to make it a snug fit.

Okay, she said.

So they flopped the sheets of ply onto the platform, lined up edges carefully, and nailed into joists. Irene could feel each hammer hit, even with fresh Tramadols. She couldn't breathe, and she was getting tears in her eyes from the pain, but she wiped them away and didn't say anything.

The wind increased, of course, just to say hello and acknowledge her presence. The sun disappeared through thicker cloud cover. But it didn't rain.

Only six sheets of ply, a small platform, twelve feet by sixteen feet, so the nailing didn't take long. They stood back to take a look.

It's really small, Irene said.

Yeah, he said. Nothing wasteful. Just a cabin. Only what we need.

I think we need more. If you want me to live out here, actually live out here, we need space for a bed, a kitchen, a bathroom, and maybe just a little bit of space to walk around. Somewhere to sit.

Sixteen by twelve is actually pretty big, Gary said. I think it's fine as is.

Where does the bathroom go?

We'll use an outhouse.

An outhouse?

They stood there in silence for a while.

What about a fireplace? Irene finally asked. Will there be a fireplace?

That's tough, Gary said. Maybe one of those freestanding ones. We could add that.

Irene could see, in one terrible moment, that they really would live out here. The cabin would not go together right. It would not have what they needed. But they would live in it anyway. She could see that with absolute clarity. And though she wanted to tell Gary to live out here on his own, she knew she couldn't do that, because it was the excuse he was looking for. He'd leave her forever, and it was not okay for her to be left again. That would not happen again in her life.

What about water? she asked.

I'll rig a pump from the lake.

Will we have electricity?

It'll be a hand pump, he said. I'll have to track one down.

I meant for lights.

We'll use lanterns.

And the stove?

Propane. I'll get a little two- or three-burner.

And the roof?

Not sure about the roof yet. Geez, Irene. I've only just started. The floor is working out, isn't it? All the rest will follow. He put his arm around her for a moment, pulled her in closer, a couple tugs of reassurance.

Okay, she said. I think I need to go back. My head really hurts. I need to lie down.

We'll have you back in a jiffy, he said. And then he was prancing around helping her into the boat, gathering the tools, etc. The optimistic time that always came before his failures. And these were the worst for Irene. All the failed business ventures, the boats he had built that had gone over budget and then not sold or not sold well. They had all begun like this, full of hope. And he was smart, well-educated. He should have known better. He should have done better. Their lives should have been better than this.

Gary had seemed so promising. A doctoral student, bright enough to get into Berkeley. He had long hair then, blond and curly. She could pull down on a curl and it would spring back into place. They played guitars, sitting cross-legged, staring into each other's eyes, singing "Brown-Eyed Girl" or "Suzanne." She felt tied to him, felt wanted, felt like she belonged. Gary had a lopsided, goofy smile, and he was always talking about his feelings, and her feelings. So easily reachable, and he promised her he would always be this way.

Alaska was just an idea. A year off from school, a little break so he could get some distance on his dissertation, some needed perspective. They would go to the frontier, soak up the wilderness. She hadn't quite believed they would really go. But Gary was running away. That's what she hadn't understood. He never had any intention of returning to California.

Gary had summer funding, to work on his dissertation, and

they burned through it quickly as they traveled through southeast Alaska, Ketchikan and Juneau, all the smaller towns, Wrangell, St. Petersburg. Looking for the idea of Alaska.

For Gary, this idea was Scandinavian, connecting to his studies, to *Beowulf* and "The Seafarer," a warrior society crossing the whale road into fjords in a new land, founding small inbred fishing villages. Small clusters of steep-roofed wooden houses right on the water that have no name outside themselves. These villages tucked into narrow bays in southeast Alaska between mountains that rose up three and four thousand feet almost right from the water's edge. From a passing ferry, they seemed uninhabited, ghost towns, relics of mining days and frontier trade or even something older. What Gary wanted was the imagined village, the return to an idyllic time when he could have a role, a set task, as blacksmith or baker or singer of a people's stories. That's who he really wanted to be, the "shaper," the singer of a people's history, a place's history, which would be one and the same. What Irene wanted was only to never be alone again, passed around, unwanted.

Gary spent his last money getting to these places, paying for rides on private boats. So excited each time they set out, and Irene was caught up in this excitement, but each new village was a disappointment. One house would have a gas pump down on a pier, and maybe a faded 76 sign in one of the windows. Another would be an engine repair place. Summer cabins and obvious hippie plantations, with stray animals and spare parts hanging around the yard and a sense that underneath one of the moldy mattresses inside, there must be some very large wads of marijuana money. Gary and Irene hippies themselves, minus the drugs, but they were looking for something more, something authentic. Gary wanted to walk into a village and hear an ancient tongue.

One larger group of houses they visited had a barber, who actually had a barber pole. It was holding up one corner of his porch. Gary liked that. It didn't go back a thousand years, but it gave him a sense he might be able to get a bath for five cents, ten cents for clean water. It went back, at least, to mining days, maybe. But all in all, the whole thing was a bitter disappointment to him. The real Alaska didn't seem to exist. No one seemed to have any interest in the kind of honest and difficult frontier life he would have liked to muse on, and none of these places was consistently Scandinavian. None of them evoked the village.

So they burned through all their money by the time they reached the Kenai Peninsula, and Irene had to get a job. In her field, teaching preschool, she could always get a job, and she liked her work. It was supposed to be temporary, but Gary had no intention of ever going back. He wasn't going to finish his dissertation. He wasn't going to make it in his field, and this search for Alaska had all been an expression of despair, the village a sign only that Gary hadn't found a way to fit into his real life.

If Irene had understood any of this in time, she might have left Gary, back when that would have been possible. But it would take her decades to figure out the truth, not only because of the distractions of work and children but also because Gary was such a good liar, always so excited about the next opportunity. This cabin another lie, another attempt at purity, at finding the imagined life he needed because he had run away from who he was.

And now he was running from her, too, but she didn't quite understand why. She could feel it, and anyone else would have called her paranoid, but she knew it was true. As simple as a shift in focus, letting her become slowly invisible. No other woman yet, but there would be. Gary was hitting the limits of how well this life could shield him from his despair, and after he failed at this cabin, a thirty-year dream, he'd have to move on to a more powerful distraction.

As Irene huddled in the bow watching the shoreline approach, she felt her life and Gary's life as suffocation. An awful weight and shortness of breath and panic, and she knew this wasn't just the Tramadol.

Rhoda faced a surly gray Persian named Smokey. Time for your pill, she told him, and he wanted to fight when she grabbed his head, but she was fast and knew how to lock his jaw open. It was over before he could blink. Now we can be friends again, she said.

Jim was not so easy. She dialed him again quick on her cell phone and hit voice mail, snapped the phone shut. Hm, she said.

Jim was in Juneau meeting with his potential new partner for the practice, a dentist named Jacobsen. That was all she knew, which was unusual. Jim tended to ramble on about details, but there were no details here, not even a phone call. Gone all yesterday, no call in the evening, gone today. He'd probably had dinner with Jacobsen, and maybe even stayed over at his house, with his family, though of course she knew nothing about Jacobsen and didn't know whether he had a family.

After work, she drove over to Jim's office and was surprised to see his Suburban in the lot. She knocked on the office door, and a few moments later, he opened it, looking tired.

Hey, he said. He was wearing the same clothes from yesterday, rumpled and a faint smell of sweat.

What happened to you? she asked. No phone call? And she gave him a big hug, happy to see him returned.

Hey, thanks, he said. But yeah, I lost my cell phone. Maybe it fell out of my pocket on the plane. Not sure. But anyway, it's good to see you again.

Well yeah. I was worried. You dropped off the edge of the earth.

Sorry.

You can make it up to me.

Whoa, he said. I'm really tired. Couldn't sleep last night.

Poor Jim, she said. Let's go home. I'll make you dinner.

I have to catch up on things here. Go for a couple days and everything falls apart.

I'll help, she said, so they sat down together and went through all the reschedulings, messages, vendor orders, questions on accounts. All on yellow Post-it notes scattered by his secretary.

She sucks, Rhoda said. This is not a system.

Down, tiger, Jim said.

When they finished, finally, and arrived home, Rhoda made a nice dinner, ling cod wrapped in bacon, a big salad with avocados and tomatoes that were riper than usual. A pleasure to cook, to cook for Jim, here in their home. She took pauses to look up at the vaulted ceiling, all the wood. Had a glass of wine. Felt a little dreamy.

It's ready, she called when she had the plates on the table, but there was no answer, so she went back to the bedroom and found him already asleep. Poor Jim, she said, and turned out the light.

Monique walked from her hotel to the Coffee Bus in the rain. Late morning, the day after returning with Jim, and she couldn't stand any more time on her own. She needed a bit of human company.

The walk was not short, and the rain was not warm. She had a rain jacket with a hood, but her legs, in jeans, were getting cold and wet. The end of summer here felt a lot like winter. No complaining, she told herself. You're the one who wanted to come. Alaska had seemed like an adventure, but really it felt pretty tame. You see a moose a few times and they start to look normal, like cows. The glacier had been cool, though.

She walked past a long strip mall, all single story, then an abandoned lot with an old car and other debris at the edge of a forest. Hicklandia, she said aloud. The ground decorated with bits of rust.

The Coffee Bus sat on an empty corner, a large gravel lot. An old white bus, perhaps a mini schoolbus painted over, and an awning coming out the side, steps leading up to a window. No drive-thru.

Hey Mark, she said once she was under the awning.

Dude, he said. Carl is like beside himself in grief. It's kind of funny you just left him at that campground.

Shouldn't you be out fishing?

Owner decided to take a break for a day or two. Wanted me to polish up the boat in the meantime and be her lackey, but that's not me.

Hey Monique, Karen said.

Monique said hey back.

Come inside and have a coffee.

Monique went around to the back door, climbed in, and sat on a stool. The inside of the bus smelled like a roaster, the air thick and rich.

So where have you been? Karen asked.

Monique told them about Seward, minus Jim, and said she crashed with people she met. She asked about Carl, who was pining away for her, apparently. She hoped they'd offer her a ride out to the campground, but they offered Rhoda.

She comes by just after noon, Mark said. Like clockwork. She'll give you a lift.

Okay, Monique said, and it wasn't long before Rhoda appeared and agreed. It was a long way out to the campsite, but Rhoda didn't seem bothered. I'd be happy to, she said, with a faint nod downward, oddly formal, a motion that could have accompanied a curtsey.

Thank you, Monique said, and walked out to Rhoda's car, something less than a royal carriage. A Datsun, a brand that didn't even exist anymore. Definitely in the pumpkin realm.

To my rescue, Monique said.

No problem, Rhoda said. Tell me about your travels. Have you been here all summer?

We've been everywhere. Up on the ferry, on to Denali and Fairbanks, finishing here on the peninsula. Carl is on a quest to become a man. A big fish will do that for him, apparently.

Rhoda laughed. Why can't they just *be* men? Why do they have to become men?

Exactly.

I've got an unhatched one myself. A dentist named Jim.

I've met him, Monique said. The Coffee Bus. Mark introduced us.

Did it seem like he didn't say hello?

It was kind of quiet.

He does that. People think he's not saying hello, but he is.

He seemed all right, Monique said. She was looking at Rhoda, thinking Rhoda was very attractive in her way. And she wanted almost to tell Rhoda the truth, right then, right from the start, to save her from Jim, but that seemed pointless. Rhoda and Jim would carry on in their small lives no matter what Monique did. You grew up here? she asked Rhoda.

Yep. On Skilak Lake. A great place to grow up. Always free to roam around.

Any run-ins with bears?

A few times.

Can you tell me? I like stories about bears.

Well there's one you're not going to believe.

Yay! Monique said. A good one. I can tell it's going to be a good one. And she turned sideways in her seat to give Rhoda her full attention.

I'm four years old, Rhoda said. One of my earliest memories. I'm wearing my red jacket, with the hood.

Little Red Riding Hood.

Exactly. I loved that jacket.

This is perfect.

I'm on the first hill behind the house, looking for blueberries. It's August, still summer, but already turning cold. Later that week, we got snow, which almost never happens in August.

Wow, Monique said.

And maybe the bears are more desperate because of the early cold. I don't know. But I'm looking down at a blueberry bush and I feel like someone is watching me. I just look up for some reason, and about twenty feet away from me is an enormous bear.

Oh my god.

Yeah, a really big brown bear. Not a black bear, which would maybe be okay. And you never see a bear this close. They don't come up to you like this. They go the other way. You startle them, and they run off. But this one was so close, it must have smelled me or heard me and come closer.

What did you do?

That's the thing. I didn't do anything. I just stood there and watched it, and it watched me. It was beautiful and seemed friendly, like a big dog. I said hi, and its head swayed back and forth a little, then it turned and ran.

You said hi.

Yeah, I said hi, and now I work for a vet. I've always had this good feeling about animals, that they don't ever really want to hurt us. We just get in their way sometimes.

You win for best bear story.

They arrived at the campground, and Monique directed Rhoda to the tent. They parked very close, and Carl poked his head out.

Hey, Monique said.

What the fuck, Carl said.

Don't be mad.

It's raining and miserable, Rhoda said. Why don't you both come to our place. You can dry out for the day, have dinner, spend the night. I'll bring you back here tomorrow at lunch.

Monique laughed. Jim would freak. That sounds great, she said. What do you say, Carl? Mope here by yourself or rejoin human society?

I'm coming, Carl said. I hate this tent.

The logs were not all the same. Some lighter-colored birch, thin bark like paper. Then darker spruce. Every variety of tree from this part of Alaska. And not one of them straight. Knots and bumps and the nubs of sawed-off branches. Gary kept picking up an end and sighting down it, dropping it and moving on to the next.

Raining again, but this time they wore full gear, thick dark green fishermen's gear, with boots. Irene warm and dry.

Maybe I should have had them planed down, Gary said.

Irene held her tongue. Sat on the edge of the platform and waited. She would do whatever he wanted for this cabin. If he decided to tie the logs together with licorice, or use cake icing to fill the gaps, she'd do it.

Gary selected four of the darker spruce logs finally, measured and sawed the ends so the corners would meet. Forty-five-degree angles, using a handsaw, and he didn't get them quite right. Yellow sawdust turning orange-red in the rain. The smell of the wood brought out by the sawing. Gary matching corners and wondering at the gaps.

Close enough, he said, but Irene could tell he was getting frustrated already. He had this immaculate idea in his head, and he was seeing the first tarnish now.

She kneeled down and held the logs together while he nailed. Big six-inch nails, galvanized. Her hands wet and cold, the bark rough.

They nailed together four corners and that was the first level of their walls. Two sixteen-foot logs and two twelve-foot logs making a low border. On the uphill side, the log came almost to the floor. The downhill log was more than a foot short.

At the roof, we'll add partial layers to even it all up? Irene asked.

Yeah, Gary said. We'll have to do that. Though I guess a roof can be tilted, too. Might look kind of interesting. And he grinned at Irene.

Irene laughed. It would have that rustic feel.

It's a deal, Gary said. We're doing a tilted roof.

Irene put her arm around Gary and gave a squeeze. Maybe it would work out. Maybe it would be okay that the cabin would look ridiculous.

Second layer? he asked.

You bet, she said. She was dizzy and had an ice pick in her brain, but she was doing her best to ignore that. Maybe she needed more antibiotics.

They measured again and he sawed the ends. The rain came down harder, blown by more wind, so they faced away from it.

Irene held the corners while he nailed, and she could see enormous gaps between the two layers. In some spots, maybe two or three inches of air between logs.

Damn it, Gary said.

The rain blowing sideways now, as if to show what would happen to these gaps. Irene slipped a Tramadol quickly while

Gary was distracted. She was almost out. She needed to ask Rhoda for more.

Damn it, Gary said again. I need a planer, but by hand it's going to take forever. All those knots and cut-off branches, all the bark. There's no way I can get through that. I should have had them planed before. I knew that. I knew that and I didn't do it.

It's your first time doing this, Irene said.

But I knew it. I just didn't have enough time. I was starting the project late. So I thought maybe I could make it work. When am I going to learn not to start shit late?

Well, Irene said, I think you're being hard on yourself.

No I'm not. I'm an ass. I'm an incompetent ass, and that's what I've always been. Every project.

Gary, she said, and she tried to put her arms around him, but he stomped off into the trees. Hard to believe he was fifty-five years old. He could have been twenty, or thirteen, or three. Having a tantrum, just like the children she'd taught for thirty-three years.

And meanwhile, Irene said quietly to herself, this gets to be my life. Because you can choose who you'll be with, but you can't choose who they'll become.

Gary was through the trees at the back of the property quickly, moving fast. The rain coming down heavy, his footsteps just as heavy, snapping deadfall. He felt like he could go forever, hike clear across Alaska into the Yukon and Northwest Territories, hike until his legs burned away and his mind cleared. He found that other cabin again, with the large even logs. He examined the gaps and still couldn't tell what they used. The prongs of his hammer and the logs themselves curved enough that he couldn't quite dig in, so he swung hard to bite into one of the gaps, tearing away at the log face. The lighter wood exposed, the surface gone almost black. He was able to free a small piece of the filler. A gray grout or cement or epoxy. It had flexibility but wasn't rubber or silicone. Slightly grainy in his fingers. He smelled it and couldn't tell what it was. And he doubted it could fill several inches of gap. Nothing would fill that. He'd have to nail up plywood. Instead of a cabin, the inside would look like a storage unit.

Gary turned and threw his hammer at a tree. It hit with too quiet a sound, nothing satisfying. So he walked over and picked it up and threw it at another tree, closer, and it bounced back at him so he jumped to the side.

He wanted to reach down into the island and tear it apart with his hands, see the lake's water rise up in the gap. That would be enough. Nothing less than that.

Well, he said. Because it was time to move on.

He hiked back to Irene, who was sitting on the edge of the platform, turned away from the wind and rain, hunched over. He should let her go back home. She shouldn't have to be a part of this. Just a few more layers of logs and they'd go.

He walked up to her and said sorry. This is just frustrating, he said. There's another cabin back there, and I don't know where they got their big logs.

It's okay. Maybe we can work something out with these.

So they made another layer, sawing and nailing corners, then stood back to look at the gaps. They stood there in the rain and tried to figure out how to make it work.

Maybe you can nail each layer down into the next, Irene said. With longer nails. That might bring them closer together. And she was thinking this was a kind of metaphor, that if they could take all their previous selves and nail them together, get who they were five years ago and twenty-five years ago to fit closer together, maybe they'd have a sense of something solid. For themselves and for their marriage, a marriage not unlike a sense of self, something fleeting and changing, important and also nothing. You could rely on it for years, just assume it was there, but then if you looked for it, needed it, tried to find some substance to it, something to grab on to, your hands closed on air.

That's a good idea, Gary said. I'll try that. Thanks, Reney.

They made one more layer, then lifted each layer off and dragged it aside for tomorrow's work. Tomorrow they'd try to make it all fit together more closely.

Monique and Carl were lying on the bed in Jim's spare bedroom. Late afternoon, after showers. Carl praying she'd have sex with him, afraid to say anything. Monique staring at the ceiling.

I'm tired, Monique said.

Hm, Carl said.

Monique cracked her toes.

You shouldn't do that. Arthritis.

Monique sighed. She stood up, unwrapped her towel and tossed it on a chair, naked now, then got under the covers.

Carl tossed his towel and got under the covers, too.

Monique turned onto her stomach, facing away from him, and went to sleep.

Carl dressed and wandered into the kitchen and living room. A rich place, great views, all wood, nice couches. He opened the fridge and freezer and looked for something good. Ice cream bars, which were a possibility. Smoked salmon, always good. But he closed the doors and looked in the pantry, wanting something else. Found a small glass bottle of maple syrup, unopened. It had a handle big enough to put one finger through, and a tiny golden cap on top. Imported from Canada.

Carl brought it to the living room, sat on a couch looking out over the Cook Inlet, darkened with rain. He unscrewed the cap and sipped lightly at the syrup, holding it in both hands in his lap between sips, like a canteen of whiskey.

The clouds over the water formed a low, dark ceiling, almost like a theater, the slanted bands of rain and light a trick of staging, all of it in motion. It was beautiful, and different now that he was removed, in this warm, dry, expensive place. Money wasn't a bad thing. Maybe he should rethink the anthropology major. Living in that tent was a preview of what his entire life would be like if he went the no-money route.

He laid his head back and closed his eyes. He'd been getting terrible sleep, the bottom half of his sleeping bag wet whenever it rained. The couch incredibly comfortable.

In his dream, Carl was being shaken by monkeys, trying to hold on to the branches in a very tall tree, but this was Rhoda, her hands all over him, and he woke to see the maple syrup spilled over him and the couch, a honey drool that had gone everywhere. Rhoda wiping at his shirt and jeans with a wet kitchen towel.

I'm sorry, Carl said, panicked.

It's okay, Rhoda said. It's funny. Let me just get a bit more so you don't drip when you stand up.

God, Carl said. I'm such an idiot.

It's fine, sweetie. Your secret is safe with me.

Ah, he said. It's everywhere.

Yes it is.

He was able to stand up, finally, and helped her dab at the couch, which luckily was a dark brown.

I'm so sorry, he said.

Really. It's fine.

So Carl slunk off to change his clothes and take another shower, but Monique was awake now and asked what happened and then laughed, of course.

Thanks, he said. I feel real big.

Don't pout, she said, but he closed the bathroom door and got in the shower. He'd had about enough of Monique.

Rhoda finished cleaning up then set out a platter of cheeses, olives, smoked salmon, crackers, capers, several tapenades. Opened a bottle of shiraz and a pinot gris. She liked entertaining. She was humming "A Spoonful of Sugar" from *Mary Poppins,* her favorite movie from childhood. She could imagine herself putting out platters of treats for kids.

When Jim came in the door, she hopped over to him and put her arms around his neck, gave him a kiss. I have a surprise, she said.

A surprise?

Guests for dinner. A bit of company. I've put out a cheese platter.

Really? Who is it?

You'll like them, Rhoda said. You've already met at least one of them. She walked Jim into the living room, where he threw his jacket over the couch and sat down.

The rain is kind of beautiful today, she said. Carl was out here watching it earlier.

Carl?

Rhoda poured him a glass of shiraz. Yeah, he's up here with his girlfriend Monique. You met her at the Coffee Bus.

Jim stood up then, which was odd. He turned toward her with his mouth open, then turned back toward the window.

What is it? Rhoda asked.

There was a pause, and she brought him his wine. Is something wrong?

No, Jim said. But he looked upset. I just prefer not to see patients outside the office. Monique came in for a filling.

Oh, I'm sorry, Rhoda said. I'm sorry, Jim. And she gave him a hug, rubbed his back.

It's all right, he said.

Jim sat on the couch again and Rhoda started fixing dinner, caribou steaks from her mother. She set them in a roasting pan with whole cloves of garlic, Maui onions, olive oil, rosemary, balsamic, and black pepper. She had potatoes boiling, and she would steam broccoli.

Monique walked out from the guest room, with Carl following behind. She was tall and kind of glamorous, in a way, though she had a weird little nose. Like an elf whose body had grown too big. Carl was out of his league, though, insecure and hopeless. Rhoda gave their relationship another few weeks at most.

Hey, Rhoda said. Have some wine. And there's a cheese platter over by Jim. We can all watch the rain together.

Hi Jim, Monique said, and Jim stood up, walked over to shake her hand and Carl's. He didn't say anything, though, which was odd. So much older than they were. It didn't make sense he should be awkward.

Jim said you were one of his patients, Monique. Rhoda said this just to break the tension.

I am indeed, Monique said. I've enjoyed the duck feet on the ceiling.

Jim laughed. I put those there for the kids.

For the hunters, Monique said, and there was silence again for some reason.

Have a seat, Rhoda said. Can I pour you a glass of wine? I have shiraz and pinot gris.

Shiraz, please, Monique said. And just some juice or water for Carl. He doesn't drink.

Thanks, Monique, Carl said.

What? You don't drink.

Yeah, but I'm not six years old.

Now's not the time to make a stand for your manhood.

You suck, Monique.

Rhoda laughed, trying to break the tension again. Sounds like the tent has taken its toll.

Yeah, Carl said. How has the tent been for you, Monique? A little uncomfortable?

Carl's just mad because he's had some alone time.

And where were you? Carl asked.

I was in Seward. Ever been to Seward, Rhoda?

Rhoda was pissed off they were fighting at her wine and cheese gathering, and she didn't know why Jim was being such a dolt, but she took this opening to try to change the tone. I love Seward, she said. The most beautiful bay, and mountains all around. I haven't been there in years. We should go, Jim.

Yeah, Monique said, you should take Rhoda to Seward.

Sure, Jim said. He was in some kind of daze, or maybe just tired. Seward sounds good, he said.

And that was it. Silence again. Rhoda wanted to kill all three of them. She turned back to her cooking and let them stew in their own weird pot of antisocial behaviors. She grabbed the lettuce, rinsed it quick, and tore it into little pieces. She cut up two tomatoes, part of a red onion, and threw in some pine nuts. She decided she didn't like Monique at all. She liked Monique the least out of the three of them. Her strange tone, telling Jim he should take her to Seward. As if she could pronounce upon their relationship. How old was she, anyway? Like twenty-two or something, acting like she owned the world?

All the while Rhoda worked, she had one ear cocked, and it was just silence over there. Absolute silence. Unbelievable. Who does that? And when dinner was finally ready and they all sat down, it was Monique who started talking.

Rhoda told me this great bear story today, she said. Do you have any bear stories, Jim?

Rhoda didn't like how Monique said Jim. As if she were talking down to him. And for some reason, he was letting that happen.

Not really, he said. Do I have any good bear stories, Rhoda?

Sure you do, sweetie. You have that one in the river, with the salmon on your back. You always tell that one.

Oh yeah, Jim said. But what about you, Carl? Have you seen a bear here?

No. I've been wanting to see one. We even took a trip up to Denali, but we didn't see one.

That's too bad, Rhoda said. Denali has a lot of bears. I can't believe you didn't see one there. That's really unlucky.

That's me, Carl said.

You're here in Alaska, though. That's lucky. And you're with Monique.

Ah, Monique said. That's sweet. Thank you, Rhoda.

So things were turning around after all. Rhoda was pleased. Monique seemed much brighter now, more friendly, and the conversation moved along normally, just four people enjoying an evening, the way it should be. Oohs and ahs over the caribou. Killed by my own mother, Rhoda said. Then for dessert she surprised everyone with homemade tiramisu.

I bought the ladyfingers, she said. But the rest is mine.

This is terrific, Monique said. What a feast.

Yeah, thanks Rhoda, Carl said. This beats the hell out of the tent.

Only Jim was still relatively quiet, which was unlike him. He'd had two glasses of wine, and usually that got him rambling.

Jim just got back from Juneau, Rhoda said. Talking with another dentist about joining the practice.

How was Juneau? Monique asked.

Oh, Juneau's nice, Jim said. The Mendenhall Glacier. Pretty hike around the lake at its foot, and if you go up the left side, you can get out onto parts of the glacier.

I'd like to go out on a glacier, Monique said. Maybe land on one with a helicopter and then lie down and do snow angels.

That sounds good, Jim said, but Rhoda could tell something was off, something wrong. She looked at Carl, but Carl was mesmerized by the tiramisu, staring down into it as he savored tiny bites from the tip of the dessert spoon. He had something going on with food.

Carl, Monique said. You don't need to fuck the tiramisu. You can just eat it. Then she winked at Rhoda.

Carl didn't even look up. Thanks, Monique, he said. More pleasure in this bowl than I've ever had with you.

Ouch, Jim said. And he laughed.

That's not nice, Jim, Rhoda said.

Sorry.

Hm, Monique said. She clearly wasn't used to negative comments. Rhoda was secretly a little pleased.

How about a game? Rhoda suggested. We could all play a game.

Do you have Twister? Monique asked.

Carl looked up. Twister?

We have it, Rhoda said. She went to the hall closet and rummaged around. Just leave the dishes. I'll do them later.

So they all took their shoes off and sat around the Twister mat.

So retro, Monique said, looking at all the bright dots. I love it.

They spun the dial and took turns. Jim ended up in a tough position, his feet far from his hands. Hurry, he said through gritted teeth. He was looking up at the ceiling, hands behind him, his butt sagging dangerously low.

Rhoda was laughing. She had an easy spot on a corner, two feet and one hand.

Then Carl spun and had to go over Jim, in an extended push-up. This got Monique laughing.

Thanks, Monique, he said.

Monique had to go forward on both hands on her spin, but it wasn't difficult.

Then Rhoda got an impossible one. She had to put her other hand clear over past Monique, and trying to do this put her face right in Monique's butt, which she wasn't happy about at all.

I give up, Rhoda said. I can't do it.

Jim crashed down. Thank god, he said.

That was too seventies for me, Rhoda said. Or sixties, whatever. But we have another old game that might be fun.

So they played Pin the Tail on the Moose, getting dizzy and heading off in different directions with their darts, no one hitting anything they'd intended. And finally it felt like a party. Rhoda was satisfied. She packed up the games when they were done, then went for the dishes.

I'll help, Monique said. It was late, and Jim and Carl headed off to the bedrooms.

Thank you, Rhoda said, warming up a bit to Monique. She had an edge, but she could be sweet, also.

Rhoda washed and Monique rinsed and dried. You have such a great place here, Monique said.

Yeah, I love it. I always dreamed of a house like this.

How long have you and Jim been together?

A little over two years, living together for a year.

How did you meet?

I was a patient.

Ah.

Jim didn't seem like much at first, but he grew on me after a while. He's a good guy. Solid and reliable. He has a good heart.

Yeah, Monique said. He seems like a nice guy. Are you getting married?

Rhoda wasn't quite ready for this question. She felt put on the spot. Monique was being friendly, though, and she didn't want to mess that up. Yeah, she finally said. We talk about it, though it's not official. We're taking our time. Planning what kind of wedding we'd like.

What are your ideas?

Well, Rhoda said, getting a little excited despite herself. I'm thinking Hawaii. Kauai, the Garden Island.

Kauai's nice, Monique said.

You've been there?

Yeah, a couple times. Hiked the Na Pali Coast, and kayaked it.

The whole coast?

You only go one way, with the current. It's not so tough.

Wow, Rhoda said. Maybe we could do that on our honeymoon.

You'd like it. It's beautiful.

Rhoda felt bad for disliking Monique earlier. They finished the dishes and she gave her a hug goodnight. It's too bad you're not here in Alaska longer, she said. It'd be fun to hang out more.

Yeah, Monique said. I'd like that.

Rhoda turned on the light in the bedroom but then flicked it off again, because Jim was already asleep. She undressed, bumping around a bit in the darkness, tipsy still from the wine, and collapsed into her pillow.

Jim lay awake beside her, listening to her breathing, waiting until he could feel the tiny jerks of her hands that meant she was asleep. Then he waited some more, just to be sure. Monique had said to meet him in the living room. He was angry, of course, but he also didn't want to miss out.

Irene lay awake panicking. The pain had become untouchable, and this meant no more thought, no more sleep, no more reason. She had to get up, couldn't just lie here.

She wanted to pop another Tramadol, but she'd already had four in less than an hour and was afraid she'd overdose. She wandered the house, pacing back and forth in the small kitchen, over to the fireplace, into the bedroom, back to the kitchen, holding her head with both hands, squeezing at it, begging for this to stop. She wasn't religious but found herself in something close to prayer. *Please,* she begged.

She walked outside, into the cold, the night sky clear. Wearing only her pajamas and a pair of boots. She hoped the cold might muffle the pain somehow, walked down their driveway to the road, her boots crunching gravel. Quiet tonight, without wind. She was shivering.

The trees all around seemed almost an audience, standing there waiting, watching her. Sentinels in the shadows, hidden away on a moonless night. She had never grown accustomed to this place, never felt it was home. The forest itself felt malevolent, even though she knew it well, the name of every tree and bush and flower. That worked during the day, naming, but at night the forest became a presence again, animate and unified, without name.

Irene turned and hurried back home, the crunching of her own boots seeming to come closer as she gained speed, and she saw the quick shadow of an owl cross her path ahead, the low swoop, silent. An omen, but one she didn't know how to read. Disappeared into the trees. No call.

She hurried inside, shut the door, and made her way slowly in the dark to the couch by the fireplace, lay down, exhausted. Wanted desperately to sleep, her eyes heavy, but the pain wouldn't allow rest. She had to get up again, had to move. Being still let the pain gather.

Carl lay awake. Monique's breathing too even and deep, not at all like how she slept. He was careful to keep his own breathing even, and he knew she wouldn't know the difference. She had never noticed him the way he noticed her. And he wondered why she would lie to him now, why she would pretend. Why bother? It was more considerate, in a way, than what she normally did.

She pretended for a long time, and when she finally eased the covers back and left the bed, she stood there a few minutes without moving, listening to see whether he'd stir. He kept his breathing even, and finally she tiptoed away, turned the handle of the door quietly, opened and closed it with almost no sound.

Carl waited. He heard nothing else. Looked at his watch, almost quarter after one. He waited another fifteen minutes, then sat up carefully at the edge of the bed, walked to the door and listened, opened it quietly and now could hear them faintly, their breathing, and see a glow from the living room, a flickering. They had lit a candle. He came around the corner quietly and now he could see her outline, her shape as she sat up and rode Jim, facing away. Carl could see only her dark cutout against the candlelight.

What surprised him was how much this hurt, an actual pain in the left side of his chest. The heart only a metaphor, he had thought, and he had thought he was through with Monique, basically, over her, tired of her meanness, but she had gotten him now, something hard and unforgivable. Watching her have sex with this old man, watching her curl her shoulders in pleasure, putting on her show in the candlelight, this was something that would stay with Carl, he knew, something he would never be able to forget. Her final gift to him, one more in a long series of mean gifts but more than all the others.

Carl returned to bed and wanted badly to fall asleep, tried to count his exhales, tried to fade out and go away, but he was still wide awake when she returned, so quiet with the door handle, silent across the floor, then easing carefully back under the covers. He kept his breathing even, knew she was listening, then finally heard the shorter breaths, the stop and start of her real sleep.

Terrible to have her so close beside him, only a few feet away. He looked at his watch, two thirty, and decided he would try to get on the boat to go fishing. He needed to get away from her. It would be cold on the dock, so he lay waiting another half hour until three, then rose quietly and dressed, walked into the night and set off down the road toward the river.

It felt better to be moving, to be outside and no longer trying to be quiet. Crunch of his boots on gravel, the fog of his breath. He swung his arms around a bit, rolled his shoulders, and tried to shake her off. Heard his voice. Shaking off the heebie-jeebies. Almost like a shiver. She could fuck all the old men she wanted. He was going to move on, finally.

The cold worked its way in, despite his walking, so he jogged for a while in his boots, heavy clumps. The only soul on that road, stars and no moon. Alaska a great stillness that extended a thousand miles in every direction. An open space, an opportunity to forget about something as small as heartache. Carl wanted to ingest the air, the sky, those distances.

Farther along, though, when he was walking again, he felt lost and slipped into the trees to hide himself, started to cry, tried to hold it back but ended up sobbing like a little boy. Monique, he said, because she was his first love. He would have done anything to make her love him.

He sat down on the forest floor and hugged his knees, buried his face in his shoulder. Waited for the crying to stop, then waited some more until he felt strong enough, stood up and hiked back onto the road, toward the river and the boat. He would lose himself in fishing, helping Mark. He remembered that aft deck filled with all of them gasping for air. Something magnificent in those fish, brought up out of nothing, something he wanted to be closer to.

When he made it to the pier, it was after three thirty and no one about, though he could see lights coming on in several of the boats in the channel. He waited by the ladder thinking of that Indian-American woman from last time, wondering whether he'd see her again, but it was a man in his thirties who finally came walking out of one of the buildings.

Mornin, Carl said.

Mornin.

Could I get a lift out to the *Slippery Jay*?

Sure.

And so Carl was on the river again, the roar of the outboard and fast white curve of the wake, the wind cold in his ears. He was over the side in no time, standing on deck, and made his way up to the pilothouse to wait.

Something right about a boat, sitting outside above the water, rocking in the waves. A different kind of home. A better home. Nothing stagnant. Maybe this was what he needed to do. Get a boat and live on it, maybe a sailboat and take off around the world. He knew why he was thinking this, though. Some grand gesture, something to show Monique who he really was. And that was an impossible game, one he could never win.

The seat was cold, and though Carl huddled and put his face down in his jacket, he couldn't get warm. He had to just wait, goose-bumped and shivering, until Mark finally appeared.

Cabron, Mark said. Que paso?

Was thinking about catching some fish, Carl said.

You've come to the right place. Scoot over.

Carl scooted, the new section of seat frozen, and Mark pushed the glow plugs for twenty seconds, then turned the key for the engine. A bit rough at first, Mark said. But then she's a kitten.

The owner came up the ladder. I'll take over, she said. Hey Carl.

Hey Dora.

You look cold, she said. Go below and warm up. Grab a sleeping bag.

So he went down the ladder, in through the galley and forward to the fo'c'sle. Dark in there, but he could feel around for sleeping bags, still warm, and a pillow, and he made a nice nest. He could hear Mark walking on deck above him, letting off the bow line, and then felt the engine lock into gear and they were moving. Leaving earlier than last time. Carl without sleep, exhausted, the light rocking and warm sleeping bags a comfort, and he faded quickly.

In his dreams, Carl was swimming underwater. A wide, deep river, sunny, and the salmon all much larger than him, watching. Their enormous eyes like moons, all of them in silent communication. They had received a message about him, something urgent.

Carl woke to small waves hitting the hull. From down here, you could feel how the entire boat flexed, nothing solid. Just a skin. The engine louder now, more revs, powering through. He didn't want to seem lazy, but he was so tired. So he closed his eyes again.

He woke to the outrageous rolling that meant they had stopped in place. He hurried to get his boots on, tossed back and forth, dizzy, then stumbled through the galley to the aft deck in time to see Mark throw an orange buoy over the stern, the beginning of the net.

Need help? he yelled.

Stay out of the way, Mark yelled back, so Carl held on to the doorjamb and watched. Sun glaring off the water, Mark letting the net unwind as Dora drove forward. The net an improbable thing, a vast nylon curtain with small white floats on top and a leaded skirt on the bottom.

The reel becoming slimmer, green nylon feeding out until finally the entire net was in the water. Then Dora shifted into neutral and Mark attached the main line to a stern cleat. Dora put the engine into gear again and tugged carefully at the net to straighten. A curtain nine hundred feet long, arcing out behind the boat, a long line of white floats with the orange buoy at the far end, far away.

The rolling extreme at slow speed, and Carl had to hold on. Mark came over, walking across that rolling deck with no problem. Watch the net, he told Carl. You can see 'em when they hit. You'll see a splash.

Carl looked but saw nothing. Hundreds of salmon could be out there, but this seemed impossible. Land was miles away, a fringe in the distance, and all this open water. It couldn't be that every small patch of water was so populated. Fishing seemed to him a great act of faith, or desperation.

The line of white floats very tight, rising out of the water as the trough of a big wave rolled through.

We're at the edge of a rip, Mark said, and he pointed. See the logs?

Carl could see several logs and smaller rafts of wood, the water darker on the other side, divided by a thin line of foam. I see them, he said.

The fish hang out along the rip. We can't be right in it, or we'd foul our gear with all the wood, but we try to stay close to an edge.

Let's go to the other end, Dora said from the helm.

She shifted into neutral and then slow reverse as Mark went to the stern. He untied another orange buoy from the rail, swapped the lines, and they were clear.

Dora shifted into forward and turned to run along the net.

Running the gear, Mark yelled to Carl over the engine. You can do this to other fishermen's nets, too, to see if any fish have been hitting.

Carl looked at the net passing beside them, and he didn't see anything.

No luck yet today, Mark yelled.

At the other end of the net, Mark used a pole to grab the yellow buoy line out of the water. He pulled in fast, clipped the tow line onto the net, unclipped the buoy, and Dora shifted into gear again, pulled at the net slowly, straightening.

Carl clung to the doorjamb and thought of all the ways to lose a hand on this boat, caught in any of the lines under pressure, everything wet and slippery and moving, and today was a nice day, big rollers from a faraway storm but no wind. He couldn't imagine doing this when it was rough, but he knew Mark and

Dora went out regardless of the weather. Dora's permit allowed only certain days for fishing, usually Mondays and Thursdays.

Dora pulled for another fifteen minutes at the net, then shifted into neutral and yelled for Mark to bring it in. Mark stood at the stern with his foot on a board that was tied to a hydraulic lever. A homemade contraption, something rigged to make the work faster. When he stepped on it, the reel pulled in, net and floats coming over the aluminum stern guide, a rounded plate with two posts. Dora stood on the other side of the net, and the two of them pushed and pulled to guide it evenly onto the reel.

Carl watching for fish, feeling he could understand why someone would spend a life out here. It wasn't the money, or despair. It was mystery. Wondering what was down there, what was in that net. They might have nothing or they might have hundreds of salmon. Or they could have anything else large that lives in the sea. You could believe in monsters if you had a big enough net. The ocean an immensity, but they were capturing a small part of it.

Mark kept his foot on the board, the drum pulling tight. Carl wondered whether the boat could buck from the pressure. The netting pulled free of the water, dripping, wrapping onto the reel. This seemed the point at which everything could break, the lines snapping or the drum crumpling. Carl stepped away from the door, grabbed onto what he could and got to the side of the boat. He didn't want to be in a direct line if something snapped and whipped back. The worst pressure came when the stern of the boat was lifted on a wave. The strain then was incredible.

Feels light, Mark yelled to Dora, but to Carl it felt as if the boat was about to break, as if it had a spine that could curl and finally snap.

A single salmon came over the top with the net, and Mark let his foot off the board. He grabbed the fish fast, yanked it out of the net in one quick downward motion.

Then empty net again, long winds of the reel with nothing, only a few bits of seaweed, like small brown sea bouquets, and finally one more salmon, silvery and narrow-faced, dark back, thrown onto the deck in obvious disappointment.

Skunked, Mark said to Dora, and Carl realized everything rode on Mark. If there were no fish, it was his fault. A day spent on the water was money spent, on diesel and the license and the cost of the boat, and the net could be put out only so many times.

Mark wound the rest of the net, until the buoy came over the top and he unclipped. Dora climbed the flybridge and put the engine in gear again, heading out to other water.

Carl made his way back to the door. Sorry about that, he yelled to Mark. That sucks.

Mark didn't respond. Still sorting on the aft deck, framed now by a white wake. He scooped a salmon by the gills, flicked his finger inside, which made a popping sound, then tossed the fish into a side bin. He did the same to the other salmon and grabbed a hose to wash down the deck. Then he came forward, and he didn't look unhappy.

No worries, mate, he said to Carl. You feel like helping me find the fish?

Sure, Carl said. He had no idea what that meant.

Come up top, Mark said, and Carl climbed the ladder after him. Dora gave a mock salute and went below.

Carl took the wheel and Mark sat beside him on the bench seat, pointing the direction to steer. Toward the boats way over there, he said.

What was that popping sound? Carl asked.

What?

When you grabbed the gills, some popping sound.

Oh yeah, just popping the gills so the fish bleed out. Easiest way to kill them, and with all the blood gone, they go into the slush much cleaner. We get a higher price if we do that.

Then Mark was talking on the radio, just chatting with his friends out here, other fishermen, asking how they were doing, making plans to hang out, inviting to the sauna. He seemed relaxed and casual for someone who hadn't caught any fish today. Occasionally he'd use the binoculars.

Steering the *Slippery Jay* was like steering a bicycle with loose handlebars. Carl would turn one direction and feel the boat still going the other way. Then it would come back too far. He was all over the place, embarrassing, but Mark didn't seem annoyed. Still chatting with his friends.

Then Mark pointed to the left. He put down the mic for the radio. Over there, he said. Change of direction. The two white boats right there.

The ones in closer? Carl asked. He turned the wheel.

Yeah.

Is that where the fish are?

Yeah. They're killing fish right there, right now.

One of your friends told you this?

Yeah.

But I didn't hear anything.

It was the conversation about beer. No code words or anything, just a feeling about what's being said. We don't want anyone else to know. Then every boat in the area would be moving over here.

Wow, Carl said.

Yeah, it's very James Bond out here, Mark laughed. He was using the binoculars again, looking at the group of boats they had been heading toward before. A couple of them are coming over. They figured it out, too. Maybe just waiting to see us turn. We'll have to get the net in the water fast.

Carl looked back for a moment but couldn't see anything at this distance. The whole business felt urgent now. Do you know them? he asked Mark.

Russian boats, Mark said. Bigger, forty-two feet, running a double D, two licenses, so they get an extra shackle, twelve hundred feet on their net.

Russians?

Alaskans now, I guess, Mark said. But Russian. Two communities here, one near Ninilchik. Good fishermen, so they don't usually need us. Must be having a slow day. They usually keep to themselves, very closed communities, all family, all fishermen and boat builders, highest fishermen per capita for any population here.

So they're the best?

Mark laughed. The Norwegians are the fish-killing sons of bitches. Out on the other side of the inlet. Towns you can get to only by float plane or boat. They bred the cows and killed the bulls.

What?

Sorry, Mark said. It's really rude and politically incorrect. Just a saying here. The Norwegians bred all the Aleut women and killed most of the men, so in those towns, everyone has a Norwegian last name, Knudsen and such. Almost no Aleut surnames. I worked in one of them one summer, as a carpenter, and they are serious fish-killers. Have it from both sides. And they follow their own laws.

What's that mean? Carl asked. The boat seemed terribly slow. Wallowing through the waves, nothing passing quickly. Meanwhile, the Russians were gaining on them, he knew. He could see the appeal of those fast aluminum boats with their gasoline engines.

There was a kid, Mark said, a teenager, who was angry about

something—and there's plenty to be angry about in a village, I'm sure, incest and such, who knows what goes on—so he stole from his aunt, nothing much, but then he stole someone's four-wheeler and took it down the beach and finally drove it into the water. He ditched it below the low-water mark. But of course no one was fooled. They took him into the center of the village and put a fish sack over him, then all the men came at him with fish bats. His own father clocked him right in the head. I'm standing there wondering if I'm seeing a murder, and I think I did. I never asked about it. I was just there to help build a house. That was it.

Holy shit, Carl said.

I'm gonna let Dora know, Mark said. She'll come up and grab the helm. Just stay out of the way, and if we catch fish, you can help me throw again.

The water no longer turquoise. A dark, dark blue today, with blackness in it, a clarity, no glacial silt suspended. Irene didn't know how it could change so completely in even a day. A different lake now. Another metaphor for self, each new version refuting all previous. Who she was today did not fit with two weeks ago, before the headaches, and who she was then did not fit with a few months ago, not yet retired, still in the classroom with the children. And who she was then did not fit with when her own children still lived at home, before they vanished from her daily life, and who she was then did not fit with how she and Gary first came to this place, full of hope, or fit the time just before that, on her own with an education and a job, free finally, a bright moment when all was possible. And who she was then did not fit the unwanted thing she had been for so many years, given cast-off spaces in spare bedrooms or even attics and, once, a basement, and who she was then—nobody, really, a kind of ghost—was not who she had been on that day, coming home, believing she still had a mother.

The air warm and flat, uncharged. The shorelines hazy, Sitka spruce at their odd, bent angles like a forest gone to ruin, survived some cataclysm, unearthings of bare rock. The knuckle rocks, they called one patch. Everything here enormous and also too small, closed in, living under this mountain.

Gary preoccupied as always, caught up in his struggle with the cabin, oblivious to her, no idea what she'd been through last night, not sleeping, no idea what she felt now, the inside of her head spinning like a gyroscope at fantastic speed. He thought she was making up the pain, thought it wasn't real. She was sitting right in front of him in the boat, facing him, but he managed to look ahead their entire trip across that lake without seeing her at all. Part of how he was letting her vanish.

When they arrived, Irene climbed out and helped pull the bow closer to land. Cold metal even on a warm day.

They hiked across blueberry and deadfall, around a small alder thicket to the platform and squares of logs they had built, the layers of the cabin. Gary set a piece of wood upright beneath where he was nailing, Irene sat on the logs to compress, and the ten-inch nail sank deep into the top log.

Then the log began to split, a crevice on either side of the nail, a ripping sound.

Damn it, Gary said. But he kept hammering until he was deep into the bottom log and the two layers were tight. He pounded the head until it indented into the surface of the wood.

Okay, he said. Good enough.

They moved to the next side, and Gary hammered again, grim and intent, his face looking old, all the lines. Losing himself in work, gone vacant. And Irene didn't grudge him this. She understood the desire to forget. At the moment, though, she was held present. Each hammer blow a punctuation behind her right eye, a red wavy streak shooting upward, like a cartoon, and she thought she might faint but she didn't. She could hold on, wait this out. It couldn't last forever. They nailed all four sides, then stood back to admire their work.

Not bad, Gary said. And it was true. The gaps had closed. No more than a half inch anywhere, or less than an inch, anyway, something caulking or grout could probably take care of.

They dragged a third layer into place, wet wood, four logs, and Gary nailed again. Irene stood back thinking this could go quickly. It might not take that long to build a cabin.

How are we doing the door? she asked Gary. And the windows.

Gary paused in his hammering and sat up straight. Breathing heavily. Yeah, he said. We need a door. And at least one window to look out on the lake.

Yeah, Irene said.

Gary straddling the log wall, one knee on the platform inside. I guess we just cut gaps. When we get to the top of where a window or door would be, I saw down through the logs.

Okay, Irene said. And we buy the actual glass window with a frame on it, and the door?

Yeah, we'll buy those first and then I'll cut the gaps.

Gary returned to hammering and Irene lay down in a patch of ferns. Sleep a heavy casing that could never quite close, pain wedged in along the edge. Rhoda would bring more painkiller this evening. She'd promised. Irene had one pill left and was holding out as long as possible. The smell of ferns and earth pungent in close, dark and rich, and she focused on this, tried to hang sleep on smell, but she couldn't escape, couldn't remain distracted long enough to forget. And it was unbearable to stay in one position, feeling the pressure build.

What are you doing? Gary asked.

Irene sat up. I need this to go away, she said. This pain. I'm getting desperate.

It seems like it should be over by now. The doctor said a few days, maybe a week at most, and you'd be fine.

I couldn't sleep last night. Not even for a minute. Not even with the Tramadol.

What?

Yeah, I'm afraid I won't sleep again until this goes away.

I don't understand.

Yeah. But it's real.

Gary came over then, kneeled beside her and held the sides of her head in his hands. You're crying, he said.

No. Just tears. That happens all the time now. Just something my body does automatically.

We have to find out what's wrong, he said. Something's wrong.

Hallelujah.

He took his hands away. Don't be like that.

Well, she said. It's about time you believed me.

Sorry. We'll find another doctor. A specialist. Maybe drive up to Anchorage tomorrow.

They stopped work for the day, Gary noticing her finally, helping her over the bow of the boat, watching her on the way back. She tried to smile. Thank you, she said over the engine, but he couldn't hear and she couldn't try to say it again.

At home, she rested in the bedroom while he cooked. Took her last Tramadol, waited for Rhoda. And she nearly fell asleep. She sank deeper and deeper, but couldn't quite get away from the surface. Then she heard Rhoda drive up. The front door opening, talking with Gary. The bedroom door, and Rhoda was beside her.

We're taking you to Anchorage, Rhoda said quietly. Jim is making calls now to find someone, and he gave you a prescription for codeine, so I don't have to steal Tramadol anymore.

Irene found it difficult to rise out of herself to speak. Down lower than she had thought. Thank you, she finally said. Jim's a good guy.

Yeah, Rhoda said. He is.

Rhoda helped her sit up then, and grabbed her arm to help her stand.

I'm not that far gone, Irene said. I can walk.

Okay.

It's my head that's the problem, not my legs. I'm not in a rest home. I'm fifty-five.

Okay, Mom, Rhoda said. Geez.

Sorry, Rhoda. You were always the one I could count on. You've always helped, even when you were little. It's just who you are, nothing to do with me or your father.

Thanks, Mom.

Then they were out in the main room, where Gary had put pasta and salad on the table.

Husband, my husband, Irene said. Prepared the evening's meal. Thank you.

Gary looked unsure what to say to that. His face knocked back a bit. A sign of guilt, she thought, one more tiny indicator of future betrayal. Face back, slight puffing of his neck at the word *husband*. Caught off guard because he believed he was leaving unnoticed, believed he could let her somehow fall away and be gone.

This looks great, Dad, Rhoda said.

It's just pasta, he said. How are you feeling, Reney?

Happy to have the two of you here with me, Irene said, looking at Gary and then Rhoda.

Jim gave you a prescription for a sleeping pill, too, Rhoda said. Dad said you couldn't sleep last night.

She can't sleep, Gary said. She has to be able to sleep.

Irene tried the pasta. Her appetite gone. She didn't care

whether she ever ate again. Closed her eyes and could feel every part of her pulling inward, as if her center were gravity itself. A rushing of flesh into nothing.

What's wrong, Mom?

The medication. I can't eat.

Mom, Rhoda said, and she came closer, took Irene's arm. But Gary stayed where he was. He had never known how to care for her, and now would be no different. Irene would be on her own, as she had been her whole life.

My mother had terrible headaches, Irene said.

Rhoda and Gary both paying attention now.

She said her head hurt, but I didn't know what that was. She would ask me to be silent, and I did that. I was silent. I didn't make a sound for days. I was only a kid, so that wasn't easy.

Rhoda and Gary silent now, and Irene closed her eyes. She wanted to see her mother's face. But what she saw was what she always saw, her mother's form hanging in the air, a shape that couldn't be her mother, and she didn't want to see that, so she opened her eyes again.

Rhoda drove away afraid but couldn't pinpoint the fear. Everyone around her acting odd. Her mother, her father, Jim. None of them being who they were supposed to be. And where did that leave her? Her life was based on them.

What about what she wanted? Did any of them give a shit about that? This pissed her off, which was better than being afraid. She yanked the wheel to the side, then yanked the other way, fishtailing her crappy car down the gravel road, and that felt a little better. Go, cockroach, go, she said.

She took the turnoff to the lower end of the lake and skidded up to Mark's house.

Hey, fucker, she said when he came to the door. It was late and he looked tired, or stoned.

That's nice.

Not one visit, she said. You couldn't stop by just once to see how she's doing?

How's she doing?

She died.

Well I guess we're better off, in a way, Mark said. The weight of her displeasure and all that. But I will miss the Christmas cakes, and a certain girlish hopefulness.

Rhoda kicked him in the shin with her boot, hard enough he fell down howling. Then she ran back to her car before Karen could get into the mix.

Pancakes and canned peaches when she arrived home, so at least that was a return to normal. Jim standing at the counter, clicking his fork against the side of the can as he went for a slice of peach.

I'm putting you on notice, she said.

What?

You're all acting weird.

All?

You and my mom and dad. You're all freaks. My brother's just a worthless shit, but the three of you are driving me crazy.

What did I do?

I don't know, she said. But it's not right. You'd better stop.

Jim looked hurt. I've been making calls for your mother, he said. That's all I've been doing.

I'm sorry, Rhoda said. She stood in place a moment to try to slow down. She felt like she was running, her heart pumping. She wanted Jim to put his arms around her to help hold her in place, but he just stood there oblivious. Something freaked me out about my mom, she finally said.

What was it?

Rhoda threw her jacket off, sat on one of the bar stools. It'll sound crazy, she said. But she can't sleep, she can't eat, she has this pain all the time, and so she's leaving us. She's going away somewhere in her head, back to her childhood, to her mother, and I feel like she's already gone.

Could be just the medications.

Could be. But it isn't. She's going back to a place that's not good for her.

Well I found her a good doctor. John Romano, the best ear nose throat guy in Alaska.

In Anchorage?

Yep. One p.m. tomorrow.

How expensive is he?

He's the most expensive, but he's also the best and he's willing to cut his fees in half for your mom. Everything will be half price, even if she ends up needing surgery.

Surgery?

Yeah, a sinus operation. It's pretty common.

Rhoda got up and gave Jim a hug. Thanks, Jim, she said. And sorry for snapping at you. I'm just afraid. Jim put his arms around her, and he put one hand on the back of her neck, the way she liked. She felt safe.

How old was she when her mother killed herself? Jim asked.

Ten. In Rossland, British Columbia. She came home from school one day and walked in and found her. But she never talks about it. A couple weeks ago, she told me what it was like, walking up to the house that day. First time she's ever told me that. How there was snow on the ground, and how the paint looked. Something's going on with her, even before these headaches. She's getting all paranoid and weird, thinks my dad is going to leave her.

He's leaving her?

No. She's just weirding out.

Hm, Jim said.

Let's not talk about this anymore, Rhoda said. Let's talk about something fun. Let's talk about what kind of wedding we'd like.

Okay, Jim said, and he let his arms fall, gave her a light pat on the back.

So Rhoda grabbed the brochures for hotels on Kauai and they sat together on the couch.

This is the one I like, she said, opening a full-size brochure of sea views and green-black mountains with waterfalls. Princeville, at Hanalei Bay. Listen to this. *Forever Starts Here. As the sun kisses the horizon and you are bathed in golden light, your vows are lifted by eternal trade winds and scattered over a million miles of Pacific.*

Doesn't sound bad, Jim said.

It wouldn't suck, Rhoda said. Eternity and all that. Look at that pool. Infinity, to go with eternity.

The rooms look nice, too. Pricey?

Rhoda put down the brochure and looked at Jim. The price doesn't matter, does it? This is our wedding. It only happens once.

Yeah, Jim said. I guess so.

Rhoda elbowed him in the ribs, but only softly, and she opened the brochure again. What about our dance? she asked. We may have to go to Anchorage to take lessons. I don't think there's anything here.

Anchorage?

I just want something classy, she said. She didn't like his responses. Maybe we should talk about this another time.

I'm sorry, he said.

That's fine.

I'm just new at this.

It's fine. We're not even engaged yet. I just like to think about it.

Jim didn't know what he was supposed to say to that. Rhoda looking down at the brochure, sad, and he felt like he was supposed to pop the question right then, to save the moment, but he didn't have a ring. And there was Monique. The situation was impossible. So he didn't say anything. He looked at the brochure, and she turned slowly through the pages, neither of them looking at each other.

Carl had run out of money. Not even ten dollars left. He had to leave the campground, so he sat in his tent stuffing his cheap wet sleeping bag into its sack, then wondered what to do with Monique's. Hers was new, silver and green, in a waterproof bivi sack. Much thicker and warmer than his, but also weighed less. An easier ride through life. Carl lay down on her bag, put his face on the built-in pillow, breathed in deep. And then he was crying out of control again. He didn't know how to make it stop. Ragged and painful, not a good kind of crying, no relief. And she had never even been nice to him. He didn't understand this.

He took off his jeans, got into her bag, zipped it tight, and curled up. Another wave of sobbing, his heart this awful lump. He wondered how long this would go on. He wanted her to come back. He wanted her to lie down on top of him, to hold him down. Monique, he said.

Hollows inside him, only hollows. No substance. She had somehow blown the center out of him. He could see her face, when they had first gotten together, when it seemed that she loved him. Her smile a little hesitant, even, as if she were nervous too.

Carl felt tremendously sorry for himself, a sorrow without limitation, and he just lay there for hours until the campground manager came to his tent and told him to get out or he'd be charged.

Sorry, Carl managed to say between sobs. I'm leaving. Just a few minutes.

You need to leave now.

Okay. I'm leaving.

Now.

So Carl crawled from Monique's sleeping bag and out of the tent into a light drizzle, exposed and cold, the sky dark. He pulled out both packs, broke down the tent. Had to blow his nose again from being such a crybaby.

His backpack was heavy, about sixty pounds, and then he reached down for the straps of Monique's, which weighed at least forty or fifty. He pulled up and got her straps to go over his shoulders from the front. Slipping a bit, his face mashed against her frame, and he locked his hands low. More than a hundred pounds of packs, and he weighed only one-fifty, so he didn't know how far he'd make. He had to turn sideways to look where he was going, then walk ahead blind, then check again.

Carl staggered out the camp entrance down a gravel road toward the highway. Drizzle and a breeze. He felt like his knees were compacting into his leg bones, his lower back crunching also, his arms burning.

It was a long way out the gravel road, and when he hit pavement, he dropped both packs and his steps afterward felt like he was leaping into the air, gravity gone. Wow, he said.

He put his thumb out just as a truck roared past. There was no way he could carry these packs three hours into town.

Several cars went by without slowing, and he realized he had forgotten about her for a few minutes. That was the key. He had to keep occupied. He needed a job. Also because I have no money, he said aloud. Maybe Mark could set something up for him.

Rhoda decided to go with her parents to Anchorage. I can skip work, she told Jim. I need to be there for my mom.

Okay, he said.

I'll be back tomorrow. We're staying the night.

So after Rhoda left, Jim picked up Monique at the King Salmon Hotel and brought her back to the house. She was wearing jeans and boots, her old down jacket. Sat on a bar stool and looked at what would have been a view if not for the sky.

Seems like you could use a new jacket, Jim said.

It was my dad's.

Oh.

It's fine, she said. I don't care. Just a little nostalgia. We're allowed a little bit.

Yeah, Jim said.

I'm bored out of my mind, Monique said. I think I have to go back to D.C. There is nothing here.

I'm here.

Yeah.

That didn't sound good.

I'm just bored. Maybe I'll take a bath.

So Jim pouted on the couch while she took a bath. She was in there for over an hour. He thought about sex the whole time, pretty much, and when she came out, she seemed brighter. She wore a white towel on her head, nothing else. Long and perfect. She walked over and sat on an ottoman, back straight, and he was thinking that even her posture showed class.

I've never been paid for sex, Monique said. The idea of being paid is kind of turning me on. I think I might do things I wouldn't otherwise do, too, and that turns me on even more.

Money? Jim asked.

Yeah, money. That'll make it interesting, I think. It has to be a decent amount, though. Go get five thousand in hundreds. That will get me through the afternoon, I think.

Five thousand?

Go now, she said. And get me some ice cream. New York Superfudge Chunk. And whatever you want. Food sex, bondage, toys, costumes, kinky shit, whatever floats your boat. Make it interesting. And bring more cash if you want tonight too.

Are you serious?

Are you over forty? Am I twenty-three? Do you have a muffin top? Did I shave?

You don't have to put it like that.

Wake the fuck up.

I don't think I like this.

Then why do you have a boner just looking at me? I think you like it. And I think we'll start today by parading you around in a dog collar. You're going to crawl around and beg before I let you start paying me. Don't come back without a dog collar.

What the fuck?

Fine, she said. I'm getting dressed. And she walked back into the bedroom.

What's happening here? Jim asked.

I'm getting dressed, Monique said. Then we're driving to the bank, where you'll get me five thousand, then to my hotel to pick up my stuff, maybe the campground, though I'll probably skip that, then to the airport where you'll buy a ticket. We can have lunch at the airport if you like. But I'm leaving this shithole.

I'm not doing that. He was standing in the bedroom doorway now, watching her put on panties, bra, jeans.

Then I'm telling Rhoda everything, she said.

That's blackmail.

Not really. I'm a trust fund brat. I don't need money. I don't ever need to work, in fact, which is my own cross to bear, something you wouldn't understand. It turns out it sucks. But this is just teaching you a lesson. You didn't seem to realize what you had here, so I'm helping you realize that.

You can walk to the airport, Jim said.

The price just went up to ten thousand.

Jim was so angry he wanted to kill her. The first time in his life he felt this. She wasn't even upset. Just putting on her boots like nothing was happening. Like he was nothing.

She looked up and smiled at him. Fists, she said. Are you thinking of hitting me? Would it make you feel better to fight? She stood up, smiling bigger now, and took a couple steps forward then kicked him, too fast for him to do anything about it. Her long leg out straight, her boot in his stomach, and he was falling backward into the hallway. He curled up and couldn't breathe.

She stepped over him. I'll be in the car.

On the way to Anchorage, the sky seemed to press down, gray and moving, darker bands of rain. Fall now, the snow coming. The trees already turning.

Rossland had been similar. A river rather than ocean, but these same wide mountain bases, thick forest, snow-covered peaks. The same heavy sky, the same cold breeze even in summer, gusting, her skin always goose-bumped. Irene closed her eyes and tried to remember, tried to stand there, tried to turn flat images into a place she could walk through again, because she had spent forty-five years trying to forget. She had wanted to erase, and that seemed a terrible loss now. Irene wasn't sure what had shifted, but something had. She wanted to remember her mother, wanted to remember her father, wanted to remember the time when they lived together.

The sound of Icelandic, not flat like English. A kind of music, longer vowels, each sound a clarity, a shape, a liquid, or a shot of breath. In that tongue, the world could become animated. More fearsome, more lovely, never empty. A tongue unchanged for a thousand years, a way back to that time. This was what Gary liked. Her connection to the ancient past, Icelandic spoken now almost the same as Old English spoken then. In this way, she had never been real to him, only an idea.

But she didn't want to think about Gary. She wanted to find her parents, and they remained shadows. If she could hear them speak. How was it possible to forget every word, to not be able to hear the voices she'd heard every day of her childhood?

Irene tried to remember the kitchen, sitting at her own small table. Yellow, painted wood. Rough-grained. Her mother at the sink, wearing a dress, though she couldn't remember any pattern, any color, and she could almost hear the water running, and she knew her mother would have been speaking. No face, no voice, her father even more distant. And so all she had left were ideas. There was another woman, she knew, though she didn't know how she knew. When was the moment she learned? And did she understand that idea, that her father was leaving them? Could any of that have made sense? The adult world a thing of mystery and weight, she remembered that much. A despair as immovable as a mountain. Her parents making their decisions, determining her fate, and now they'd gone even farther away, into myth. Stories transformed, impossible to know what was true. Another woman, and her mother hanged herself, and her father left forever and she never saw him again. But what story to make any sense of this?

They came down out of the mountains and drove along the water, Turnagain Arm, a long fjord, sheer rock on either side, white-tipped. Following the path of some ancient glacier that might have filled this valley and bay, though Irene didn't know whether that was true. The water was like a river, in standing waves six feet high, the "bore tide" so extreme it actually had a sound, a low roar. In winter, the ice choked here and broke, deep rivers and ravines carved through piles of blocks the size of cars and even houses. No one out on this water.

She wondered whether Iceland was like this. She'd never been. Still had relatives, but none who had ever seen her. They'd be strangers, and she'd no longer be able to speak. Until ten, she'd spoken only Icelandic at home, English at school, but then that language died for her.

She had lost the stories, also, children's tales. Her memory now was only of figures in landscape. She had lost their movement and words, their purpose. A figure in the forest, the sense of that forest, frightening, or a figure on the sea, some kind of small boat, an ancient ship. A stone house, but she couldn't be sure even of this. It could have been a wooden house with a stone hearth.

And songs. There had been those, too. Hopelessly lost.

But she did have things she knew. Her mother had experienced some awful pain in her head and asked for silence. What she didn't know was the source. Was it grief, at her husband's leaving? Did it last a very short time, only at the end, or did it go on for years? Was it only medical, something like what Irene had now? And was there such a thing as only medical? Once something took over your life, didn't it become who you were, even if it was only a physical thing?

Irene closed her eyes and tried to exhale the pain, let it slip lower. Was she inventing all of this about her mother? Had her mother really ever complained of a pain in her head? Irene had no image, no moment of her mother rubbing at her forehead, no proof. And she didn't trust the tricks of her own mind. Whatever she wanted to remember, she would begin to remember, until she wouldn't know what was real. She had a memory of her father, for instance. They rode a sled together, a wooden sled with metal runners. They walked up a giant hill of snow, her father carrying the sled, and they were laughing. When they reached the top, her father lay facedown, his hands on a steering bar. Irene lay down on top of him, her body small and light, and wrapped her arms around his neck. Her father let out a whoop and they started moving. Irene yelled in fear and delight, and they flew at incredible speed down that slope. But then there were different versions of the ending. In one, they flipped and slid and rolled and landed in a pile together, laughing. In another, they went so fast Irene's body became airborne, and she struggled to hold on to her father's neck. In another, they flipped and hit hard and she cried. No one of these endings was more real than the next, and so it seemed the entire thing was made up. Most likely, there had never been a sled at all. She had no other memories of it. The entire scene too idyllic, a winter scene. An attempt to have a memory with her father.

He was young when she last saw him, in his early thirties. Blond hair, not the usual dark hair of an Icelander. A small face, burned by the sun. A forester, leaving each day with his axe. Almost a figure out of one of the children's stories, and this was what she feared. That she had invented every part of him. Did he really leave every day with his axe? Did he wear a green scarf wrapped around his neck?

She did remember his arms and his hands. Strong forearms, tanned and veined. His hands rough, callused. She could see them on the dark wooden table at meals. She knew that was real, a memory. It was when she tried to see his face or hear his voice that she became lost.

Do you remember your parents? she asked Gary.

What? Gary seemed startled.

Sorry. I'm trying to remember my parents when I was a kid. Their faces, their voices. Do you remember yours?

Yeah, of course.

What do you remember?

Well a lot of things.

Give me one.

Geez, Irene. I don't know just offhand.

Just remember one for me.

Yeah, Dad, Rhoda said from the back seat, smashed sideways into the king cab. I'm curious, too. You never talk about anything from your childhood.

It's like the Inquisition, Gary said. I'm just thinking about our appointment and where we'll stay tonight. But fine. A childhood memory. Something from Lakeport. How about a hunting memory?

No guns, Irene said. You're too stuck on guns. All the stuff you shot when you were a kid. Give us something else.

Yeah, Rhoda said.

Geez. All I can think of right now is hunting or fishing.

Give us something in the kitchen, Rhoda said.

Gary puffed his cheeks. All right, he finally said. It's not one particular time. I just remember my dad sitting at the table by the window, looking out at the lake, pouring cream of mushroom soup from a pot onto his pancakes. And I remember him making colored pancakes for me. Blue and green and whatever I asked for.

What did he say? Irene asked.

What?

What did your father say to you when he was making the pancakes or pouring the soup over them?

I don't know.

That's what I'm asking, Irene said. I want one moment when you remember exactly what he said, or what your mom said, and how their faces looked at that moment.

Why are you asking this, Mom?

Because I can't remember my parents, not even one moment.

No one said anything then for a while, so Irene looked out her side window at rock and trees, the rough flanks of mountains. These rocks tell us as much about ourselves as our memories do, she said.

The rocks a kind of sign of all that was true in the world, Irene thought. In layers and bands, identifiable, organized, but all of it was in fact meaningless. Formed under pressure for millions or billions of years, heaved upward, bent and sheared, all to no effect. The rocks were only what they were. There was nothing awaiting them, and they were not part of a story.

We live and die, Irene said. And it doesn't matter whether we remember who we are or where we came from. It was another life.

I don't think that's true, Mom.

You're still young.

I'm still trying to remember, Gary said. And all I can remember are the tense moments. Those are the only ones that stay. Playing pinochle, and my dad had a lay-down hand, but I didn't understand it, so I said something like, Wait, how did that happen, and then my dad said, Are you accusing me of cheating? I remember he said exactly that, and I remember how his face looked, unforgiving. He'd already decided, and whatever I said or my mom said didn't matter.

You remember, Irene said. You really do remember.

Yeah. And other moments, too, but only tense ones for some reason. My dad offering to pay me five cents per walnut to pick them up out of the front yard, and my mom saying, Doug, that's too much, and how worried she looked, and how that made me feel afraid for some reason, like something terrible was going to happen. My earliest worry about money, I think. I remember what her face looked like then.

Irene put her hand on Gary's shoulder. Thank you, she said. I believe those. And I don't know why I can't remember even one myself.

You must have at least a few, Gary said.

No. I really don't.

I have a zillion memories of you guys, Rhoda said. When I think back, it's like you never shut up.

Gary laughed. Thanks, honey.

Irene smiled. She had never wanted to be a mother, not really, but she had gotten lucky with Rhoda. Not so lucky with Mark.

The road ahead, as they neared Anchorage, was clogged with motor homes, the last of the summer visitors. Some pulled over to look at waterfalls or the inlet. They were gathering back at Anchorage for the long drive down through Canada to the lower forty-eight. Snowbirds, heading back to Arizona and Florida.

What I can't remember, Gary said, is my father ever talking about being part Cherokee.

He was part Cherokee? Rhoda asked.

Yeah, he was one-fourth. His father was half. You didn't know that?

I didn't know either, Irene said. What the hell.

I never said anything?

No, Rhoda and Irene both said.

Well he didn't either. I found out from my mom.

You're both freaks, Rhoda said. My parents are freaks. And I'm part Cherokee, apparently.

Only a sixteenth, Gary said. Sorry it isn't more.

Gary turned on the radio then and they listened to old Beatles songs.

They had planned to stop for lunch before the doctor's appointment, but with the traffic, they didn't have time. Irene walked into the office dizzy from hunger as well as the meds. She hadn't had anything to drink, either.

She was seen immediately, right at her appointment time, which was a new experience. Dr. Romano tall, dark, and handsome, grayed hair, a cleft chin. He had beautiful hands, full lips. Like some Roman statue.

He listened to Irene report her history and symptoms, then he put down his pen.

We'll figure out what's wrong, he said. Sometimes an infection in the sphenoid sinuses won't show up in an X ray. They're too far back, tucked in under your brain, so they don't show up easily. I'd like you to do a CAT scan.

When can I do that? Irene asked. I'm guessing I need to come back here to Anchorage. I was really hoping to figure out something today.

I've already made the appointment, Dr. Romano said. And they're next door. You can go right now.

Irene felt herself getting choked up. Not being treated like garbage by a doctor was a new experience for her. Wow, she finally managed to say. Thank you.

Within fifteen minutes, she was lying down in the scanner, trying to keep her head still, trying not to move too much from breathing. She kept her eyes closed so she wouldn't panic from claustrophobia, but she could feel the cold presence of the machine in close as it whirred and clicked.

Gary drove them to lunch afterward. A greasy diner off the highway. Irene ordered halibut fish and chips.

They sat at a plastic table waiting for their food, looking out at the traffic. That was amazing, Irene said.

Yeah, Rhoda said. I can't believe how quick it was. What a difference.

Frank should die a slow, painful death.

Irene, Gary said.

He should. He treats everyone like crap, and he's incompetent. He should die.

Maybe a little extreme, Mom.

Irene smiled. Okay. Frank shall live. But I'm just so happy with Dr. Romano. He'll figure out what's happening, and I can get better and move on. At this point, I don't care how awful the surgery might be. I need this pain to go away.

Did he talk about surgery? Rhoda asked.

Just told me the basics. It's a week of lying down and having your nose packed, which sounds like hell, but then it's basically over, just a few follow-up appointments.

Hm, Gary said. He was clearly uncomfortable hearing about this. He'd always been squeamish. Every time something happened to one of the kids, it was Irene on her own, from diapers to broken bones to drugs. Gary always found a way to disappear.

You'd better take care of me if I have the surgery, she said.

What? Gary asked.

You know what I'm saying. You always run when there's anything unpleasant. But if I have this surgery, you're going to be at my bedside every morning, noon, and night. I'm going to cough up phlegm and blood into your hand and you're going to like it.

Geez, Irene.

I'm serious. None of your weak shit this time.

Mom, Rhoda said. I'm sure Dad'll be there for you, and I will too.

You'll be there, Irene said. But your dad will run. Hey, our food's ready. I'll go get it.

Sorry, Dad, Rhoda said when her mom was gone.

It's okay. She's just going a little crazy. Nothing new.

That's not fair, Dad.

Who cares. Fair never matters. No one's keeping track, as it turns out.

Dad.

Whatever.

Irene returned with a tray of fish and chips. You've been talking about me.

Well yeah, Rhoda said.

Irene dabbed at her fish with a napkin, which soaked through immediately. Enough oil? she asked. Then she took a bite with some ketchup. Frozen, she said. They're using frozen halibut. Who uses frozen halibut?

It tastes all right, Gary said. Good enough, anyway.

Good enough, Irene said. Good enough. Your mantra through life.

Mom, Rhoda said.

And then they just ate. No one felt like talking more. They drove to a Motel 6, checked in, and went to their room.

I need to lie down, Irene said. She took another codeine and tried to sink into sleep. Rhoda took a nap on the other bed, asleep quickly, her breathing rough and heavy in the small room. Gary had gone off somewhere on a walk, disappearing again.

Irene was afraid of surgery, even the possibility of surgery. She'd asked about risks, and Romano said there was a risk of blindness, of hitting the optic nerve. That and possible death from the general anesthesia. And the bones in her head could become irritated and grow after the surgery, blocking everything off again. She didn't really understand that, how a bone could grow, but apparently it could. And she wouldn't be able to breathe through her nose for a week while it was packed. Meanwhile, her throat would be filling with blood. She felt claustrophobia already just thinking about it. Imagine not being able to swallow or breathe.

Gary tried to clear his head by walking. He felt accused. For years now, and what had he actually done? No crime that he was aware of. The crime only of association, of being there. His marriage a thing of pressure and weight.

He didn't like walking in a city, even a city like Anchorage that was mostly one-story and spread out and not really a city. Dirty and empty, endless strip malls. Car and truck dealerships, industrial supply, nightclubs with no windows, fast food and gun shops. A sunny afternoon in a dead place.

Irene was working at him, had been for a while now. He didn't know why. But she wouldn't let up. The constant complaints. He was weak, running away, never there for her, always a failure, always a disappointment. She thought the cabin was idiotic, thought his life was idiotic. And what was her goal? Just to make the two of them miserable?

Gary took off his jacket, warming up from walking fast. Hopefully the doctor could make the headaches go away. That would be an improvement. The crazy factor would decrease considerably.

He tried not to think about her, tried to just walk. Mud-spattered pickups and campers rolling past, clogged at street-lights. He liked his trails at home, the path to Mark's house, path over the first ridge, longer trails up the mountain. More to explore on the island, too, a lot more to explore. But first he had a cabin to finish. He was running out of time.

Gary stopped and closed his eyes and tried to see it, tried to stand inside his cabin, the log walls, an old iron stove in the corner, nickel legs. A rough table, bench seats covered in hides, a bed at the end of the room, his biggest bear hide over that. Timber wolves hanging either side of the doorway, the one window leaded. A rocking chair for looking out this window, maybe a pipe. Maybe he'd take up smoking a pipe.

Gary sighed and opened his eyes, walked on. A lot of work still before he'd be thinking about that rocking chair. And very little help from anyone. Every part of the project would be a struggle. That was the truth.

Gary found himself back at the motel room before long, opened and closed the door quietly.

I'm not asleep.

Sorry, Irene. I wish you could sleep.

Me too.

He lay down beside her, put his arm over.

Thank you, she said, happy to have him back. Easier to get through the time, listening to him fall asleep.

Irene watched the clock while Gary and Rhoda napped, and finally it was four p.m. They piled into the truck for the four-thirty appointment.

Romano put CAT scans on an illuminated white screen. Irene

could see her own brain, all the soft tissues in addition to bones. Very different from an X ray, everything revealed.

These dark patches right here, Romano pointed, are your sphenoid sinuses.

Irene could see they were tucked under her brain, far back from her nose. A place hidden from X rays by surrounding bone.

Dark means they're empty, Romano said.

What?

That's good news, really. And your frontals are clear. That was the other possibility for the pain behind your right eye. Maxillaries in your cheeks also clear, though I doubted you had anything there. You would have had more facial pain.

I don't understand, Irene said. There's nothing there, just like in the X ray?

That's right.

There has to be something.

I'm sorry.

But what are these terrible headaches then? Irene could feel herself breaking down, and Romano put a hand on her shoulder.

I'm sorry, Irene. From what you describe, I think you did have a sinus infection, probably your frontal sinuses. But they seem to have cleared, and I don't know why you still have the headache.

There's no other explanation?

Not in my field, Romano said. I'm not a neurosurgeon. It could be the infection and headache, if that's what it started as, triggered something else, or it could have been the stress from the headache and not sleeping. Is there anything else you've been worried about lately, any other cause of stress?

Huh, Irene said. Just thirty years of marriage going down the toilet, my whole life with it.

I'm sorry, Romano said, and it was clear Irene had gone too

far. She never told anyone anything about her life, as a general rule—some sort of Icelandic code.

I shouldn't have said that, she told him. I normally wouldn't say that. I just wanted surgery. So everything could go away. The pain is real. The headaches won't stop, and I'm scared of them. I don't know what to do. I need to make them stop.

You need to stop taking the codeine, Romano said. You've already been on it long enough to become addicted, and that can cause new problems.

But I can't sleep. Even the codeine isn't enough sometimes.

You have to stop today. No more painkillers beyond aspirin or Advil. And I'd recommend seeing a psychiatrist. You might ask about medication for anxiety. That could help you sleep, and more sleep might take care of the headache.

Okay, Irene said, nodding, thinking there was no way in hell she was going to see a shrink. And thank you. I'm sorry.

No need to apologize, he said. You're in pain, and I'm sorry I can't help.

Irene walked to the exit counter and waited to pay, but the receptionist told her there was no charge. This made Irene start to cry, the kindness. The pain had her always on edge, ready to spill over for any reason. But she dabbed at her eyes and walked into the waiting area, trying to figure out what to tell Gary and Rhoda.

They could see her eyes were wet. They both stood right away and came over to hug her.

It's not my sinuses, she told them. We still don't know what's wrong.

Jim received a call from Rhoda. They were coming home tonight, not staying over in Anchorage. She sounded tired on the phone.

I'll have dinner ready, he said. What would you like?

Anything. I don't care. I have to go. Sorry.

So Jim drove to the store. He needed to make something nice for Rhoda. Maybe even Baked Alaska. Tried to think of what she liked most and drew a blank. He had no idea what she really liked to eat. All the dishes she fixed, they were all for him, all the things he liked.

He'd been selfish and taken her for granted. He could see that now. And he'd just paid a lot of money to have her not find out. Not a cheap fuck, he said out loud.

The problem was, he still missed Monique. Despite how things ended. She was the most beautiful woman he would ever be with. That was a certainty. There would never be anything better, and he had half his life still to live. That was depressing. Rhoda was safe, though, and available. He'd get a ring, and maybe they'd even have kids, all of which made him want to yank the wheel and flip into a ditch.

Jim tried to hold it together. Rhoda would be able to tell if he was still upset when she got home. He'd have to pretend it was just concern for her and her mom. He could come out of this looking better than ever.

Thanks for fucking me over, Monique, he said.

He parked and went inside, to the seafood section. Enormous king crab legs, even whole crabs, six feet across. Like aliens, crawling along the bottom in darkness, cold as space, under mountains of pressure. A world that shouldn't exist, far away and untouchable. You could bring a crab up, but you couldn't go down to them, couldn't join. And this was the truth about Monique. He could have her for a short time, and his money could make it seem almost that he could fit into her world, but she was untouchable. Even if he had been her age, he would have ended up like Carl.

Fuckers, Jim said.

What's that? asked the man behind the counter.

Oh. Sorry, Jim said. I'll take some crab legs.

Then there was the problem of what to go with the legs. Nothing sounded good to Jim. He didn't care if he never ate again. But he decided on a big salad. Rhoda liked salads. And he got all the goodies. Marinated artichoke hearts, pine nuts, cranberries, avocado, tomatoes, shaved Gruyère, the works. Then the fixings for Baked Alaska. Also some Ben and Jerry's for backup, though not New York Superfudge Chunk. Cherry Garcia would work.

Jim slumped over his cart in the freezer section and just held on. His face down close to the lettuce. He wasn't going to cry over her, ever. He had to focus on his breath, let it calm, slowly calm. He'd be all right. He was a dentist, after all. He made more than any of the other fucks around here.

At the moment, though, Alaska felt like the end of the world, a place of exile. Those who couldn't fit anywhere else came here, and if they couldn't cling to anything here, they just fell off the edge. These tiny towns in a great expanse, enclaves of despair.

He needed to pull himself together. There was no line at checkout, and he was home quickly, carrying his groceries to the kitchen. And it was only as he was putting the bags down that he realized there had been a change. He had been unfaithful, and even if he married Rhoda now, he had opened the possibility of other women, and he knew he would act on this. He would continue cheating. There was no way to stop it once it was possible. He would find other women, most likely his patients. Or his staff. He could advertise for another hygienist, another secretary to help with the front office. He could tell Rhoda he was doing this instead of bringing in another partner. A way to expand. But he'd be hiring an affair. That's all he'd be looking for, one at a time, just hire and fire. He didn't know how he hadn't thought of that before. Rhoda would catch on eventually, but then he'd just move on to the next wife, if he had to, and the next set of affairs. None of it was a crime. And if he had her sign a prenup, there'd be no damage done.

The question, really, was what his life was about. He didn't believe in God, and he wasn't in the right field to become famous or powerful. Those were the three biggies: faith, fame, and power. They could justify a life, perhaps, or at least make you think your life meant something. All the crap about being a good guy, treating people well, and spending time with family was only crap because it had nothing to anchor it. There was no cosmic scorecard. Having kids seemed to work for some people, but not really. They were lying, because they'd lost their lives and it was too late. And money, by itself, didn't mean anything. So all that was left was sex, and money could help with that.

Jim stood at the sink, washing lettuce, and realized this was it. He would devote his life to sex. Get in better shape and have as many women as possible. He wished he had discovered this earlier, before forty-one, because it would have been a lot easier earlier, but it still wasn't too late. He had a good ten years at least before his life dissolved into something he didn't care to think about.

He tore up the lettuce, cut tomatoes, sliced the avocado, threw in the other bits, got a pot of water ready for the crab legs, then had to stop because he didn't know when she'd be home. And he decided to skip the Baked Alaska. Too much effort.

Carl spent all day at the Coffee Bus. Karen gave him free coffee, and when she found out he had no money, gave him free sandwiches, also. He sat against the side of the bus, a backpack on either side. Nodded hello to the customers and wrote postcards. He wrote one of them to himself.

Dear Carl, Hoping to see you again soon. You seem a little lost. It's been a while since we talked. I think we have to admit at this point that things are not going well. We both have dreams, but are they leading us in the same direction? Ha ha, Carl.

Carl filled in his address and decided to send it along with the other cards. All of this assumed he'd have enough money at some point to buy stamps. He was waiting for Mark to show up so he could ask for a job.

But Mark did not show up, and at 8:00 p.m., Karen locked the bus.

Fishing ended at seven, Karen said. But they have to get to the dock and unload. Be a while before he shows up, so I'll just bring you home and you can talk with him there.

Thank you, Carl said, and climbed into her VW with the backpacks.

Where's Monique?

Carl had been sitting here all day with the two packs, so it was odd that Karen was asking now.

Dumped me, he said.

Karen nodded and pulled onto the road. Sorry about that.

It was inevitable, Carl said. She never liked me. But she could at least come pick up her stuff. Seems a little rude to have me schlep it around.

Yeah, Karen agreed. Then she mumbled to herself. Whisperings and head jerks, low grumbles, aha expressions, the whole bit, like a full conversation with another person. Carl sitting in the seat beside her, only a few feet away, completely ignored. He wondered whether she was on something, or damaged in some way. He hadn't noticed this about her before. But he didn't want to interrupt.

Karen drove a slalom course on the gravel road to the lake. Drift to the right side of the road, then a small jerk and drift to the left, then back to the right again. Carl was grateful to arrive.

Karen went in and started cooking, off in her own world. Carl carried the packs one at a time and settled in the living room. Unfinished plywood floor, an old and dirty couch, but comfortable enough. The air surprisingly cold. No heat or insulation, the wind coming in from somewhere. Carl had taken off his jacket but he put it back on, flipped the hood up. Same as being outside.

Carl was hungry. The sandwiches and coffee not enough. A kind of torture to sit here on the couch, knowing food was nearby. He couldn't just get up and grab a snack. There had to be some smoked salmon. Food within reach but untouchable, though in her mutterings would she even notice?

Mark finally drove up and walked in.

My brother from another planet, he said to Carl. Hail.

Avast, Carl said, trying to rise to the occasion.

Did you bring Monique?

She dumped me.

Ah, Mark said. Have you heard my calculus joke?

No.

E to the X is walking down the street with C, and they run into an integration sign.

What?

You didn't take calculus?

No.

Well never mind, then. It's a long joke. I told it to a girl at the cannery today, though, and she got it. She speaks five languages.

Sorry, Carl said.

Mark went over to hug Karen, and they had some odd little ritual involving ear massage. Apparently Mark's ears got cold on the boat and Karen's hands were exceptionally warm. Too embarrassing to watch, so Carl sat down on the couch again, facing the other way. He could hear slurpings and murmurings but tried to just look at the trees and bits of lake between the trees.

Carl felt how poor he was. He had to sit here because he had nowhere else to go. If you were poor, you had to ask favors and hang out and wait and spend time with people you didn't want to spend time with. All the while, you were essentially invisible. Carl was not going to do this anymore. He was going to change his major, even if it meant an extra year of college. And he was going to tell Mark about Jim and Monique. That was the one weak spot of the rich. They had secrets.

Mark finally made it over to the couch, finished with the ear massaging and whatever else. Hombre, he said. There's a guy at the cannery who can say "Who farted?" in eight languages.

Huh, Carl said. He never knew what to say around Mark.

And he couldn't figure out how to segue from that to, Can you get me a job?

He can say it in Thai.

How was fishing? Carl asked.

Rough, Mark said. Ten-footers. Cut way down on the catch. No one could do volume. We did only a thousand pounds.

That sounds like a lot.

It's not.

Could you have done more if you had help?

Mark gave him a squinty look.

Okay, Carl said. That was pretty obvious, I guess. I'm broke and I need a job. Any chance of joining you on the boat?

Mark patted Carl on the shoulder, which made him feel real big. Sorry, he said. It's impossible to get on a boat. You have to live here and know everyone and be around every summer. You have to have experience. There's a line of guys trying to get on. And it's the end of the season anyway.

Okay, Carl said. That makes sense. But he felt disappointed. No way in. He stared at the skinny trees, dwarfing out near the lake. They got shorter and shorter the closer they were to the water. A forest for the little people, like Carl himself. I'm a wee man, he said to Mark, using his fake Irish accent.

Hey, Mark said. Go easy, man. You can find something, just not on a boat.

I have to find something now, unfortunately. I have less than five dollars at this point. I maybe should have set something up earlier.

Yeah, Mark laughed. Maybe. But hey, I can probably get you a job at the cannery.

Really?

Yeah. Eight bucks an hour, not a lot, but you don't need any experience. You can start at the wash table, just pulling out membranes and getting the last bits of blood. Takes five minutes to learn.

Thanks, Mark. That'd be perfect.

Let's celebrate with a bowl.

Carl was going to say no, as he always did, but then he thought what the hell. Marijuana wasn't going to kill him. Okay, he said.

My man, Mark said, and he packed a bowl and got it lit, small puffs. Then he took a long drag, held it in, and passed the pipe to Carl.

Carl didn't like the smell, or the smoke, and he hated to break his record. He'd never tried anything, not even a cigarette or an alcoholic drink. A point of pride, and it would be over now. But what the hell. He sucked in the hot smoke, acrid and constricting, and coughed, his breath gone short.

Mark was laughing, and Karen came over to laugh, too.

Popped his cherry, Mark told her. Right here, in our humble abode.

Karen took a hit then floated away back to the kitchen.

Carl waited for a feeling, a different perception, anything. He was hoping for visions, maybe the walls dissolving. But nothing happened. Mark passed him the bowl and he sucked in again, held it like Mark told him, then exhaled and coughed again.

Is it good? Mark asked.

I don't feel anything, Carl said.

Nothing? Mark asked.

Nothing.

Try another hit.

So Carl tried again, but really there was no effect other than a low-grade headache at the back of his neck and a foul taste in his mouth, a tightness in his lungs.

Try again, Mark said, so Carl tried a fourth hit, but then he gave up.

Sometimes nothing happens your first time, Mark said.

Carl wasn't sure there'd be a second time. It was all disappointing. Monique is fucking Jim, he told Mark. And he looked over to the kitchen, to Karen, who was looking at him now. I saw them do it in the living room when we stayed over there, and she's been disappearing a lot.

Mark was packing another bowl.

Rhoda's Jim? Karen asked.

Yeah, the dentist.

Mark lit up and took a long hit, then passed the bowl to Carl.

No thanks, Carl said. That's enough for now.

Mark shrugged and held the bowl up in the air for Karen to come over. She took a drag and handed it back.

So that was it, the big revelation, the much-anticipated moment. Carl's secret information hitting the world like a meteor.

Dinner's ready, Karen said.

Milky with silt, and calm. You could imagine it was only ankle-deep. As Gary cut the engine and they glided toward shore, Irene could hear seagulls on a rocky perch farther up the lake. The smallest of the islands, exposed rock covered white in guano. No wind today, sunny and still, the last good weather of summer. Next week, the first of the fall storms forecast.

Irene looked over the side to see blue-gray stones emerge below the hull. The milky water somehow clear in close, a looking glass, magnifying the stones, bringing them closer. It seemed they should already be touching. The boat bumped, finally, its bottom scraping, and Irene hoisted her backpack, climbed carefully over the side, rubber boot sucking close to her ankle and shin in the water. Slippery. In her backpack, a tent and sleeping bag, pots and pans, clothing. Gary carrying a Coleman stove, another tent. Setting up camp so they could work longer days. From when they rose each morning to when they went to sleep, they would work on the cabin.

Irene careful over the slick stones, a few steps onto shore, more stones but dry and gray, small tufts of grass, miniature freshwater tidal pools of algae and mosquitoes, a cloud of them around her now, going for her knuckles and wrists, any place of bone and blood close to the surface. A narrow band of grass and rock along the shore, then the taller grass and wildflowers no longer in bloom. Most likely there was purple iris, prickly rose, shy maiden, pink twin flower, pyrola, others yellow and white she couldn't yet name. Deadfall and ruts all through here, Irene hoping not to trip under the weight of the pack.

The alder thicket a third band up from shore, bright green in the sun, all the earth green. The growth thick in here, cobwebs lacing the air. Irene tried to keep her steps light, to avoid any jarring. Her husband behind her, the sound of his faster steps, snapping of small branches.

Perfect day for setting up camp, he said as he passed, and she didn't reply. She kept her head down, red fireweed in a large patch, the tops already bloomed. A sign of fall coming, the beginning of the end. Six weeks until snow when the tops bloomed, and they had opened a while ago, though she had forgotten to notice exactly when. After enough years here, you could begin to fear that flower, so it was odd she hadn't noticed.

Irene passed through low alder to the edge of the larger forest, where their cabin tottered too far inward on one side, too far outward on another. The entire thing ready to topple. They'd brought a load of two-by-fours, to set up braces.

Irene walked back to the boat, passing Gary who grinned and jigged his eyebrows. Good eats, he said, carrying a plastic tub of food.

Irene wanted to respond, wanted to make this easier. But she couldn't. Off medication, every edge was sharp. She had to move carefully, had to avoid speaking or facial expressions.

She grabbed half a dozen two-by-fours from the boat, stepped slowly up through tufts and ruts, set the wood down and returned for another load. Nothing was wrong, so she needed to just wait for the pain to go away.

What a beautiful spot, Gary said. I love this place.

It is beautiful, she said, wincing. But Gary was all movement, didn't see. He dropped off a cooler and spun around quick for the next load.

Tools and supplies, enough food for two weeks, a toilet seat for an outhouse, more nails and a window and door, two-by-fours and a come-along for pulling the walls into shape: they were making their full assault now.

One last load of wood, then Gary cleared a spot for the tent, near a stand of birch, behind the cabin. Can you help me put up the tent? he called out, as if she weren't standing nearby on a windless day. It was the excitement. He wanted to do everything at once.

So she helped, a big tent, enough room for the two of them and all their clothing and gear.

What about the food? Irene asked. How do we keep it away from bears?

No bears out here, Gary said. It's an island.

Bears do swim.

Yeah, but not just to come visiting. It's a long way from shore.

Only a couple hundred yards on the close side, right?

Something like that. Let's just put the food in the tent for now. Help me with the cooler. So they put their food next to their sleeping bags.

Now the other tent, Gary said. They looked for level ground, feeling their way through the undergrowth. Large patches of club moss, spongy and soft, lady ferns, shield ferns, an area with more shade.

Seems okay here, Gary said. We're not sleeping in this one, so it can be a little bumpy.

Irene helped unroll another tarp and tent, helped drive in stakes and spread the rain fly. If only the cabin could be this easy. She and Gary loaded tools and supplies, everything except the wood, into the tent, then stood back and looked at their little camp.

Not bad, Gary said. Outhouse is next.

Irene looked at the lake, so calm today, the mountains reflected. Peaks clear, upper snow patches outlining ridges, the edge of the Harding Icefield. Sunny and warm, maybe seventy degrees. She'd taken her jacket off. The kind of day when all could seem possible.

It shouldn't be far from the cabin, Gary was saying. We'll need to use it through the winter.

Let's just build it on the back of the cabin, Irene said. So we don't have to go outside at all.

Irene.

What? Every time I have to use the bathroom, I have to wade through a bunch of snow?

The snow's not too bad here.

Is it the kind that's not cold and wet?

Irene.

Irene yourself. Build the damn thing on the back of the cabin, just sticking out from the wall. Put a door on it.

We'll smell the outhouse all winter.

Then so be it. If we're going to live like shit, we should smell shit.

Gary turned away from her. The kind of moment he was looking for, she knew. Enough fights about this ridiculous cabin and he could justify leaving. Put her in an impossible situation and then say the marriage was impossible. The beauty of it was that he could lie so well to himself he'd still think he was the good guy. He'd actually believe he'd done everything he could.

Look, she said. You can build it ten feet away, with a short hallway connecting. Put a door on both ends. Maybe that way we won't smell it.

Gary considered. He walked along the back wall of the cabin, turned in place several times, pacing things out. Okay, he said finally. I can do something like that. But we have to move the supply tent to make room.

Crisis averted, and if it was this easy, she wondered whether she could refuse the entire cabin right now. Just say no to the whole idea and go home. But she knew that was not possible. Because the cabin was not about the cabin.

They pulled all the tools and supplies out of the second tent, found another spot farther back, put it up and loaded again. The afternoon passing, Gary looking at his watch.

It's getting late, he said, and we haven't even started the outhouse yet. Punishment, indirect. Letting her know the consequences.

Yeah, Irene said. Bummer it's not June.

Gary tight-lipped after that. Grabbing the shovel to chop a pathway through the growth, a narrow aisle to a larger square for the outhouse, about four feet by four feet. His T-shirt darkening from sweat.

Irene finally pulled the cooler from their tent, sat down on it to watch him work. Digging to China, tearing a hole in the earth to let her know how he felt. No different from a little boy. She should grab him and make him take the tit, rock him until he fell asleep.

It aggravated Irene that she'd had to take care of this man for thirty years. The weight of his complaints and impatience, his failures, and in return, his vacancy. Why had any of that seemed okay?

Irene couldn't watch him anymore. She got up and walked into the trees. All shaded here, cooler, the trunks close, every tree with rakes of slim dead branches, thin curved fingers, leftovers, perhaps, from when they were much younger. Snapping against her as she broke through, all the green and new growth much higher. Spruce and birch, trees you could tire of after enough years in Alaska. The occasional cottonwood with its rougher bark, a few aspen.

Narrow pathways like alleys opened up, and she followed these, game trails. Small patches of moss and fern, the forest quiet. Irene a hunter or hunted, either way the same feeling, the same awareness of the forest, the same waiting for sound or movement, the same awareness of breath. It was time to hunt again, to bring her bow out here. But she was accompanied now by this new thing, this new betrayal of body, something she couldn't fight, couldn't track, could never see because it didn't exist. Irene climbed higher, hitting plateaus and slopes all hidden by forest, until she had reached a hump with no higher to go, still surrounded, still no view, a panorama that was there but blocked on every side.

Sunday, and Rhoda and Jim both had the day off, so they slept late, had sex, napped again, then just lay there. Jim with his eyes closed, Rhoda with her head propped on his chest, looking at the view. Slow rollers coming up the inlet, a clear and sunny day. Slim black spruce in the flats before the beach, standing individually. They'd always seemed like people to Rhoda, vagabonds heading toward the sea, each walking alone. She could imagine a lower branch as a hand, holding a small suitcase.

The trees look like people, Rhoda said.

What? Jim asked.

The spruce out there, like people, a little bit shaggy, like the Whos of Whoville.

Huh, he said.

You're not looking.

Okay, he said, and propped his head with a pillow. Rhoda readjusted lower on his chest. The trees out there? he asked.

Yeah.

I guess I can see that. Small ones for the kids, bigger ones for the adults. They're about the right height.

And where are they going? she asked.

Sounds like a loaded question.

Hm, Rhoda said. It wasn't. I wasn't thinking of that.

Sorry, he said.

My parents are so weird. Promise me we'll never be like them.

That's easy.

Rhoda laughed. They are freaks.

You're the one who said it.

When do I meet your parents?

I don't know, Jim said. They moved to Arizona.

That's all you ever say about them.

Well I don't go down there, and they don't come up here.

That's sad.

No it's not. It's an accidental relationship, unchosen. I never would have chosen them as friends. I don't even like them.

That's really sad.

Not for me. I don't care at all.

Hm, Rhoda said. She didn't like this side of Jim, cold and unconnected to anyone. It didn't sound true, and it certainly didn't fit her vision of having kids and cozy family scenes. Accidental and unchosen.

Am I accidental and unchosen? she finally asked.

Rhoda, he said.

Really. Is it just because I'm here, and available?

No. I love you. You know that.

Rhoda propped up and looked into his eyes. Really? she asked. Can you promise me that?

Absolutely, he said, and pulled her close for a kiss.

Okay, she said, and settled back against his chest. Some of his chest hair was turning gray. A change just in the last year since they'd been living together. And his stomach going soft, a little mound. A thickening at his sides. Eleven years older than her.

I'm worried about my mom, she said.

Yeah. I thought Romano would find something.

I don't know what's wrong with her. I don't know how to help her.

Hm.

Rhoda could tell Jim wasn't really interested in this subject. Too messy and complicated. You don't want to talk about this.

I'm fine, Jim said. Really.

I try to understand her, and I just can't. Maybe it's retirement. I know she misses her work and feels pointless now. And they don't have as much money as they wanted for retirement, so she probably worries about that. But there's something else, too, something more important going on. It's like she's making her own secret deals with the gods.

Whoa, Jim said. That sounds a little grand.

I'm serious, though. She's decided the world is against her, and it's like she's getting ready for battle. She's all paranoid. And then I try to say something, and she knows I'm not in there with the gods. I don't get to decide anything. I only get to watch it all happen, so I don't matter.

That's not true. You matter to her.

I used to. But I don't now. I think the pain in her head is from getting ready to go to war. And I know the war is with my dad, but I can't figure out what it's really about, because I'm not in it.

Rhoda, Jim said. I'm sorry, but I think you're going off the deep end yourself. You're making too much of this. She has some kind of pain, probably from being a stress case. Or she needs to get used to retirement, like you said. But that's it. She'll get over it.

I don't think she will. And Rhoda realized this was true. She felt very sad suddenly. She didn't believe her mother would recover from this. Because whatever was wrong was pulling in every part of her life. That was the key. It was reaching across time. I don't think she'll get better, she said to Jim. I really don't.

Jim held her then, both arms wrapped around her, and she closed her eyes and wanted to find some way to stop everything, but it was all darkness, a void, nothing to grab onto. When are you going to marry me, Jim? she asked. I need something solid. She couldn't believe she had just said that, said those words aloud. But she had.

There was a long and ugly pause, and she could feel his breath and heart quickening. I love you, Rhoda, he finally said.

Not enough. When are you going to marry me?

The wash table was a cold aluminum trough, a wading pool of blood and saltwater. Carl's hands aching from the cold, fingers sore. The salmon came to him gutted and beheaded, but he needed to grip thin, clear membranes with his triple-gloved hands and pull them out, then flick onto the floor. Four or five tries for every membrane before he could find it, and sometimes it wasn't there.

The chu-chunk of the beheading machine a steady rhythm, every few seconds, another fish coming his way, and he was starting to panic. Too many fish, a backup at the wash table. Metallica blasting on speakers above.

Three others were working the same job, all faster, but the fish were piling up, filling the blood bath. The woman across from him, another college student, wasn't actually grabbing any membranes, so that was stressing him out. She'd give the fish a light caress on each side, to wash off the blood, then give a peek inside the gutted area of the body, where the membranes were hiding, and throw the fish onto a white plastic chute in the middle of the table, sending it on to the inspectors. Each time she threw, she managed to splat the tail against the chute, flicking slime and water onto Carl's face. She had it perfected. And she'd throw three fish for every one of his.

The inspectors two more women, similar age but not in college, at the end of the trough. They were supposed to give a quick check and sort the fish. Any with gashes or broken spines thrown into a side bin. Any other species of salmon in another bin, because they were packing sockeye only. But they'd pull a membrane or push out a blood spot or pluck a bit of gill if the fish wasn't clean, and they didn't seem to care that they had to do this with every one of this other woman's fish and none of Carl's. They chatted the whole time, locals, having to shout over the Metallica. They'd worked here for years, and they had a low opinion of the place.

Dude, you can't get fired from a cannery, one said to the other, especially this cannery. This is as low as it gets.

They chatted about men and money, and they'd had this job so long they didn't have to pay it any attention. But Carl struggled with every fish. First the membrane, trying to find an edge somewhere down by the asshole, then looking for two blood pockets up near where the head had been removed. He had to push hard with a thumb to get this blood to pop out. Then checking for any leftover pieces of gill and trying to scrape the extra blood from the backbone. Impossible to get all of it, and he had no tool. Just a rough cotton glove over a plastic glove over another cotton glove. Because theoretically, everything had already been removed by a person with a gutting spoon on the conveyor belt. So that was the person Carl resented most.

Carl resented everyone upstream of him, though. They were all skilled, all higher paid, and all had easier jobs. One stood with a shovel and helped move fish from enormous slush tanks. This guy spent a lot of time just standing there watching the fish go by. Then someone lined up the fish so their heads faced the same way. This is the job Carl would have liked. Then a guy made one quick slit from asshole to gullet. One flick of the knife for each fish. Then the beheader. He moved the fish only a few inches, lining up the head for a heavy set of blades. A guillotine, and dangerous. But he wore a lanyard that was attached to the table and kept his hand from scooting too far forward. And he moved the fish hardly at all.

Only men at the head of the stream, until the next station, ripping out the guts. A woman did that. The guts traveled on a small conveyor belt to another woman who sorted the roe, the red sack of eggs, into a small plastic basket. Like a diviner, reading futures from each plop of guts onto her table. Then she'd scrape it clean with a quick swoop before the next plop came.

After that, knives and men again, one quick slit to open the blood along the spine. Then a woman with a spoon to scoop out all the blood and a man with a spray nozzle to wash it down. All of this on a wide conveyor belt, light blue plastic, and the fish exited with a flop into the wash table trough. Every flop spattered the guy standing to the left of Carl, and the guy flinched every time. Worst position in the plant, and though Carl had to pee like a madman, he wouldn't leave, because he knew the guy would step to the side and Carl would get stuck there.

So the problem was either the woman with the gutting spoon or the man with the spray nozzle. One of them was supposed to be getting the membrane and the last of the blood, but they just sent the fish on as quickly as possible. The salmon kept piling up at the wash table until they were in danger of spilling over the sides and the conveyor was backing up, and there was no water within reach for washing. A mountain of carcasses and no way to wash, and Carl thought he might scream.

Sean, the manager, appeared at the clean aluminum table beyond the inspectors and barked for fish to be sent his way. So the inspectors grabbed fish from the wash table quick and scooted about fifty. Sean glanced inside each one then passed it along to where it was boxed in ice, ready to be shipped. Another sign that Carl's job was entirely pointless. The boss sending all these fish along in a bypass, after Carl had endured over an hour of rubbish, at five a.m., about quality control in the plant. There was a bucket of hot chlorinated hand wash behind Carl that he could dip his hands into, for instance, and this would help keep the fish cleaner and increase shelf life, but he could never risk walking over to this bucket to warm his hands, because then the guy next to him would step to the side and Carl would be splatted by every arriving salmon. A roving inspector checked temperatures and made sure everyone was doing their jobs, but he stood by the woman across from Carl and seemed to think that her nothing peek into the carcass was sufficient.

To Carl, all of life's lessons were apparent here. Everything he should have learned already in college. Everything he needed to understand about his future. He made the list in his head as he pushed at blood and scraped for membranes:

1. *Don't work with other people.*
2. *Don't work a manual job.*
3. *Be glad you don't have to work as a woman.*
4. *There's no such thing as quality control. All the other terms of business are bullshit also. The business world is where thoughts and language go to die.*
5. *Work means nothing except money. So find a job that means more than this, something ideally that doesn't feel like work.*

But the most important lesson was that Carl needed to leave immediately. There were no prizes for sticking around in a shitty situation. He would call his mother tonight and beg for a ticket home. He didn't care what it would cost him in the end. He was not going to spend even one more day in this place.

Everyone went on break, finally, fifteen minutes after four hours of salmon. It took Carl five minutes to take off his raingear bibs and pee, then he stood outside, by the campfire. A metal pit in the dirt, no flames but a few coals and lots of smoke. The smoke coming Carl's direction most of the time, dousing him. He and his fellow fish processors stood in a circle staring at the coals, one of the guys talking about his bar fight and brief jail stay. He'd been released this morning just in time for work.

My ex comes in with this known crack dealer, and that means this guy is spending time with my kid. I know who he is, and he knows who I am. He comes right over, and I don't do anything. I just sit there as he rants.

Carl had trouble making sense of this story, because the guy looked so mild-mannered. Same age as Carl, a bit thicker and stronger, light red beard, but he didn't look like someone with an ex who was with a crack dealer.

He yells up in my face for maybe half an hour, some incredible length of time. I thought he would stop, but he didn't, so I finally said, Let's take it outside.

Let's take it outside, Carl repeated aloud. What a cliché, he was thinking, grinning a bit, but no one shared this moment with him. Odd looks from the teller and others, only a brief pause in the story. Carl an outsider, as usual.

I slip my beer bottle in my pocket, something he doesn't see, and when we're outside, I break the end against the railing and tell him I'm ready.

The group was impressed, Carl could tell. Carl was not impressed. He couldn't believe he was hanging out with these knuckleheads.

So he doesn't fuck with me when he sees the bottle. We just circle around and he doesn't dare get close. And then the cops come, and it's my friend Bill. I'm just like, do you want me to put the handcuffs on myself? He's already had to do this a couple times, and he's like dude, how do you get into this shit? So it was cool. I spent the night at the station, and they let me out in time for work.

Everyone looked at the coals another minute or so, no comments about the story, then it was time to go in, the break over. Back to the guts.

Carl in pole position this time, splatted every time a carcass hit the pool. He tried not to flinch. Cold slime hitting his face and left ear, in his hair. It's only slime and blood, he told himself. It'll wash off. He tried to figure out some small way to hurt this business and his coworkers, but he couldn't think of anything. He was inconsequential. He could do the non-job the woman across from him was doing, but since he was standing here anyway, he decided to keep removing the membranes and blood. Only another four hours. His right hand cramped up, cold, but he could ignore that.

He needed to call his mom, say good-bye to Mark and thank him, and also figure out what to do with Monique's backpack.

The salmon began appearing with heads. Gutted and gills removed, but heads on. Some change in the plans, and Carl hadn't been notified, but his job still the same. The eyes wide, dilated, silver-rimmed. Hooked lower jaws on some of them, almost like beaks. The males, perhaps. He wasn't finding membranes.

Something's different, he yelled to one of the inspectors over the music. I can't find any membranes.

These already came through the line yesterday, she yelled back. Head and gills. But the order changed, and now they're without gills.

Cool, he said.

Yeah, she yelled. It's great. Why not do everything twice. Motto of this cannery.

You sound like a disgruntled employee.

Bite me.

Carl tried to laugh, but the way she said it was actually kind of mean, and she wasn't looking at him anymore. The other peons at the wash table gave a quick look up, no sympathy, and looked back down at the fish.

A pause in the line, enough time for the peons to catch up, and then half a dozen smaller salmon came by, whole. Not gutted or beheaded, the upstream folks just watching them pass by. Carl was confused, but he gave a quick wash in the blood pool and passed a salmon along. Smaller, lighter, a little bullet. A different species, but he didn't ask anyone. Who cared what it was, anyway.

And then they all shifted over to another long table on the other side of the warehouse. Plastic wheelbarrows full of halibut. Flat ghosts. Sideways mouths and thick lips, open, expressions of despair. Their tops dark mottled green, camouflaged, ugly. A beast from another time that hadn't imagined humans. Floor-dwellers, safely hidden away in the deep, swallowing whatever came near, and they could have gone on like that for the next hundred million years. Carl didn't want to be a part of this destruction anymore, so he stepped off the line and found Sean, the boss.

I'm sorry, he told Sean. I can't do this. I need to go home.

You have to finish the shift, Sean said.

I can't. I need to leave now.

Then you leave without pay.

No, Carl said. You're paying me for my six hours, forty-eight dollars cash right now, or I'm going to hurt you. I'm serious. I hate this place and everyone in it, and I'll take all of that out on you. So pay me my fucking money now.

Sean smiled. Fuck off, he said. Then he turned his back on Carl and walked slowly away.

So Carl stood there enraged at the latest sign that the world would not bend to his will, then went to the rack to hang up his raingear. He pulled off the rubber boots, changed into his shoes, and left. Carrying his own backpack and Monique's, he staggered up the beach to a campground where motor homes had gathered for dip-netting. Empty boat trailers, four-wheelers and dirt bikes, nets and garbage and tents. They had a long-drop outhouse he had used before, and this would be perfect for Monique's stuff. He wasn't going to carry around her shit anymore.

He had to wait, and a fat old man came out, finally, swinging the wooden door wide. Carl left his own backpack outside on the ground, stepped in with Monique's and closed the door. The light dim, air thick, and he didn't want to get any shit on her backpack, because he was planning to keep it himself, so he stepped outside and set it on the ground, opened up the top and pulled out an armload of her clothing. The panties he'd been all excited about once upon a time, her T-shirts and socks and jeans, scarves, sweaters, all this crap, and he stood over the long-drop to toss one item at a time. Fuck you, Monique, he said to the toilet. And fuck you, Alaska. Thank you very much for a delightful summer. The old man had finished the pile below with very light brown shit, covered now by her clothing. This is what Alaska is, right here, Carl said. A place where people shit. Just a bigger toilet.

He saved her expensive sleeping bag and other small bits of gear. A headlamp, a tiny stove, a knife. But every last scrap of clothing went in the hole, and he felt better, a lot better. Her pack lighter now, something he could carry in one hand.

So then he was on to the phone. Called his mother collect. I have to get out of here, he said.

What about Monique? she asked.

Left me for a dentist. An old guy, like forty or something.

Oh pumpkin.

Yeah, he said, tears forming, feeling sorry for himself. Hearing his mom's voice brought out all the self-pity.

You'll find someone else, she said.

Yeah, he said. He could hardly speak, his chest tight, and this whole scene struck him as ridiculous, laughable. But you can't fake feelings, and he was grateful to have his mom, someone in the world who would help him out. She said she'd deposit cash in his account within an hour so he could get dinner and a bus to Anchorage in the morning, and she'd book a flight. Expressions of love, and then he was walking to the beach to pitch his tent. He had wanted to find Mark to thank him, but now he just didn't care. He was through with Alaska.

The first fall storm. Gary leaned into blasts of wind and rain as he tried to nail the next layer of logs. Time. He hadn't finished on time, and now he would pay the price. A thirty-degree drop in temperature, the sky gone dark, a malevolence, a beast physical and intent. You could see why the ancients gave names. The lake a corollary beast, awakened also into whitecaps, breaking waves, cresting six feet high, pounding the shore. The wind in blasts, compressed, colder and colder, born in the icefield, accelerated in the wind tunnel over Skilak Glacier, funneled by mountains.

Atol ytha gewealc, Gary called out, the terrible surging of the waves. Irene in the tent, so he was alone and could speak. *Bitre breostceare,* bitter heart-care, *hu ic oft throwade,* how I often suffered, *geswincdagum,* in days of toil, *atol ytha gewealc.* He had always wanted to go to sea because of that poem, but never had. This storm now perhaps the closest he had come. *Iscealdne sae,* ice-cold sea, *winter wunade,* in winter inhabited, *wraeccan lastum,* in paths of exile, and this was true. He had lived almost his entire adult life in exile, in Alaska, a self-exile as good as any sea, and he wanted now to experience the very worst this storm could throw at him. He wanted the snows to come early, he wanted to suffer. He wanted to pay a price. Bring it on, fucker, he yelled into the storm. *Isigfethera,* he yelled. Icy-feathered.

He tried to catch a glimpse of the boat at the shore, but the rain drove into his eyeballs, pinpricks, the air so thick with water he couldn't see more than fifty feet. The boat driven onto the shore already, battered and pounded against rocks, but it was aluminum and would survive, unfortunately. Better if it were wood and smashed, its keel broken, no way ever to leave, better if the island were uninhabited by others, no one to go to for help. Gary wanted to be desolate, alone, not even Irene to witness. He wanted her to disappear, vanish, never have been. Bitter woman, sulking in the tent, contriving punishments worse than any storm.

Gary held the wood in place and kept driving nails, compacting the wood, forming a wall that would keep out nothing. Wood a satisfaction because it was once alive. A way to strike back at the earth, a way to mete out his own small punishment.

He stood on the platform swaying and catching his balance in each new blast, anchored by his left hand on the wood. Holding nails in his teeth, more in his pocket. Taste of galvanized steel. Arms and shoulders ropy now, fit, corded from work, enough time out here. Muscles a way to remember and return, hard work the only solace. So he pounded for hours, cut new logs, sawed their ends and lifted into place, hammered again. Rammed braces below, trued the walls a bit, didn't care they would never be true. The platform become a cage, a place of battle.

The tent a different battleground entirely. Old lump seething, waiting. But none of this was true, of course. He could see he was just getting himself worked up in the storm. Real life not so simple. His relation to the lump not so simple. But it was good to stand out here and blow a bit, and now he was hungry for lunch.

Hey Reney, he said as he unzipped the tent. Room for an old man in there?

He heard what sounded like a grunt, ducked in fast and closed the zipper.

Wow, he said. The storm's for real.

Don't get our stuff wet.

I'm being careful, he said. And he kept to the edge near the flap as he stripped off his coat and bibs and boots. Good to have a tent with full standing headroom, he said, but he could see it was catching a lot of wind. Irene lying down in her sleeping bag. Still not feeling well? he asked.

No.

Were you able to sleep?

No.

Is it because of the tent moving around in the wind?

Yeah, that and the pain. And not being home.

Sorry, he said.

It's okay. I know we have to be out here building to finish before the snows.

Gary crawled over to his own sleeping bag beside her. Midday but dark. It won't take long, he said. I promise. We'll be in the cabin and have a roof.

Irene didn't say anything in response. She was curled facing the other way.

So he lay in his sleeping bag, looked up into blue nylon, faintly backlit. The movement berserk, the sound unbelievable. Like living in a hurricane. Lying here, you could start to feel afraid, even though nothing was wrong. The tent wasn't going to blow down. The storm wasn't going to come in. They were safe. But if you spent enough time living in this confined space, you could begin to believe anything. You could feel the end coming. Terror fabricated from nothing, from nylon and wind. The mind that frail.

You could go crazy lying in this tent, he said to Irene.

Yep.

Maybe you should come outside for a bit.

Nope.

It's not so bad out there. Cold but not that cold. And the raingear works.

No thanks.

She was losing it, he could tell. Going a little nuts in here. But there was nothing he could do, really. They couldn't take the boat out in this storm even if they wanted to. So he closed his eyes and tried to catch a little shut-eye. Then he'd have some food and go back out to build. It was a simple cabin. It shouldn't be taking so long. He needed to just nail it all up.

He tried not to think about the cabin. He could never sleep if he spiraled off into thoughts. And he tried to ignore the sound of the tent, but after about twenty minutes, he gave up. He grabbed the peanut butter and jelly, made a sandwich, and put on his raingear as he ate.

I'm going, he said.

My regards to the storm.

Ha, he said, and stepped out into the blast, zipped the tent quickly. He turned his back to the wind, feeling a quick chill even through raingear, and jammed the last of the sandwich. Finished chewing, put some nails in his mouth. A little galvi for dessert, he told himself, and he liked this part, hunching into the wind and grabbing a hammer. He could have been a Viking heading off into a storm wearing only hides and a sword and shield. Or maybe a war hammer, a big piece of iron on the end of a stick. He could have done it. He would have been tough enough. Rowing and sailing, the blast of spray with each wave, days or even weeks on the water waiting for land to appear. And when it did make itself out of the fog, they'd sneak along that coast looking for a town, something small, perched on a headland or hidden up in a cove. And they'd blast ashore right onto the beach, the prow hitting sand, and leap over the side with their hammers and swords and spears and slaughter the men who had come to meet them. The feel of bringing a hammer down on another man's head. Like nothing else, Gary was sure. Brutal and true. Like animals, nothing deceptive. Just the stronger killing the weaker.

And then they'd run into town, dirt streets and hovels, sticks and thatched roofs, and they'd know that all the men were already dead. Women and children, and Gary standing before a hut with a woman inside. She'd be afraid. Her legs bare, and he realized he was slipping into bad movies here, that no one would have bare legs in that environment, wearing hides only on top. No G-string or Wonder Bra animal hides. But he felt turned on anyway, imagining a woman lying there on hides. He would strip her bare, tear the hides off her.

Gary was really feeling turned on, even though he knew it was dumb, especially for an Anglo-Saxonist. He looked toward the tent. It had been a long time, and rare he felt anything at all. But he knew Irene would think he was crazy, getting a boner out in a storm, coming in wet and cold expecting to do something about it. So Gary walked around to the front of the cabin, leaned against the log wall, his back to the outrageous wind, and opened his pants. He closed his eyes and saw himself spreading this woman's legs. She was still fighting, trying to pluck his eyes, so as he entered her, he was pinning her arms down.

He felt himself tighten and come onto the wall of the cabin, pathetic little spurts, his hips bucking, and he pressed in close to the wood, his eyes still closed, pressed in against the wall and just waited until his breath calmed.

Then he bent down to wipe his hand on some ferns, grabbed a bunch to wipe off the end of his dick, and buttoned up. He didn't bother to clean off the cabin. Irene would never notice, especially with all this rain.

Gary walked around onto the platform again and grabbed his hammer and nails. He felt tired now, ashamed of the violence of his imaginings. Raping a woman. This wasn't who he was, and it shouldn't excite him, either. It had just been so long since he and Irene had had sex. He didn't know why that was. The pain in her head, certainly, but even before that. He didn't understand marriage. The gradual denial of all one desired, the early death of self and possibility. The closing of a life prematurely. But this wasn't true, he knew. It was only the way it seemed right now, during a bad time. Once Irene got better and returned to her old self, he'd feel differently. He stood in the wind and rain, facing it, eyes closed, and tried to feel close to her, tried to feel what was best, the sense of the two of them providing mutual comfort, animal comfort, not being alone in the world, but at the moment, he just couldn't feel any connection at all. He didn't care to see her ever again. And maybe that was his fault. Maybe it was who he was. Maybe he was incapable of that kind of connection. But he didn't like to think about this. So he put an arm over a wall, cranked down on it with all his weight, and hammered a nail into the top log, kept hammering until he had driven it through, compressing into the next log, compacting the layers, and then he moved back a foot and drove in the next nail.

Rhoda was trying to save a golden retriever, a dog locked in a shed for weeks without food. There had been enough water to keep her barely alive. Red-gold hair filthy and matted, ribs and spine protruding, a skull with slack hanging skin. Still good-natured despite everything. Licked Rhoda's hand, looked at her with love, then had to put her head down again, no energy left. This killed Rhoda, the abuse of animals. She didn't understand how anyone could do this.

You're a good girl, Rhoda said as she set up an IV drip. We're going to fix you right up. A bit of struggle, frightened at the prick of the needle, but Rhoda stayed close and calmed her. You're beautiful, Rhoda said. We'll make you strong again. But she knew the dog might be dead by morning. She hated this part of her job.

So she went on lunch break. She had to get out of here, and it was almost two o'clock anyway. Full raingear just to get to the car. Coming down in buckets, the wind insane. Cold, too.

She wondered about the wisdom of driving anywhere in this, idled in the parking lot and tried again to call her mother, but couldn't get through. She'd given her mom a cell phone, but there was no cell phone service on the island, maybe. They should have tried it before, not waited until a storm. What if something went wrong out there? No way off the island, no way to call anyone.

Damn it, Rhoda said. She tried a couple more times, then backed out and drove slowly onto the spur highway. She wanted a chicken pot pie. Comfort food. Fattening, but she needed something.

Another run through a parking lot with puddles, then she was settled in a booth drinking hot tea and waiting for her pie. She felt lost, alone. Rainy days did that to her, but there was also the abused dog dying, her parents unreachable on that island, and Jim not wanting to marry her. And her best friends had all left over the years, moving to places like New York and San Diego and Seattle, better places. No one stayed unless they were stuck. So there was no one to talk to. Her mother, but she couldn't reach her mother.

Rhoda put her forehead down on the table and just stayed like that until the pot pie arrived.

Tired, darling? the waitress asked.

No, just unmarried and unloved.

Ah, darling, the waitress said, and gave Rhoda's shoulder a squeeze. The way I look at it, men are like that pot pie, but God forgot to put in the filling.

Ha, Rhoda said. Thanks.

No problem, darling. Just let me know if you need anything else.

Rhoda lifted the top carefully, set it aside on the plate, portioned crust with filling, not wanting to run out at the end. The pie was good. Gravy for the soul. She felt like crying, but held back. Was it too much to ask for, to get married? She was willing to give everything, her whole life, so was it really too much to ask in return?

Jim was the one who'd asked her to move in. Easy access to sex. Maybe that's all she was to him. The drive across town an annoyance, and her apartment small and dark, with old carpet. Maybe asking her to move in was just a way to not have to see that apartment again. She was only providing a service. Sex and food and house cleaning, a few errands and help with secretarial crap. She should be getting paid.

She took a bigger piece of crust, because she wanted it, even though the ratio would be off at the end. Everything was supposed to be different. He was supposed to love her and want to take care of her. The care should follow the love. It should be obvious.

Rhoda closed her eyes and stopped chewing, stared into the empty dark space behind her eyes for a while. She could feel her mouth pulled down in a frown, and she didn't care if anyone saw. Her face heavy, her cheeks old. She finished chewing and swallowed. Nothing inside her except longing. For a home and a husband and the end of worry about money, the end of worry about her mother. She would give up her time to get to the other side. Not live these weeks or months if she could fast-forward to when things would be better.

Darling, the waitress said, and Rhoda opened her eyes. Only dessert is going to fix that one.

Rhoda smiled. A sundae, with everything.

You got it.

Rhoda already felt a little full, but she finished the last bites of her pie to clear the decks for the sundae. Expensive lunch, and she ran out of crust, but oh well.

Her waitress was right. What she didn't understand about Jim was where his filling was. Nice golden crust on the outside. A dentist, with money and respect. When she first told people she was dating him, they were all impressed. His house fit the dream, too. A buttery life.

And he could be funny. He made up little songs, even, songs about her, though it had been a while now. And he didn't watch sports or any TV at all, so that was good. He didn't have disgusting guy friends or really any friends, so that was maybe more a negative than a positive. He didn't hunt or fish, so she was spared that. He wasn't building some ridiculous car in the garage. He wasn't sneaking porn on the side or addicted to computer games. But what was he living for? What did he care about? She used to think it was her, and their future together, a family. He used to talk about kids, but maybe she had been the one talking about kids. She had no idea what he wanted, and if she didn't know that, maybe she didn't know who he was at all.

This thought stopped her for a moment. She stared down at the stained restaurant carpet and wondered what it was she loved. Was it only an idea? Did the love she felt have anything to do with him?

The cheap carpet had fleur-de-lis patterns, mock royalty. The divider wall trimmed with a strip of light brown plastic where it met carpet, the heads of the nails showing. She hated cheap, and depressing, and cold, and lonely. That's all she was. Just someone who hated these things and was running from them. She didn't have any filling either.

Here you go, the waitress said, and Rhoda couldn't even respond. She felt like none of it mattered. She stared at the sundae, half a banana on each side, though she hadn't ordered a banana split, and the three flavors of ice cream that had been served for fifty years or longer, with the four sauces, and three cherries on top. A formula for happiness, no different from a husband and house and kids, the three mounds, and somehow it was supposed to fill you up or make you sick trying.

The Coleman stove had a back to it, a windbreak, but when Irene tried to put it up, the stove blew over, spilling fuel, the wind too strong. Plenty of propane stoves available now, and they were still using one with wet fuel. She'd be bringing fumes into the tent. The wind was something you could learn to hate. Pressurized and vindictive.

Irene's hood blew off, her head exposed now to the rain, but she jammed the lighter right against the burner, flicked again, and it caught. A quick flash of warmth on her hand. She adjusted the knob and the flame held, though it was blown so much it was never a full ring, one side or another snuffed.

Irene pulled the hood of her raingear back on, turned away from the wind, and shivered. It should be visible. You should be able to see the wind. It had weight and heft, an intent born purely into the world, unforgiving. It would blow until all the world was smooth and nothing left in its path.

The six-gallon water jug was heavy, so Irene only tipped it, filled a pot, placed the pot on the stove and put a lid on. The water should come to a boil in about two hours. That was her guess. Another impossible part of their stupid plan. Why don't you make some pasta, Irene? Sure thing, big daddy, coming right up. Wouldn't want to slow down your pile of sticks.

Irene hunched over as low as she could, her face close to a patch of horsetail, thin spindles, segmented. Only a foot high now, she said to the plants, but you used to be higher, didn't you. They looked frail now, on their way out, but once they had grown as tall as redwoods, in a time when other plants hadn't yet figured out how to grow above two inches. First with a vascular system. The lives of plants like humans, full of struggle and domination, loss and dreams that never happened or happened only briefly. And that was the worst, to have something and then not have it, that was certainly the worst by far.

Irene ripped out all the horsetail, tossed it aside. Time to move on, she told the plants. You've stayed past your time. Then she stood up, braced against the blast, and tromped over to Gary, to the hovel.

Gary was sawing down through the front wall, a jerky motion, stops and starts.

Can you push out against the wall? Gary yelled. The saw's jamming up.

So the wall was folding back already, pinching the saw. What would it be like when he removed a section? Irene knew he hadn't thought that far ahead, though. She leaned into the wall beside him. Smell of sawdust even in all this wind, huff and puff of Gary beside her, sound of saw teeth ripping. He liked this, she knew. And maybe she shouldn't grudge him. She held on to the top log, rough bark, laid her cheek against it, and could feel the whole wall moving.

A concentration again behind her right eye, a fault line, the bones of her skull like tectonic plates moving, grinding at the edges. Her only goal each day now was to get through the day, her only goal each sleepless night to get through the night. Reduced to existence, to bare survival, and there was something good about that maybe, something honest. But she still felt other things, too, light drifting notes somewhere out there: loneliness, for instance. She missed Rhoda. She hadn't stopped feeling entirely.

Irene wondered if this was what had made her mother's end possible, the fading away of feeling. She had always imagined the opposite: her mother in a fit of passion, distraught at losing her husband to another woman, unable to imagine her life without him. But what if she simply hadn't felt anything anymore, after losing everything? That was a new possibility, something Irene couldn't have guessed. And it felt dangerous. You could end up there without having noticed the transition at all.

Lean harder, Gary yelled. It's still jamming up.

Sorry, Irene yelled back, and she pushed harder into the wall, her feet slipping on the ply. She doubted any cabin had ever been built like this, having to push at the walls, walls so frail they bent in the wind. Even the first pioneers, with their rough tools, would have done better.

Pushing harder pressurized her head, brought the pain to a new intensity, the cold and wind and exertion a perfect combination. That was the other possibility: suicide to end the pain. A very simple equation. Not worth living if you only felt pain, so if the pain seemed unending, the logical thing was to end your life. But she would never forgive her mother for that. Her mother should have loved her, and that should have been enough. Irene would never do that to Rhoda.

Irene had to stop pushing for a moment, the pressure in her head too intense, the entire thing a balloon.

Keep pushing, Gary yelled.

I can't, she told him. My head.

Gary stopped sawing, the saw left jammed in the wood, hanging there. He straightened up and had to grab the wall with one hand to keep from blowing over. Irene hunched against the wind.

You can't work? Gary's lips pulled back a bit, angry, impatient. But then maybe he realized how that sounded. Closed his mouth, looked away. Sorry, he said.

Yeah, me too.

Sorry, what? he asked. Couldn't hear you over the wind. The wind buffeting, pumping in blasts, a rising howl each time it accelerated.

I said, Yeah, me too.

Oh.

She could tell he was afraid to ask what that meant.

Gary looked down at the wall, at where he was sawing, the wall curving back, pinching the gap. I think I have to brace this better first, he yelled. If I get the braces ready, can you push while I nail?

Yeah, she yelled. Why not.

Gary climbed over the back wall, going for the pile of two-by-fours. Irene slumped down inside the cabin, out of the wind for the most part, ducked her head down, her chin inside her jacket, folded her arms, closed her eyes.

A fair representation of her three decades in Alaska, slumping down in raingear, hiding, making herself as small as possible, fending off mosquitoes that somehow managed to fly despite the wind. Feeling chilled and alone. Not the expansive vision you'd be tempted to have, spreading your arms on some sunny day on an open slope of purple lupine, looking at mountains all around. This was her life, and she wanted it to pass. At least right now.

Thick rain came down again, and she remembered the pasta water but didn't want to get up.

Gary sawed away at the lumber pile. The braces would be knees jutting inside the cabin from every wall, impossible to walk around inside without running into them. First house in the world designed like that. Irene the lucky wife.

But she shouldn't be so small-minded, ungenerous. That wasn't who she wanted to be. So she stood up, sailed across the platform, climbed over the back wall, and went to tend the water. Lifted the lid, saw no bubbles. Hadn't expected to see any.

She hiked over to Gary. A patch covered in sawdust now, bright and reddish in the rain. Water's not boiling, she yelled. Too much wind. How about I make PB&J?

Yeah, Gary said, not looking up, concentrated on sawing.

So Irene turned off the stove burner, left the pot of water sitting there for next time. The storm forecast to last a week, maybe two, so it might be a while. At the tent, she kneeled just inside the opening, careful not to drip on a sleeping bag, and made sandwiches. Made four, to get them through the afternoon. Almond butter and lingonberry jam, not bad.

Soup's on, she yelled from the tent. Kneeling like she was at some altar, but worshipping what god? An outpost for the faithful who hadn't yet decided on a name. Still fashioning their god, finding their fears and their corollaries. Most importantly, what would the god do? Irene didn't want an afterlife. This life was more than enough. And she didn't need to be forgiven. She just wanted to be given back what had been taken. A lost-and-found god. That would be good enough. No other fancy qualities, nothing mystical. Just give back what had been taken. Can you do that? she asked.

No answer, of course. The tent as wild as any flames for reading signs, but you'd have to want to see. You'd have to be half-dumb or from an earlier time. That was the problem with now. You couldn't believe, and it was awful not to believe.

Gary fell down beside her, another would-be penitent on his knees. Well, he said. I got a couple frames knocked together.

The House of the Lord shall be built, Irene said. Hallelujah.

What?

Sorry, Irene said. Just a joke. Here on my knees, I feel like I'm in some kind of church.

Huh, Gary said. You're right. Unbelievers going through the motions, like Anglo-Saxon Christians. We even have the storm blowing outside. They'd give a Christian burial but lop off the head just in case. Then they'd go lop off some living heads.

Sounds good, Irene said. If I stayed out here long enough, I could probably be driven to murder.

It's not that bad.

I'd rather be unconscious, but other than that, yeah, it's pretty good.

Irene.

She chewed her sandwich and didn't say more. She didn't feel like talking. For a moment, things had seemed bright. And that moment had lasted about half a minute. The tent a void before them, beckoning. She wanted to lie down again.

We need a roof, Gary said. We get to that stage and everything will seem a lot better.

The almond butter was too salty, the sandwich gumming in her mouth. I miss Rhoda, she said. She used to visit every day or two, and now she can't.

Once we're done, she can come out and visit us.

You've separated me from everyone. And I don't mean just now. I mean for thirty years. Separated me from my family, from your family, from friends we could have made here, from the people

I worked with, who you didn't want coming over to the house. You've made me alone, and now it's too late.

Whoa, Irene. Slow down there. You're hitching up a hissy eighteen-wheeler.

You've destroyed my life, you fuck.

Fine, he said. I've destroyed your life. Gary left his uneaten sandwich, stalked off to hammer at his own ill-shapen temple.

And what was the point? Irene asked. Why did everything have to be taken? Retired from work, her children grown, friends and family fallen away, everything that her marriage had once been, who she had been. All gone. What was left?

She finished her sandwich then stood in the rain and wind that had no power to purify, empty water, and walked to the cabin, climbed over the back wall, stood beside her husband to push so he could fit a clumsy brace, a couple pieces of two-by-four tacked together. She didn't speak and he didn't speak. They only worked, first one side of the window and then the next, Gary down on his knees, driving his shoulder into the lower wall, pushing the logs back to the edge of the ply, driving nails.

Irene knew she should feel sorry, but she felt nothing. She left Gary to carve out the window, a void in the wall that would become their only view, something that seemed an obvious symbol of the narrowing of their lives, and returned to the tent to lie down.

The tent so loud above her over every other sound, she finally slept, faded away into the only real shelter.

When she awoke, it was night and Gary was in his sleeping bag beside her. Are you awake? she asked.

Yes.

What are you thinking about?

The Seafarer. *Calde gethrungen,* he recited to her, *waeron mine fet, forste gebunden, caldum clommum, thaer tha ceare seofedun hat ymb heortan.*

And what's that mean? she asked. You want me to ask.

Pinched by cold were my feet, fettered by frost, by cold chains, *caldum clommum,* there the anxieties sighed hot around my heart.

Yeah, you have it tough, she said.

Who are you to know?

The storm came from a colder place, an early fall promising an early winter. The Bering Sea weighing down on them, the Arctic close enough to be felt. Already the leaves had turned, and it was still September. Aspen become yellow and gold. Rhoda hadn't noticed the transition. It seemed that overnight the leaves had changed, the motor homes disappeared. The streets felt empty, thick bands of rain sweeping across, no one on the river walk as she crossed the bridge. River swollen and fast, salmon already rotted away, their desperate run finished. Darker in the mornings now, the light disappearing quickly.

For more than a week Rhoda hadn't been able to reach her mother, and this was all she could think about now, her mother and father out there on that island in the storm. Cold now, near freezing, and they were living in a tent, building a cabin. They couldn't be building in this weather, though. All day and night lying in a tent, waiting. They'd go crazy. Or one of them could be hurt, and it was too rough to take the boat for help. Rhoda didn't know whether anyone else was still out there. Only summer cabins now. In the past, half a dozen families had lived year-round on Caribou, but now her parents would be the only ones.

Rhoda found it difficult to go to work. She couldn't focus. She arrived almost fifteen minutes late, said hello to Dr. Turin and Sandy, the front office manager, and took off her raincoat. Walked into the back room and said hello to Chippy, an arctic ground squirrel some nut had raised as a pet. His tail too small, like a chipmunk's. Bear burrito. Tundra rat. But he had gotten lucky somehow, transcended his fate. He'd have heating all winter, skip hibernation, feast on cat food and watch TV. How would his little brain make any sense of that?

Rhoda looked through the day's schedule. Mostly flea baths. Light now that drop-ins had gone south. She had a lunch date with Jim. He was taking her somewhere nice—a surprise, he'd said—though there were only a couple nice restaurants in town, so the surprise would be somewhat limited.

A buzz from Sandy, and Rhoda went out front to collect a pug named Corker, brought him back and set him in the tub. He was looking for a limb to grab, she could tell, but she stayed behind him, kept him dominated.

She'd been dominating Jim, too, for the past week. An accident. She'd given up hope, realized it wasn't going to work, and somehow that put her in the stronger position. She felt like the walking dead, sleepless and worried about her mom and dad, feeling unattractive and doomed to spinsterhood, and somehow that was setting Jim on fire. It was too stupid to even try to understand, because in the end, he would still take her for granted, same as he'd been doing all along. The only reason she wasn't leaving was that she had nowhere else to live.

Corker hunched down, trembling, and Rhoda hoped this was fear as well as cold. He'd had his share of getting his way. Time for him to feel something new.

The flea shampoo always irritated Rhoda's eyes, made her red and puffy, so at the restaurant, she'd look like she'd been crying. She gave Corker his final rinse, he shook and didn't do a very good job of it, she toweled him off, and she could see her father having a heart attack out there, gone to build in the rain, pushing himself, picking up some big log and then just keeling over. Her mother trying to help him, calling out for anyone, but her voice lost in the storm, no help nearby, no phone. Her mother would have to drag him down to the shore, try to get him into that boat with waves pounding at it, waves over her head maybe, and she'd be knocked down, her leg broken, maybe unconscious, and Rhoda wouldn't even know. The storm would blow for another week, her parents lying facedown in water, dead, or thrown on the beach, waves breaking over, their bodies white and bloated, blue lips.

Damn it, she said. How could you do this to me? Then she realized she could buy a satellite phone for her parents. That would work. She'd be able to reach them. She didn't know why she hadn't thought of this before.

She left Corker in the heat lamp area to dry and thumbed through the yellow pages. Half a dozen calls later, she was told no one would have a sat phone in stock but she could order one online. So she checked and found it was almost $1,500, plus air time at $1.49 per minute if you bought 500 minutes, so another $750.

Yikes, she said. She would have to ask Jim. That was the only way. She needed the phone, and she deserved to be paid for all the domestic service she had provided. Though maybe she was being a little hard on him.

At noon, Jim called and asked her to meet at Kenai Landing. He was running late. So she drove out, almost fifteen minutes away. An old converted cannery. Mark had worked on boats here when it was in full operation. Now only one of the two large warehouses still processed fish. The other had been converted to boutique shops, the machinist's shop and hen house converted to hotel rooms, a smaller warehouse become a restaurant.

The wind sharper here off the Cook Inlet. Colder. Heavier rain. She parked as close as she could but had to run a hundred yards. In this rain, it all looked like a cannery still, an industrial camp, cold gray warehouses and grim work. A hell of a place to meet for lunch.

But when she swung open the door, Jim was waiting there and had a big grin, obviously happy to see her, so that was nice. Sorry about the rain, he said.

They shed their raingear and sat at a booth. Jim ordered king crab legs for both of them, a treat. How's work? he asked.

Jim never asked about her work, but she decided not to look a gift horse in the mouth. Someone brought in an arctic ground squirrel, she said.

As a pet?

Yeah. He claims Chippy is real smart. Has plans for teaching him various card games this winter, I think.

Jim laughed. Takes all kinds.

And that's something we do have here.

Ha, Jim said.

Then it was oddly silent. She couldn't think of anything to say, and he seemed preoccupied. Looking down at his napkin and silverware. He was a weirdo, plain and simple. She didn't know why she hadn't seen that before.

Jim slid out of the booth, slow and awkward, stood a moment, looking at the ground, then got down on one knee. He was holding a small box in one hand.

Rhoda, he said, looking up at her now, and she couldn't believe this was happening. He hadn't given her any chance to prepare.

He opened the box and showed her the ring, a large princess-cut diamond with smaller diamonds on either side, not a setting she ever would have picked, but there it was, a big diamond. Will you marry me?

He looked afraid. And she felt afraid suddenly. All she had wanted, and none of it was happening the way she had imagined, but it was happening at least. This miserable restaurant, mostly empty, a rainy day, and she smelled like flea bath, her eyes all irritated, but what the hell. Yes, she said. Yes, of course. She stood and he held her and they kissed, the way it should be. The ring on her finger now, looking at it on his shoulder as she held him, her husband, or fiancé. Soon to be. She wanted to tell her mother.

I have to tell my mom, she said.

Yeah, Jim said. We can tell your parents.

But she's on that island. Rhoda let go of Jim and sat back down. The waiters and waitresses were clapping now, from across that huge empty space. Thank you, Rhoda called out to them, and tried to smile.

Rhoda, Jim said, sitting back down on his side. It's all right. You'll be able to tell her soon.

I want to tell her now. I want my mom to know.

Jim looked over his shoulder at the restaurant staff, gave a little wave. Rhoda, they're going to think something is wrong. You look so unhappy.

I think I'm going to cry, she said, and then she did. She put her hands up to cover her face.

That ended the clapping, and no one came over. Rhoda tried to make it stop, but she wanted her mother to be here, and she was afraid something might have happened. I'm afraid they might be hurt, she told Jim. There's no way to reach them.

Rhoda, can you stop crying? I don't want these people to think the wrong thing.

Fine, Rhoda said, pulling her hands away from her face, dabbing at her eyes with her napkin. I won't embarrass you, since that's what's important now.

Rhoda. It's not like that. They just won't understand.

I'm going back to work, she said. And she stood up, grabbed her purse and raingear.

Please, Jim said.

I'll see you this evening. I'm driving out to their house after work.

In all this rain? It's forty minutes out there, and then the gravel road.

I'll see you this evening. She marched out the front door without looking at the waitstaff, who were all staring at her, she knew, and ran through the rain to her car, a place where she could cry all she wanted, all the way back to work.

And when she arrived, she wiped her face with Kleenex and no one thought anything was wrong, since her eyes were always puffy here. She could hide. She gave a gray terrier a bath and wondered why she felt so miserable. She loved Jim. She was happy to marry Jim. It was all she wanted, really. But somehow not being able to tell her mother was ruining everything, and she didn't understand that. She felt empty and lonely and scared when she should be feeling happy.

The afternoon dragged on forever, flea bath after flea bath. She had small bites all up her arms and could feel several in her hair. The smaller dogs, especially, were just flea sponges.

She had to work late, until after seven, time creeping along and no call from Jim, no visit to see how she was doing. She bundled up, hurried through cold and rain to her car, and took the highway toward the lake. The sun low, setting so much earlier now than even a few weeks ago. She ran the heater, had the defroster going on the windshield.

Rhoda was angry Jim hadn't called or visited, but she tried to stay positive. They'd get married this winter on Kauai, maybe Hanalei Bay. But Rhoda felt tired thinking about any of that. All the years of dreaming, and now that it was happening, she couldn't even focus on it. Thanks, Mom and Dad, she said. And thanks, Jim.

So much water on the road. A truck came blasting past and threw up enough spray she couldn't see anything for a moment. Driving blind at sixty. She slowed down.

The bullet-riddled signs for the lake appeared, finally, and she turned onto gravel. She didn't know why she was coming out here. They weren't going to be home. She should be with Jim. But she just had to check.

No one else on this road. A long, lonely curve of gravel in the middle of nowhere. The summer traffic ended. Trees blown and bent. Pieces of gravel hitting the underside of the car, the windshield swamped and then clear and then covered again, fogged all along the edges.

She pulled up to her parents' house and ran to the front door, but no one had been around for a while now. Small branches on the walkway. She banged on the door, but of course no response. Looked down to see weeds in the planter boxes. Colder here than in Soldotna. Dark and windy, close to the mountains and glacier. Rhoda didn't know what to do. She needed to know her mother was safe.

She leaned against the front door, put her cheek against it, and closed her eyes. She needed to think, but the inside of her was only fear. She could go to the boat ramp. Maybe she'd see something there.

So she drove to the campground. Her dad's truck in the lot, and nothing else. The sun had set, blocked by rain and cloud, almost no light left. She walked in near darkness down the ramp to the water's edge. Breaking waves, just as she had imagined, white flashes nearly as high as her head. Steep and packed close together, louder even than the wind as they crashed ashore. The rain stinging her face, cold and slushy, turning into snow.

Damn you, she yelled across the lake. No way to reach them even if she found a boat. Only a few miles away, and sealed off from the rest of the world.

Gary noticed a change in the sound of the rain hitting the tent. Softer now. The first snow, a kind of prayer answered. No roof yet on their cabin, but the snows had arrived. He wouldn't have thought of it this way before. He would have railed and raged at the early season, felt cheated by time. But now he understood he wanted this. He wanted the snow.

He sat up in his sleeping bag, unzipped quietly.

I'm awake, Irene said. You don't have to be quiet. I'm always awake.

It's snowing, he said.

I know. It's been snowing for hours now.

I'm just going to take a look. He pulled on his pants and shirt, stood in the entranceway of the tent to pull on boots and rain-gear. The tent still blown by wind, whipping and lurching, but no longer the heavy sound of the rain.

He stepped outside into a deeper cold than he had expected. Not quite October yet, but it felt like October. Not wearing enough beneath his raingear, but he'd only be out here a short time anyway. He bent into the wind and snow and walked toward the water's edge, wanted to see the waves. Dark out, black, but the waves would be breaking, showing white.

The undergrowth thick, deadwood everywhere. Alder branches lashing at him. The snow cold on his cheeks, melting when it hit. Big flakes, delicate. He wished he could see them.

Through alder to the tufted growth near the shore, thick grasses, and he could see the white of the waves now, fainter than he had imagined, and feel the windblown spray on his cheeks.

Nap nihtscua, darkened night-shadow, *northan sniwde,* snow from north. This is what Gary loved. *Hrim hrusan bond,* frost-bound world, *haegl feol on eorthan,* hail fell on the earth, *corna caldast,* coldest of grains. His favorite part of the poem, because it was the unexpected shift, a surprise. After all his suffering at sea in storms, the seafarer wants only to go back out again. *Nor is his thought for the harp nor for ring-receiving nor the pleasure in woman nor in hope of the world, nor for anything else, except for the surging of the waves.*

A desire from a thousand years ago, a longing for *atol ytha gewealc,* the terrible surging of the waves, and Gary understood this, finally. He hadn't understood it in grad school, because he'd been too young, too conventional, believed the poem was only about religion. He hadn't yet seen his life wasted, hadn't yet understood the pure longing for what was really a kind of annihilation. A desire to see what the world can do, to see what you can endure, to see, finally, what you're made of as you're torn apart. A kind of bliss to annihilation, to being wiped away. *But ever he has longing, he who sets out on the sea,* and this longing is to face the very worst, a delicate hope for a larger wave.

Gary shivered with cold but wanted to face the elements more purely. He pushed back his hood, unzipped his rain jacket, laid it in the grass at his feet. Full shock of wind, all his warmth taken. Pulled off his sweater and then his shirt. Barechested now, and he raised his arms into the storm, yelled at the wind and snow, a madman. A man alive, he thought, and wondered whether he was expecting some kind of rebirth, redemption. But he hated that he had any thoughts at all. He wanted to be swept clean of thoughts, wanted his mind to stop. So he stepped forward into the spray, onto the beach, slippery stones covered in slime, kept his arms raised and walked slowly, ceremonially, his body shaking out of control, wracked. He slipped and had to put a hand down, recovered. Legs pounded now by waves, blasting into him, the first shock of a wave hitting his stomach, and he leaned sideways into the oncoming water, arms lowered now, bracing, hit again by a wave, knocking him back and he fell, went under, one arm jarred all the way to the shoulder from impact with rock, and then he was clear again, then drenched by another wave. He yelled, whooped and hollered, felt better than he'd felt in years, stopped trying to stand, just sprawled in the rocks, held his breath each time he was covered, shook free in the trough, yelled again. He didn't even feel that cold anymore.

The world came in different sizes, though. That expansive feeling, that sense of extension, of connection, could moments later feel smaller, hard and cold, and Gary didn't know how this worked. The moment was over, before he had ridden it as far as he would have liked, and if he stayed here now, it would not come back. He knew that. But he stayed anyway, because he didn't like that rule. Was it a rule of the world, or just a limitation of self, and how could you ever know the difference?

Why can't I stop thinking about this as a moment? he asked out loud. Why can't I just live it? Why does it have to end after five minutes?

Consciousness not really a gift. He'd had these thoughts thirty years ago, when he first arrived, and there'd been no progress. All that had changed was his commitment. Back then it'd been full of belief, and now it was more determined, coupled to annihilation, not expecting anything in return. Nothing better to do, he told the waves.

The water more than just a medium, more than wave and temp. It felt abrasive against his skin. It had body and impact. It hurt to stay here, despite the numbness. So that's what got him to crawl away, finally. He couldn't stand. The rocks hurt his knees, even through his jeans. He crawled out of the waves and onto the beach, into tufts of grass, spiky and rough, felt around with his hands until he found his shirt and sweater and raincoat. He didn't put them on. Just held them in his hands as he crawled over deadfall and blueberry, patches of moss, whatever else covered this ground. He made it to the tent, unzipped, his hand numb like a club, and crawled in.

You're shivering, Irene said. Your teeth are chattering like they're going to splinter. What did you do out there?

Went for a swim, he said, and fumbled at the buttons on his jeans, trying to get his wet clothing off.

Went for a swim.

Yep. I need help with my pants. Can't get the buttons. Hurry, please.

That's great. But she crawled over and helped. Her hands hot on his skin. You're freezing, she said. Don't think of trying to get in my bag with me.

Thanks, he said.

Thank yourself. You've been doing stupid shit like this for too long.

Out of his jeans and boots and socks, Gary found a towel to dry off, found his thermal underwear, top first, then bottoms, got into his bag. Found his stocking cap. The mummy part of his bag over his head, he pulled the drawstring. He'd be okay now.

Here's what I have to tell you, Irene said.

Let's skip it.

No. Your idea that you've deserved more than you've gotten, that's the problem.

I don't need a lecture. I'm aware of my failings.

No you're not. None of your life has measured up. You think you were destined for more. You think you were worth more.

I know who I am.

No you don't.

Fuck you.

Not that easy. You think you deserved someone better than me.

Maybe I did.

Irene hit him then, a hard punch that glanced off his forearm. He went into a tuck in his sleeping bag and she kept hitting him, not saying anything, just hard punches over and over to his body. Didn't punch his face. Still holding back. Why hold back? he asked. Why not punch me in the face?

Because I love you, you fucker. And then she was weeping.

Gary turned over to face the other way. Let her weep. Maybe she would leave. And he knew that was wrong, but he just didn't feel whatever he'd need to feel to counter it. Maybe he was missing some basic human faculty, whatever it is that connects people to each other. But what he wanted was to be left alone. And was that really a crime?

When Gary woke in the morning, Irene was gone. He was stuffed up, having to breathe through his mouth, throat sore. His head hurt. So he turned over and tried to go back to sleep.

He could hear hammering, the wind died down, the tent no

longer berserk. Irene working on the cabin, but he wondered what she was doing. She could be breaking it apart, not building at all.

This got him up, the idea that she might be destroying the cabin. He pulled on a dry set of clothes, his bib overalls and an old dry pair of boots, his wet raincoat. Unzipped the tent and stepped into a land gone white. The snow not deep, maybe an inch or two, but breathtaking the way it transformed. Distance and depth defined, the upward-facing leaves white, the stems beneath in shadow. Even the spruce, the collective effect of the topside of each needle and topside only made white. The world outlined and remade entirely, the light itself changed. Yesterday might as well have been six months ago.

Wow, Gary said. This is beautiful.

Irene paused in her hammering, looked around, hooded in green raingear. Yes it is, she said. But she didn't look at Gary. Went back to hammering.

Gary stepped over to the cabin, walked in the back door, fully cut out and braced. On the forward wall, the space for the window, not quite square. Layers of log above it, the last layer at eight feet. Irene standing on an aluminum stepstool, driving in the last nails.

Thanks, Gary said. Looks like we're ready for a roof.

Yeah, she said. What's the plan?

I was going to do it with logs, Gary said. But I don't see how that's going to work. It'll just leak.

No response from Irene. Being careful, he could tell. Had a lot to say but was holding back, which was fine by him. She finished a nail, five blows. The wind sifting through the trees, much lighter than before.

So I think I'll buy some sheeting in town. Not the look I wanted, but we're late, and we need a roof. Wind's dying down, so we should be able to get to shore, maybe tomorrow or the next day.

I like that plan, she said.

We need to put it at an angle, Gary said, for the snow to slide off. We'll make the back wall higher and get some two-by-eights for roof joists to run from the back wall to the front. That should hold it, I think.

Irene stepped down from the stool, looked out the hole for the front window, standing there with her shoulders slumped, holding the hammer. Sounds good, she finally said. That'll work.

She still wouldn't look at him, and Gary felt almost like he should make an effort here, say something to close the distance, to make peace. Maybe apologize for last night, for saying he deserved someone better than her. But she was the one who had attacked him, and he didn't feel like making the effort right now. He felt chilled. He thought for some reason of Ariadne and the passage in Catullus where *in her bride's heart revolves a maze of sorrow,* maybe because of the way Irene's shoulders were slumped. He couldn't see her face, but she looked like all was lost, staring out into the snow. He couldn't remember the Latin. Ariadne was watching Theseus take off in his ship, abandoning her, just as Aeneas would do to Dido and Gary himself had been thinking for years, perhaps decades now, of doing to Irene. And maybe now was finally the time to let their marriage die. It might be better for both of them. A thing ill-conceived from the start, something that had made both their lives smaller. Hard to know what was true. Part of him wanted to apologize, wrap his arms around her, tell her she was all he had in this world, but that was only habit, not a thing you could trust.

I'll go cut the logs, he said.

Rhoda found Mark at the go-cart track. He and his friends always went on the first day of snow so they could spin circles and crash into each other. Fishing was over, and they had nothing to do now except drugs and stupid shit like this. Rhoda clung to the chain-link fence and yelled to get his attention, but of course there was no way he could hear her. The putting of a dozen engines. Mark wearing a camo jacket and a Russian hat with earflaps. His friend Jason wearing a pink Hello Kitty jacket just to be an ass.

The course was rimmed by stacks of old tires, then fence, then the broken-down motor homes of half a dozen fishermen who lived here year-round, Mark's buddies. The kind of depressing hell Rhoda wanted no part of anymore. The kind of place where she had spent all of junior high and high school, smoking pot and having sex at the edge of gravel lots. She wanted to forget any of that had ever happened.

She grabbed a piece of gravel and threw it at Mark as he flew around the corner. It bounced off the front of his cart. He skidded to a stop, then saw it was her, grinned, flipped her off, and hit the accelerator. Tok, wearing a Red Baron scarf, slammed from behind, threw Mark's cart sideways into the barrier. Tollef, Tok's brother, came around fast and rammed Mark again, Mark whiplashing against his seatbelt. He was yelling and stomping the accelerator, trying to get out of there, made it maybe twenty feet before Hello Kitty whipped by and leaned over to cuff him on the back of the neck. But then Mark made it clear and was chasing them down.

Rhoda walked through a gap in the fence to the small set of bleachers, the only spectator. She'd had sex with Jason once on these bleachers, disgusting to think of now. That had been in the snow, too, though much colder, middle of winter. It hadn't become her life; that was the important thing.

She waited through another fifteen minutes of crude gestures and obscenities, doughnuts and collisions, the life of the penis. Waited until they'd had their fill and sauntered back to the entrance, shouldering each other and going for wedgies. Then they walked past, without stopping, Jason with a little smile. We're going to Coolie's if you want a beer, Mark said over his shoulder.

Hey. I came here to talk to you.

Sorry, he said. I'm otherwise engaged. He said it in his Brit voice and of course got a laugh.

I need to get out to Caribou Island. You can arrange a boat.

Mark stopped, at least, and turned around. His friends kept going. Why do you have to go out there?

Our parents, she said. Remember? The people who made you and raised you? They've been out there this entire storm, in a tent, and there's no way to contact them. I need to know they're all right.

They're fine, Mark said and turned away.

Listen, Rhoda said, but her voice had gone weak. She was starting to cry. I know you don't like me, but I'm really worried about them, and I need your help.

Mark surprised her then. Turned around, walked over and gave her a hug, patted her on the back. Okay, he said. I'm sorry. I'll get a boat. When do you want to go?

Today?

It's too late for today. How about tomorrow, ten a.m., I'll meet you at the lower campground?

Thank you, Mark. You can be good, see?

Can't make a habit of it, he smiled. See you tomorrow. He jogged ahead to catch up with his friends.

Then she remembered. Hey, she yelled. I'm getting married.

Mark waved his arm in the air to acknowledge, but that was all. Didn't turn around.

So Rhoda returned to work and asked for the time off. She got through the rest the day and went home to Jim. An enormous complex of exercise equipment in the middle of the living room, painted metallic light blue. Jim wearing spandex shorts and a wife-beater, pulling a bar down behind his neck.

Wow, she said. What the hell is that?

This is the future me, Jim said. I figure I have at least ten more good years.

Okay, she said. She wasn't sure what this was all about. You'd better have more than ten. I'm only thirty.

No problemo, he said. You'll be living with a hardbody soon.

She watched him finish his set. He was out of breath and red-faced by the end, splotchy, his arms and shoulders looking old and slack.

You're not thinking of other women, are you?

What?

This sudden getting in shape thing, right after you ask me to marry you. Kind of seems like a panic response, making yourself attractive again so you're not limited to one mate.

Rhoda.

I'm serious. You said you have ten more good years. Good for what?

Jim stood up and flopped his workout towel over his shoulder. Rhoda, he said. You're the only woman I want. Okay?

She tried to find anything in his eyes, any sign of a lie, looked at his mouth, also.

Rhoda, I love you.

Okay. She gave him a hug. I'm just stressed out about my mom still, I think. I'm going to Caribou Island tomorrow. Mark's taking me.

In this weather? You go out on Skilak at the wrong time and you could die.

The storm's passed. There's not supposed to be any wind tomorrow morning. Maybe not even any snow.

You shouldn't go out there. Just wait for them to come in. They have to come in soon for supplies. They've been out almost a week.

Ten days.

Well that's my point then. They'll come in.

Rhoda didn't feel like talking about this. She went to the fridge and started pulling things out for dinner. Chicken she needed to use up, olives, feta, red onion. Maybe some couscous. She could hear Jim huffing away. Hard to believe the new muscles were for her.

Cooking always helped. Especially in a kitchen like this. A good stove, six burners. The couscous in water on the back row. Then she poured olive oil in a pan, added minced garlic, got the chicken breasts going. Chopped the red onion. She could calm down when she was cooking. Her breathing could slow. She'd been panicking without even knowing it. Panicking all day, probably.

Hey, she called out to Jim.

Yeah?

I need a satellite phone. They're expensive. But I need to talk with my mom. It's been freaking me out.

How expensive are they?

Fifteen hundred, or maybe a little less. Plus seven-fifty for minutes.

Ouch.

I need it.

Okay.

The chicken was browned, cooked most the way through, red onions translucent. She poured in the tomato sauce, olives and some of their juice, let it come to a boil then turned down to simmer. Added pepper, couldn't think of what other spices went with Greek chicken. Poured in some balsamic, then added Madeira. Probably not right for this dish, but what the hell. Drunken chicken. She poured herself a glass of cabernet.

I'll take some in a minute, Jim said. I'm hitting the showers.

Rhoda drank her wine and stared down at the chicken, the olives dark in the sauce. Something had changed. Somehow the air a little cooler, maybe, thinner, more isolating. Just the two of them here in this house. Maybe because there had been a goal before. The proposal. Rhoda could see how marriage might feel lonely. A new feeling she couldn't quite describe or even reach. Something at the edges, something she didn't like. She could imagine long periods of time in which they wouldn't say much to each other, just moving individually around the house. And she wondered whether this was where kids fit in. Having a child would provide a new focus, a new center of attention, a place for the two of them to meet. Maybe that was how it was supposed to be. You focused on each other until you decided to marry, then you focused together on someone else. And then what happened when your kids grew up and left? Where were you supposed to focus then? There was something terrifying about not having a focus. Your life could never be just what it was. That was frightening. No one wanted that.

In the morning, Rhoda drove to Skilak. Heavy skies, cold, twenty-eight degrees, but very little wind, only occasional light snow, a few flakes and then it would be clear again. The trees white, with black shadows. No green. She knew they were still green, but she couldn't see it. The winter color palette of white, black, brown, and gray, arrived earlier than usual.

She wanted to call Mark to confirm, but he would consider that nagging. She turned off the loop road toward the lower campground and coming over a rise could see water, gray and very small waves. Pulled into an empty lot, no one around, looked at her watch, a few minutes before ten.

Rhoda bundled in her snow jacket and hat, winter gloves. Wearing long underwear, also, and boots. It would be cold out on the lake in the boat. If the boat and Mark ever arrived, of course. She walked down to the ramp, to the water's edge. A fine layer of snow, undisturbed. No one had used this ramp today. Her parents most likely the only people out there.

The lake already freezing at its edges. Clear thin panes of ice among the rocks. Delicate and translucent, most of it broken already into small triangular shards. Rhoda tapped at them with the toe of her boot.

Okay, Mark, she said, and pulled out her cell phone. Let's hear the story. But when she called, he said he was only a few minutes away, so she decided to be nice. Thank you, she said. See you soon.

Rhoda had grown up on this lake. This was supposed to be home, this shoreline. These trees. The mountains, the way the heavy clouds moved in and made the summits an act of memory. But it didn't feel like home. It felt as cold and impersonal as a place she had never been. She didn't understand why her parents had settled here, and she wondered why she hadn't moved away, like her friends, to a better place.

Mark came down the gravel road in his old truck, pulling a trailer. He gave her the shaka sign and a grin, pulled a wide half-circle in front of her, then backed the boat to the water. An open aluminum boat, something less than twenty feet, with an outboard. Exposed to the cold, but big enough to be safe.

Mark hopped out and Rhoda gave him a hug. Thanks, Mark.

Whoa, Mark said. It's just a boat.

I know, but I'm worried about them. And I'm thinking, also, that they'd use the upper campground if they came in today. We may miss them if we launch here.

Well we're here now, Mark said. We'll just zip over to the upper campground if we don't find them.

Okay, Rhoda said. She didn't want to argue, but she wished they could drive around to the other ramp. It wouldn't be that hard to do.

Mark was already unbuckling straps. Then he grabbed a small cooler out of the back of his truck, and fishing poles.

What's that for? Rhoda asked.

A few brewskis. And a fishing pole in case I'm waiting. Never know when Nessie might be hungry. Six hundred feet deep. We have to have some sort of Sasquatch motherfucker down there.

Rhoda wanted to laugh or smile or something, but she felt tense. This trip a kind of opportunity, perhaps, but she just didn't have it in her. She needed to see her parents safe first, and then she could do the chitchat.

Right, then, Mark said, and he grabbed life jackets. Here's yours. Not that it'll do much. We'd freeze before anyone got to us.

Thanks, she said. Thanks, Mark. I appreciate this.

He backed the boat into the water, left her with the bow line while he parked. Then they climbed aboard and were off, Rhoda in the bow, the wind sharp. Waves very small, no more than a foot, but the boat felt loose and wobbly at speed. Occasional spray over the side.

Rhoda searched off the port bow for any sign of a boat crossing to the upper campground, but she didn't see a thing. No one else out here. The lake always larger than she expected. Rimmed by low shoreline and trees all along this end, impossible to tell distance. If you stood on one shore, you could think the other shore wasn't far. It was only when you came out to the middle that you could judge size, but even then the perspective kept changing. Caribou and the other islands hardly visible at first, and then slowly they grew. Frying Pan Island first, with its long handle, Caribou behind it. Past them, a shoreline rockier, she knew, with boulders and cliffs, much prettier. Each of the bays over there was large enough to feel like its own lake, and yet from here they looked like nothing. Then the headwaters up to the glacier and the river that linked to other lakes beyond. It had been years since she'd been up there.

When they were kids, their parents took them camping on the far shores. Steep pebble beaches backed by forest and mountain. She and Mark hiked a rocky headland, with views of bays on both sides, and looked for wolverines. A nearly mythical creature. She didn't know a single person who had seen one, and so as children, they were constantly hunting the wolverine, and they scared each other with tales of what would happen when they'd find it. The wolverine would sometimes play dead, or offer up its neck, but if a bear went for that, the wolverine would attach to the bear's underside, bite its neck and rip its razor claws all along the bear's belly. This was what she imagined as a kid, reaching down for a dead wolverine and having it rise up and rip out her stomach. She wasn't scared of bears, because she had seen those, and she loved animals, but she had never seen a wolverine.

Remember the wolverine stories? she yelled to Mark over the engine.

What?

She repeated.

Oh yeah, Mark smiled. You used to scare the crap out of me with those.

Rhoda smiled too, then looked ahead again at the islands approaching. White now with snow, and she couldn't remember how many years it had been since she'd last visited.

Calmer on the back side of the islands as they curved around Frying Pan. Flat water, no spray. Small waves again around the other side, and several cabins tucked into the trees. She had expected to see her parents' boat by now.

The chop a little rougher, and Mark slowed. The island steeper, rising to a hill. No boat along the shore. Rhoda couldn't find her parents.

Slow down, she yelled to Mark. They have to be somewhere in here. She was searching the trees, starting to panic. There was no boat. So they could have left for the upper campground already. But they also could have gone down in the storm, drowned, or their boat washed away and they were stranded and maybe something had happened. It was nothing out here. No other people, no help.

In there, Mark yelled and slowed.

Where? Rhoda asked. What is it?

I see the cabin, he said, and then Rhoda saw it too. Like ruins, some cabin from a hundred years ago, burned out, its roof missing. A big hole for the front window. Rough logs covered in snow. Thin logs, like sticks. It didn't look at all like she had imagined. So small. But that had to be it. A blue tent and another tent, brown, hidden mostly by the low brush.

They must have gone in today, Mark said.

Yeah, we should have gone to the upper campground.

It's not the end of the world. We'll go there next. But we should take a look around. I'm curious.

Their boat could have been taken away in the storm, Rhoda said. They may be here. I hate this. I hate not knowing what the fuck is happening to them. They could be dead for all we know.

No need to shit yourself. I'm sure they're fine. Mark raised the engine partway out of the water, turned it off. They drifted in slowly, and then he was using a paddle.

We have to be quick, Mark said. This sucks for parking. And I'd better stay with the boat, actually.

Rhoda looking down at the water, trying to guess how deep. She didn't have waders. But she had to check whether her mom was here. So she stepped in, sank past her knees, the water a shock how cold it was. The stones were slippery, but she worked her way ashore carefully, over rocky beach and up through grass and snow.

Mom, she yelled. Dad. Past undergrowth and alders, she came to a woodpile with fresh sawdust, so they'd been working after it stopped snowing. Their boot prints visible. Mom, she yelled again. Are you here?

The cabin lopsided and rough, small, unbelievable they could want to live in that. It looked abandoned from a much older time, open now to the sky, but had fresh plywood for its floor. An open space in the back. They'd be putting a door there. The growth beaten down all around here. A Coleman stove with a pot on it. The two tents, and now Rhoda really was afraid. She didn't want to unzip a tent, for what she'd find inside.

Mom, she said again, quieter this time. Stood in front of the larger tent and could feel her heart racing. Unzipped it quick and saw their sleeping bags, clothing, food. No one inside. No body. Nothing wrong. So she stepped to the other tent quick and unzipped it, and no one there, either. Thank god, she said. And she closed her eyes a moment, let her breathing calm down, let her heart slow.

They up there? Mark yelled from the boat, his voice faint. This cabin was tucked back a ways.

No, she yelled. No one here. They must have left this morning.

Supplies in the second tent. Tools. She couldn't believe they had lived out here in the storm. And it looked like they were doing it, really building this cabin, intending to stay through the winter. Rhoda kneeled on the path, closed her eyes and just took a moment. She was so afraid. When the lake began to freeze over, there'd be a time when no boat could make it out here and the ice wouldn't be solid enough to walk across. They'd be isolated, no way to reach them if something was wrong.

Irene at home, looking around at everything, didn't know what to take. The lights were off, neither of them in the habit now of turning on light switches. Portraits of her family on the walls. Old portraits, including family she had never met. Stern faces, living more difficult lives. Photo albums on the lower shelf of the bookcase. Her children's art from all the years, handprints to color by numbers to Mark's drums made of elk hide and cottonwood. He'd sawn rings from hollowed-out stumps. Held summer solstice rituals here with his friends in high school, drumming all night around a fire on the beach, dancing with a bear skull on a stick. The last that she had known him, before he went off into his own life.

Rhoda had not gone as far away, but every wall held a sign of when she had still lived here, when their lives had been spent together. Even the secretive times, in junior high, when she'd first started having sex, were recorded here, in photos of dances and posters for school plays. All those years together added up to something, right? But what could be taken to an unbuilt cabin, to a tent? This place in its entirety, the walls and windows, the yard and forest, all of it would have to be moved.

I can't do this, she said to Gary. She could hear him bumping around in the bedroom as he packed more clothing into a duffel.

What?

She raised her voice. There's nothing I can take that will make that cabin a home.

I think you're making this more complicated, Irene. We're just grabbing our stuff, then we're going to town for the sheeting and more two-by-fours and a few other supplies, then trying to load up and get back out there before dark.

Today?

What?

You're planning to go back out today?

Yeah, that was the plan.

That wasn't the plan. You didn't bother to tell the help.

Irene.

I'm spending tonight here, in my bed. If you go, you're going without me.

Gary emerged from the bedroom, stood in front of her. The weather could get bad again, he said. This is our window. This is the time.

I'm not going today.

Gary slammed his hand on the counter. Fine, he said. Then he turned around and went back into the bedroom.

Irene sat down on their couch. Ringing in her ears, her blood pumping hard. She tried to calm, and her heartbeat slowed a bit, but then it clenched tight four or five beats, moments when she could feel its exact shape, hanging from its arteries, jerking in her chest. Panic. Panic as if she were about to be killed, and yet she was only sitting on a couch in her own living room. The light soft from outside, no wind, no storm, just another gray, overcast day, her husband in the other room, and they weren't going back to the tent tonight. She needed to calm down.

If we can't make it a home, why are we doing it? she called out to Gary.

No answer. Because his life was the given, beyond question. Hers was the accompaniment; it didn't really matter.

Irene lay out fully on the couch, propped her head with a small pillow, closed her eyes and spun in blood. Beating endlessly, pressurizing, her body a hard case she wanted out of. She wanted peace. Not to be trapped anymore. Trapped in this body and with Gary in this life and its regrets. Her life an accumulation of all that was closing in, fronts gathering all along the edges, coming closer. Even getting through the next five minutes.

Gary, she called out. She wanted to warn him.

Yes? His voice so ungenerous. How could she say what she needed to say? That they were going too far. That something would be lost. That they wouldn't recover from this.

Never mind, she said. Closed her eyes again and rested, the air around her sifting downward until she heard the popping of gravel outside, someone driving up. She hoped it would be Rhoda, but didn't go to the door. She didn't feel like moving.

Mom, Rhoda called.

Here on the couch.

Rhoda at her side then, leaning down to give her a hug. Warm and alive, real love, not the grudging love of Gary. Flesh of her flesh, the only permanent bond. A marriage could turn into nothing, but not this.

I'm getting you a satellite phone, Rhoda said. I couldn't stand not knowing if you were okay.

Hey rents, Mark said from the doorway. How goes the frontier life? He switched on the lights. The miracle of electricity, he said.

Hey Mark, Gary called from the bedroom.

Are you sick, Mom? Mark came over to the couch.

Just resting.

Holding court, Gary said, passing by to the kitchen.

A crime, I suppose.

You two have to stop fighting, Rhoda said. You're getting a little cabin fever, I think.

Ha, Irene said.

Don't start, Irene.

Well it's nice to have all four of us here, Irene said, and got up off the couch, felt dizzy. When's the last time that happened? she asked. And when will it ever happen again? This may be the last time we're all here as a family.

That's not true, Mom, Rhoda said. You won't be in the cabin forever.

Ask your father. But we should have something to eat. Some lunch. We should all sit down at the table.

I need to get the sheeting, Gary said. And the joists.

After lunch, Irene said.

I need to go now. I need to get this done.

Irene walked over to the cupboards, found a couple cans of chili. Gary standing beside her at the counter, writing a list. I'll just heat these up, she said.

Look. I don't have time.

C'mon Dad, Rhoda said. It's just lunch.

All the obstacles to a man's work, Mark said.

Gary walked into the bedroom and came out with his jacket. Angry and impatient as always. I'll be back in a couple hours, he said. We can have dinner together. And then he walked out, long strides to his truck.

Huh, Mark said. I would have offered to help. And I can't come back for dinner. I need to return this boat.

Irene gave Mark a hug, but he was uncomfortable, pulling away quickly. I'll be fine, he said.

Sorry, Irene said.

It's all good, Mark said, but he was edging for the door. What made the men run? They could have had lunch together. Was that too much to ask? To be a family for an hour?

How's Karen? Irene asked.

Mark's lopsided grin, holding back. You never ask about her, Mom. You don't like her.

That's not true.

Yeah it is.

He's right, Mom, Rhoda said. You always avoid her.

This isn't true. None of it. I only want you to be happy, and if you're happy with her, then that's great.

But you don't actually like her, Mark said. That's my point. You think she's dumb.

This isn't true. Why would you think that?

Whatever, Mark said. It's fine. I need to go.

Stay for lunch, Rhoda said.

I promised I'd return the boat. I need to get back.

Running away, just like your father, Irene said. Why can't you stay? It's just lunch. Why do the men in the family always run?

I don't know, Mark said. Maybe because we're creeped out? If I stay even one minute longer, I'll scream. I don't know why that is, but that's just the way it is. Sorry. It's nothing personal. And he had the door open now, escaping.

Nothing personal? Irene asked.

Later, Mark said, and he shut the door behind him. Irene went to the window, watched him walk away fast to his truck and boat.

She felt Rhoda then behind her, arms around her. It's okay, Mom.

Irene watched Mark drive away. She didn't understand what had just happened. I'm a terrible mother, she finally said.

No, Mom.

I don't think I knew that until now, Irene said.

Mom, it's just Mark.

But you said yourself that it's me. I avoid Karen. That's true. I don't like her. I do think she's dumb. And Mark knows that.

Rhoda let go then and sighed. She sat down at the table. Maybe we should have something to eat.

Okay, Irene said, and she went for the can opener, her hand a bit shaky, just a bit. Not something Rhoda would see. She opened up two cans of chili, emptied them into a pot and lit the burner. Then she stood there and stared into the chili, stirred occasionally with a spoon. The sound of the burner. She didn't want to think of herself as a terrible mother. Not on top of everything else. What if everything going wrong with Gary was her fault, too?

I'm getting married, Rhoda said.

What? Irene turned and Rhoda rose from her seat.

Jim proposed, Rhoda said, and she showed Irene her ring.

Rhoda, Irene said, and pulled her close for a hug. This is wonderful. She held Rhoda close and didn't want to let go. The beginning of the end for Rhoda, her life given and wasted on a man who didn't love her. That's what would happen, a cruel repetition of Irene's life, and what could Irene say now? But Irene didn't know anything for certain. That was the thing. Maybe Jim did love Rhoda, and maybe their marriage would be good, and maybe Rhoda would be happy.

Okay Mom, Rhoda finally said. I need to breathe.

Sorry, Irene said, and she let Rhoda go.

I'll check the chili, Rhoda said, and she turned away from Irene to give a stir, poured it into two bowls.

Irene was surprised by how she felt. She wanted to be happy for Rhoda, but she didn't feel happy at all. And she couldn't let Rhoda see that. This is wonderful, she said again as Rhoda placed the two bowls on the table.

Thanks, Mom, Rhoda said. But she sat and looked down at her chili as she ate. She wouldn't look at Irene. So Irene wasn't hiding anything here. Rhoda could tell.

I'm sorry, Irene said. I just don't want anything that's happened to me to happen to you.

What are you talking about, Mom?

Can you look at me when we're talking?

Rhoda looked up. Geez, Mom.

I'm sorry. I can't seem to get along with anyone.

Well you might think about that.

How can I think about anything else? You're my daughter. Rhoda was looking down again, and Irene hated that. I want you to be happy. That's all.

Well that's good, Rhoda said. Thank you.

Your father never loved me.

Rhoda put down her spoon and looked up again, annoyed. Mom, she said. We've talked about this before. You know that's not true. Dad has always loved you.

That's the thing, Irene said. He never has. He thinks he deserved someone better than me. He's admitted that now, out in the tent. And he wanted to be left alone. That's what's true about him. I was just easy, something that happened, and it would have been a hassle to cut me loose. He'd prefer to be without me, but he's never bothered to put together the effort to do that.

I'm not listening to this, Rhoda said. It's just the pain in your head, and maybe this stupid cabin thing, too, having to live out there.

The pain has made everything clearer, Irene said. I can't sleep, and it feels like I can't even think, but for some reason, I'm seeing everything more clearly than I ever have before. Irene was leaning forward, both forearms on the table. She felt excited.

That's really scary, Mom. You should listen to yourself.

Rhoda, you have to pay attention. What I'm telling you is important.

Mom. Rhoda was looking right at her now. You have to stop. Listen to yourself. You sound like a bag lady talking about aliens, like you have the secret and you've figured it all out.

A bag lady?

I'm sorry, Mom. It's just that you sound like you're going a little crazy. None of what you're saying about Dad is true. He loves you. He's always loved you.

Irene stood up. She was trembling. She grabbed her chili bowl and threw it at the window above the sink. A louder sound than she had expected as the glass shattered, but still not enough. Not satisfying at all. She wanted to bring the whole house down. He doesn't love me, she said. I should know. I'm the one living it.

The window glass jagged, an open view now of trees and snow. The light strange, no clear sense of where the sun was, no direction for light or shadow, the snow reflecting. No sense of time. A day that could stretch on forever.

I don't feel safe, Rhoda said. I think I need to leave.

Run away like the men, Irene said.

That's not fair, Mom.

Fair. That's funny.

That's the problem, Mom. You're sunk in some kind of pity fest. And you don't fight fair. Throwing your bowl through the window. How am I supposed to respond to that?

You make it sound like it's an act.

Well isn't it?

You should stop now, Rhoda.

Here's the truth, Mom. There's nothing wrong with you. Your husband loves you. Your family loves you. And there's nothing wrong with your head, either. You're just freaking yourself out. Why are you doing this?

You don't believe me?

No, I don't. I don't believe any of it.

Irene felt a strange calm then. Rhoda standing before her, worried, condescending, understanding nothing. And yet Rhoda was the person she was closest to in this world. She stepped forward and gave Rhoda a hug, held her tight. I'll only tell you this once, she said quietly. I'm alone now.

Mom.

Shh. Just listen. If you don't wake up, you'll be alone like this too. Your life spent, and nothing left. And no one will understand you. And you'll feel so angry, you'll want to do far more than throw a bowl through a window.

Rhoda pushed away. What the fuck, Mom.

That's all I have to offer you. Just the truth.

You're scaring me, Mom.

Well maybe you're starting to understand.

Everything was working against Gary now. Irene, the weather, time. Old troll brought her bow, said she wanted to hunt. Arrow tips wide fins of razor blade, a compound bow with pulleys, a frightening amount of power, and she seemed in dark enough a mind to consider using it on him.

The wind colder again, building. Another low-pressure system, hardly a break since the last. Gary had expected some warmer weather after the early storm. A kind of Indian summer. But this was starting to look like fall would be short. Another day below freezing.

Not another soul anywhere on this huge lake. The boat heavy with canned goods, loaded to the gunwales. A barge making its way slowly into white, the sky coming down.

All that held them was a hollow in the water, the theoretical weight of that, a depression in the surface. If they dipped an edge, the water would rush to fill the vacuum and they'd sink right to the bottom. Gary could feel the weight of the boat loaded down, could feel its desire to sink. The inanimate world full of intent, and Gary acutely aware how frail his life was. Waiting, hoping to pass safely, and he could do nothing more.

I could have loaded us down a bit less, he called out to Irene. We're heavy.

Irene turned to look at him a moment, as hostile a presence as ever, then looked forward again.

A slow passage, so slow it felt almost like Gary's will was all that was powering them, but finally he was able to turn toward shore. He came in slow, aimed carefully, but they were too heavy. They hit rocks fifteen feet out, stopped dead.

It's not deep, Irene said. I'll just get out here.

She was over the side and sank to her thighs. Not wearing waders. She grabbed a flat of chili, heavy he knew, and took a step toward shore then slipped and went down. Dropped the canned goods, went in to her shoulders, thrashing with her arms. Stood back up, dripping, and didn't say a thing. Just grabbed another flat of cans out of the boat, stepped forward again and made it this time to shore. Entirely soaked and must have been freezing.

Gary didn't know what to say. He couldn't think of anything safe. He put the engine in gear and tried to ram a bit closer but was caught. So he turned off the engine and climbed over the bags and flats to the bow, handed another flat to Irene, who had returned.

We'll go back after unloading, he said. So you can take a hot bath and get some warm clothes.

She looked old, very old, the lower part of her hair wet, her face wet. She took the plastic-wrapped flat of soups and turned away again.

Gary swung his legs over and lowered into the water, a shock of cold. Grabbed a flat and stepped carefully on the slick rocks below, made it to shore, cracking through thin panes of ice.

If you want, you can relay everything up to the tents and I'll do the trips to the boat, he said.

Irene paused a moment. All right, she said.

He was going to have probably fifty trips over the slick stones. Not having a dock or a better beach was something he hadn't considered enough when he bought this place. One more example of his poor planning. But they wouldn't have to do this often. Another boatload would last them to the hard freeze, then he'd buy a used snowmobile and bring supplies on that. Some kind of cargo sled. This entire place would be transformed. An open flat plain of white, no boats, and it was coming soon.

Gary could imagine walking out across the ice, the island no longer an island. The air still, no sound. Peaceful.

Irene gone a long time from shore. Changing her clothes, he was sure, and that was a good idea. Might save them a trip back home, too. Gary carried more flats of canned goods. His legs numb, his feet not feeling the rocks well.

Irene reappeared in dry clothing.

Feel better? Gary asked, but there was no answer. Irene picked up a flat of baked beans and walked carefully into grass and alders. The snow coming down heavier now, the world vanishing. No mountain, and the lake shortened. Closing in, leaving only the two of them and their work.

Back and forth, slogging through the water, Gary's legs no more than stumps. He removed all the canned goods, the tubs of putty, everything heavy. Then pulled himself aboard and was able to motor in to shore.

Eagle has landed, he said to Irene, trying to cheer things up, but she was impervious. Grabbed another flat and walked away.

Gary finished unloading, then helped carry up to the cabin. Irene just setting things randomly in any spot.

How about a little planning? he said. We need to organize this stuff. But she didn't respond.

Fine, he said, and he looked around. No room in the tents, and they needed the cabin clear for construction. So Gary stacked against the back wall. Soups and baked beans on one end, chili and canned veggies on the other. Bags piled between. If a bear came along, they'd be in trouble, but a bear seemed unlikely out here. Plenty on the far shore, but he'd never heard of one on this island.

By the time he was finished, Irene was sitting on a log.

That's it? he asked.

Yeah.

We should try to place a couple joists, Gary said, looking around, but he could see the light was fading, the world going dark blue. Looking like winter. He could see his breath in the air. Or maybe it's a little late for that.

I'll heat up some soup, Irene said.

Thanks, he said. He walked down to the beach to fish out that flat of chili she dropped. Stepped into the water, newly cold, the waves about a foot high now, the water blue-gray and opaque. Couldn't see even his own feet, but he'd brought the shovel, so he poked around with that, could feel the tip on rock. A new kind of fisherman, a prospector, almost, prodding at the deep to find what could be unburied. What if he could go deeper? He'd follow this rocky slope all the way to a hundred fathoms, the low valley, where he'd dig deep into silt, make great piles like sand. Who knows what could be uncovered then. The Lake Man, they'd call him, and he'd find everything that had ever been forgotten. A childhood alongside an old shoe, a rusted-out engine full of someone's thoughts from a summer afternoon. He'd find everything that ever was here. There's something about water, he said aloud. What is it about water?

Gary pulled the shovel along the bottom like a rake, a farmer tending soil, feeling for that flat, for a rectangular shape softer than rock. He stepped deeper and went for another row of rock, shuffling sideways, combing the area, and finally found it. Eureka, he said. The Lake Man recovers all.

He tugged with the shovel, pulled into shallows until he was able to reach down and grab. Carried it up to Irene to show her.

I got that case of chili, he said.

Irene didn't even look up. Kneeling before the stove, gazing into a pot of soup. Getting darker now, her face lit by the stove.

What the fuck, he said. Are you ever going to talk to me again?

You wouldn't want to hear what I have to say.

Fine, he said. You're probably right. I've heard about enough of your crap.

Gary went into the tool and supply tent to clear a space. Kneeled at the opening and stacked everything high on one side. Then went to the sleeping tent to grab his bag and pillow. I'm sleeping in the other tent, he said.

Irene like a monk over the soup. As if this meal were made of signs.

Gary stripped off his wet boots and pants and socks, put on dry clothing. Could feel his feet tingling back to life. I'll take my soup now, he said. I'm sure it's hot enough.

So Irene poured half the pot into a large plastic bowl and Gary grabbed a spoon and hiked down to the water's edge. Found a good rock and sat looking into the darkness falling over the water. No longer snowing. In the far distance, on the opposite shores, no longer a clear divide between water and sky. The boat bumping in the waves, scraping occasionally on rock.

He wanted to live out here. He wanted to spend a winter, wanted to experience that. But he could see now it would be only one winter. In the spring, he would leave this place, leave Irene. He didn't know where he would go or what he would do, but he knew it was time to leave. This life had finished.

Irene lay alone in her tent. A quieter night than usual, no wind. And she tried to imagine what it would be like in winter. Not so hard to do, really, after living at the edge of this lake so many years. As she walked out onto it, she'd find fault lines in the snow. A thin dusting, faint ridges raised up where the ice had cracked. No other footsteps, no tracks of any kind. Irene the only figure on a broad pan of white.

Early winter, the temperature minus fifteen. The mountains would be white, the lake and glacier. Only the sky a new color, rare winter sun, rare midwinter blue. The sun above the peaks moving sideways, unable to rise any higher.

Irene would carry her bow, her footsteps the only sound. The world prehistoric. Wind shifting the snow like sand, small dunes and hollows. The water close beneath.

Irene imagined herself not properly dressed for the cold for some reason. Wearing what she had worn inside the cabin, finished now: a blue sweater, thin down vest, wool pants and boots, a knit cap, white and gray. No gloves. Her hand holding the bow was cold. She walked toward the glacier, toward the mountains, away from the island. Walked slowly. Then stopped and looked around.

Without her footsteps, no sound. No wind, no moving water, no bird, no other human. This bright world. The sound of her heart, the sound of her own breath, the sound of her own blood in her temples, those were all she would hear. If she could make those stop, she could hear the world.

The water beneath her was moving, and that must make a sound. A dark current beneath ice, no surface to break, no ripples, but even that must make a sound. Deep water, layers and currents, and when one layer moved over another, something must hear that, some tearing of water against water. And over time, the changes in those currents, the shifts, the lake never the same from moment to moment. All of that must be recorded somehow.

Irene could imagine herself continuing on over the thin crust, holding the bow in her left hand, letting the other hand warm in her pocket. Continuing over light dunes of snow, pausing in an area of large flakes. The size of fingernails, individual snowflakes, their branches visible, lying at angles, razor-thin. They looked ornamental, contrived, too large and individual to be real. She squatted down for a closer look, touched a flake, then wiped her hand across the surface revealing the black of the lake, the color of ice over the depths. A vacuum of light. And no way to peer into it, the surface clear but so dark as to be essentially opaque.

The cold would press in. Not dressed for this, not prepared. Her legs and back cold. She'd be shivering soon. The sun so bright and without any warmth.

Gary, she said. And she stopped. This big lake, so flat, only the small drifts of snow. She looked at the far shorelines, turned a slow circle, tried to see it all at once, the immensity of it.

And then she would walk toward the nearest shoreline, wanting the cover of trees. The distances deceiving, elongating. At the edge of the lake, ruptures and monuments of ice, their peaks covered in snow, mountains of another scale. She stepped over a ridge, a giantess, slick ice beneath her boots and then rock, large pebbles, the beach. Into the trees quickly, home of winter birds: spruce grouse and willow ptarmigan, white-tailed ptarmigan. She'd seen small flocks of redpoll feed in temperatures colder than this.

No trail here. She stepped over deadfall, pushed through bare patches of alder, grown thick, food for ptarmigan, into the taller white trunks of birch, the evergreen Sitka spruce, tall and thin with branches bent at odd angles.

Irene looked for signs of life, saw and heard nothing. Her footsteps cracking. The forest nonconcealing, open to the sky, too bare, too stunted to cover. Wallow and swale, the flats and hollows, pushing again through denser growth right into a devil's club, spiny knob rising out of the forest as high as her shoulder. She cried out, her left hand impaled with spines. Twisted cane with its knobby head, thick with spines. And now she saw there were many more here. A thicket, so she had to backtrack, go around the wallow, find higher ground again.

She would find a stand of white birch, easier going, more space between trunks, make good progress, the snow not too deep. A rise, finally, the flank of the mountain, dragging the bow behind her. The cold air heavy in her lungs. As she came over a small hill, she could see the mountain above, white above the treeline, rumpled and old. She'd climb until she reached the top. Many miles, and she'd never done this in winter, but it didn't seem difficult now. It seemed almost as if she could be carried upward, as if she could float above the ground. Only the bow was holding her back, weighing her down, so she let it drop from her hand, didn't watch it fall, didn't look back, climbed faster, a new urgency, pulling at small branches with her hands.

Irene felt dizzy, lightheaded, the climbing a kind of trance, watching the snow in front of her, always perfect, small hollows around every trunk, everything contoured, the world traced and made softer.

Nothing more after that. Irene lost the vision. Could no longer see herself, could no longer see the winter. She was back in the tent, alone, thinking the world wasn't possible as it was. Too flat, too empty.

Irene curled on her side in her sleeping bag, waited for sleep, which never came. The night an expanse. Hours of focusing on her breath, counting her exhales, trying to slip away. Then turning onto her stomach, her knees sore from the sideways positions.

Early morning, the wind coming up. Still dark out. She lay on her back, no longer trying for sleep. Just let the pain pulse through her head, drifted around in it, felt tears leaking from her eyes but couldn't find any emotion attached. A general sense of grief, or despair, something empty, but not what you'd call a feeling. Too tired for that. Waiting for light, for the day to start so at least she could get up and there would be activity. Something to pass the time.

She closed her eyes again, and when she opened her eyes sleepless hours later, the blue nylon of the tent was just visible, and so this was the beginning of the day. Another half hour of waiting and it was light enough to rise and dress.

Cold and overcast as Irene emerged from the tent. She walked over to the cabin, looked out the open space for the front window, shivering in the wind. She needed to get working to warm up.

So she stepped over to Gary's tent. Get up, she called out. Gary. It's time to work. I'm cold. I need to start working.

Okay, he answered finally. She envied him his sleep. Waking into a new day separated from the last. For Irene, her entire life was becoming one long day. She wondered how long she could survive. At some point, if you never sleep, do you die? Or does just lying there for hours, resting with your eyes closed, count somehow as partial sleep, something you can do for years on end?

Gary came out of the tent with his boots unlaced, jacket unzipped, head bare. Mostly gray now. Stumbled off a few feet and took a piss, faced away from her. Which reminded her of the outhouse. They still had an outhouse to build. No more squatting behind bushes in the snow.

Gary shook and zipped, stepped away, laced his boots, grabbed his hat from the tent. Cold, he said. Wind coming up.

Yeah, she said. I get to saw the ends of the joists. I need to get moving to warm up.

Okay, he said. What about breakfast?

We can have that later.

Okay.

They walked to the pile of two-by-eights and brought one into the cabin through the back door, stood on stepstools. Gary along the high back wall, holding the joist over his head, marked a pencil line for the cut.

Then Irene worked at the saw, feeling her upper body warm. Under different circumstances, she might enjoy building a cabin. A good distraction, a sense of accomplishment. The angled piece came off and they walked back to test the fit.

Pretty good, Gary said finally. Good enough. We can cut the others at the same angle.

Irene tried to just work and not think about anything else. The ripping of the saw through wood, the way the wood grabbed at it, clenched it, stops and starts, and she was thinking of winter again, wondering at what she had seen. Did it mean anything? Saying his name, standing there on the ice looking all around. Or brushing away the snow, seeing the black of the ice, or running into devil's club, all the spines. It hadn't been a dream. It was a waking vision, and yet she'd felt the sting of the spines, seen the twisted club heads all around her. Carrying her bow. And had she been out hunting? How can we not know our own visions, our own daydreams?

Gary saying something. Irene tried to come back, focus. What? she asked.

I said we won't be able to fit both ends. Or maybe we can. Let me think.

Irene stopped sawing. Waited. Looked down at sawdust in the snow. Her toes cold, her knees cold against the ground. She got up in a squat, but that felt unstable for sawing, so she kneeled again.

I'm not thinking well, he said. I need some breakfast. We should have breakfast before we start.

Irene at fault for his inability to think. Nothing new there. She went to the Coleman stove and put the teakettle on a burner. Hot water for oatmeal and chocolate or tea. Neither of them drank coffee. In many ways, their strange lifestyle had been good. No TV. No Internet. No phone. Just the lake, the woods, their home, their kids, going into town to work and buy supplies. It hadn't been a bad life, on the surface. Something elemental about it. Something that could have been true if it hadn't all been just a distraction for Gary, a kind of lie. If he had been true, their lives could have been true.

Gary in his tent, resting or warming up while Irene waited for the water to boil. She wondered whether she could be softer, forgive him for everything, let it pass. Accept what her life had been. Something reassuring about that. But in the end, you feel what you feel. You don't get a choice. You don't get to remake yourself from the beginning. You can't put a life back together a different way.

The water boiled, finally, and Gary emerged for his oatmeal and hot chocolate, sat down in the doorway, a space for one. So Irene ate her oatmeal kneeling at the stove, thinking you really can't put a life back together a different way. That was the problem. Knowledge came too late, and by then, there was no use for it. The choices had already been made.

I see now how to do it, Gary said. I just needed a little food in my stomach. We'll angle one end of the extension pieces, then hold them in place and mark a line for where to join. That'll work.

Sounds good, Irene said. She hadn't been listening, and she didn't care. She began sawing again, her shoulder getting sore.

Gary taking a break, making plans while she worked, or maybe only daydreaming. So she stopped. You can finish these, she said, and walked to the tent to lie down, her head spinning. The pain as sharp as it had ever been, like someone sawing through her skull, but she didn't care much about that. It just was. The pain had become like breathing. Nothing convenient about breathing, but we keep doing it.

She could hear Gary moving faster but also jamming the blade more often. Impatient. Wanting to get the roof on. But Irene could see now that the tent was more comfortable than the cabin ever would be, so she was in no rush.

Okay Irene, Gary called out. I'm ready to measure the extensions.

Irene didn't move at first. Just seemed too difficult to get up.

Let's go, Gary said. We can put up all these joists today and maybe even get the roof on.

Okay, Irene said. She crawled out of her bag, put on her boots, and stepped outside. A perfect workday, really. Cold and overcast, but not coming down on them, not too windy. She walked over to the pile of joists and looked at her husband. A stranger's face. No friendliness.

I'll go in first, he said. You'll be on the back wall.

Okay, she said, and followed with her end. Stepped onto a stool, held her end high.

Make sure you're level with the top, he said.

It's there, she said. Just mark it.

I'm doing that, he said.

They set the joist down and he nailed the two pieces together. Hard hammer blows, loud.

They raised it again, and Gary nailed his end into the log wall. Damn it, he said. I don't know how I'm supposed to do this.

Irene could see a nail at the base going in crooked, another angled from the side. Maybe you need brackets, she said.

Yeah. I realize that now. But I don't have brackets, and there doesn't happen to be a store out here. Damn it.

So she kept holding her end while he drove in four crooked nails.

A long morning and afternoon with the joists, Gary growing steadily more frustrated and angry. His hat off and jacket unzipped from the exertion, his hair in ruffs that stood at odd angles and bent in the breeze. Jammed his thumb, cracked one of the ends, threw his hammer at the ground, got through the day in small fits and rages. Told her to hold her damn end still.

But finally the joists were in place, slanting down from the back wall to the front. Gary stood on a stool in the middle of the platform and pulled himself up on one, testing the strength. That'll hold, he said. Let's get the roof on before dark.

Irene hadn't said a word in hours. They grabbed a piece of aluminum sheeting and leaned it against the front of the cabin. Brought out stepstools and hoisted the sheet into place.

It's not quite long enough, Gary said. That's why I got the smaller pieces. So we can let this overhang a bit. That'll help keep the rain off the walls.

Irene did as she was told, held the sheet while he went inside to nail. I'll have to get some goop for the nail holes, he said. So Irene knew it would drip on them, probably all winter. No bed, just their sleeping bags with large wet spots from the drips. Or maybe they'd sleep under a plastic tarp, the edges of the plywood wet and muddy, her pillow on the floor. That's what she had to look forward to, she knew.

Let's grab the next sheet, he said. Evening, only an hour or so of light, racing against the dark now. No lunch. Only that oatmeal for breakfast. Irene felt dizzy and insubstantial, like she might be able to drift above the ground, float just below the level of the trees. Held another sheet in place while he nailed, and another, cold aluminum. She wore only thin canvas work gloves. The temperature dropping, something below freezing. Shivering now.

As they hoisted the last full sheet, Gary was getting excited, the end in sight. She held while he went inside to nail. His head poking up through the joists, one arm slung around to nail from above.

Only the back row now, he said. We'll have a roof over our heads tonight.

It's getting dark, she said.

We'll do it by flashlight.

So Irene brought out flashlights from her tent. We should have headlamps, Gary said. I wish you would have bought headlamps. And these flashlights are cheap. We'll be lucky if they last. Irene at fault again. If they didn't get the roof on tonight, it would be her fault.

Irene brought her stepstool around to the back wall, tried to plant the legs firmly enough so she wouldn't totter. She stepped up and Gary handed her a sheet. The smaller sheets much lighter, but still difficult to raise over her head. She was tired and hungry and cold and her head was knifing. She pushed upward but wasn't tall enough to get the sheet to flop over onto the roof. It only pointed into the sky.

Damn it, Gary said. Just drop it.

She let it fall into an alder bush.

I'll have to do this myself. Bring your stool around front.

Irene went to the front and helped heave the piece onto the roof, then held it in place while he went inside. His head poking up between the joists, he grabbed the sheet and slid it upward. Fucking flashlight, he said. We needed headlamps. I can't hold the piece and hold a nail and a hammer and a flashlight. I don't have four fucking hands.

I'll hold a flashlight from here, Irene said. And if you give me a stick or something, I might be able to keep the piece from slipping.

Fine, Gary said. Just hurry up. I can't hold this forever.

Irene looked around the woodpile for a stick, trying to hurry, but she didn't see anything. Starting to feel panicked. Gary waiting.

Just get the boat hook, he shouted. Go to the boat. I can't fucking hold this much longer.

She walked as fast as she could to the boat, running when possible, the flashlight beam jumping around grass and snow. The boat bumping and scraping in small waves. She climbed over the bow, her flashlight beam bright against all the aluminum, and found the boat hook, hurried back to the cabin.

Here it is, she called out. She used the boat hook to push at the lower edge of the sheet. Other hand holding the flashlight, afraid she might fall, standing on the top step of the stool.

Okay, Gary said. He adjusted the sheet a bit. Now hold it there and keep the light on it.

Gary nailed the sheet along the joists, then asked for the next.

I'll need help lifting it onto the roof, Irene said.

Fine, Gary said, and he came around, tossed it up by himself. Just hold it now, he said.

He was back inside and nailing, and they did two more sheets, utterly dark, the beam bright off the aluminum, the roof a kind of reflector. They could have been building a spacecraft, Irene thought, something meant to rise up into this night and take them away from the world. A strange thing they were doing out here. A man and his slave, building his machine.

Gary heaved the last piece in place, went around inside, and then wasn't sure what to do. This one closes the gap, he said. I can't get my hand outside to hammer. I shouldn't have put those two-by-fours in yet to block the side gap. Hold it and just wait a minute.

Gary moved his stool outside the back wall, then the side wall. Damn it, he said. Not quite tall enough. The ground's too low.

The ground's fault, Irene thought. If they had better ground, it would know to rise up. She held the boat hook and flashlight, tried to stay balanced on the stool. This was her part in the circus.

Gary let out a little grunt-scream thing of frustration. No planning, ever, his entire life. Just throwing himself from one obstacle to the next, blaming the world and Irene.

Fuck, he said. I'm gonna have to climb onto the fucking roof. I can't do it any other way.

Irene didn't say anything. Just did her job.

Gary brought his stool beside her and let out another little scream of frustration. Nothing to grab on to, he said. So he took his stool back inside. Give me some room, he said. Move the sheet.

Irene let the sheet slide down toward her.

More, he said, so she let it slide farther, then saw his hands on the joist. He yanked himself upward and got one leg onto the roof. Growling, working that leg out farther, pushing down with his heel, trying to leverage. Finally pulled up sideways and made it.

I need the hammer, he said. It's inside.

What about the sheet?

I'll hold it. Just get the hammer.

Irene stepped down, walked around quickly, handed him the hammer, and returned to her station. Gary slid the sheet into place, she held it with the boat hook, and he nailed.

Okay, he said. We have a roof. Then he looked around. Not sure how I'm getting down, he said.

I'll get out of the way, Irene said, and climbed down off her stool.

Nothing to hold on to, he said. But because of the slant, I should be able to hang off the back. Go around with the flashlight. We have to find a safe place for me to jump down.

Irene ran around quick, shone her light all along the back, moved a pile of garbage bags, their food, and found a mossy patch that seemed soft. This looks good, she said. A bunch of moss.

Okay, keep your light on it. And he lowered himself off the back, hopped down a few feet, easy enough.

Let's tack up the window, he said, so the wind doesn't come in. We can leave the back door for now.

Are we spending the night in there?

Yeah, of course.

With all the gaps? Wind and snow are going to come in, right?

It's not perfect.

Why not use the tents another night?

Why are you like this?

Like what?

Get that light out of my face, he said, slapping it away. And don't pretend you don't know what you're doing.

I've been helping you, she said. All day and now at night.

You help, but you've also been letting me know what you think of me, every few days, how I've destroyed your life, separated you from everyone. So maybe it's time I let you know what I think of you.

Stop it, Gary. Don't do this.

No. I'm going to let you have it like you've been letting me have it.

Gary, I'm trying here. I'm building your cabin in the dark. I haven't had any food since the oatmeal this morning.

My cabin, Gary said. See? That's what I mean. Our whole lives, my fucking fault. No choice of yours. Not your fault you have no friends. You're a social misfit. That's why you don't have any friends.

Stop, Gary. Please.

No, I think I'm enjoying this. I think I'm going to sink my teeth into this.

Irene started crying. She didn't mean to, but she couldn't help it.

Cry your fucking eyes out, he said. If it weren't for you, I would have left this place. I might even have become a professor, finally. But you wanted kids, and then I had to support the kids, and build more rooms on the house. I got trapped in a life that wasn't really me. Building boats and fishing. I was working on a dissertation. A *dissertation.* That's what I was supposed to be doing.

The unfairness was too much for Irene. She couldn't speak. She kneeled on the ground and cried.

Misery loves company, he said. And all you wanted to do was drag me down with you. You're a mean old bitch. You don't say it, but you're thinking it, always judging. Gary doesn't know what he's doing. Gary hasn't planned a thing, hasn't thought ahead. Always a little bit of judgment. A mean old bitch.

You're a monster, she said.

See? I'm a monster. I'm the fucking monster.

The satellite phone arrived by UPS in the afternoon. A yellow Pelican case, watertight, the phone tucked inside, padded in foam. Power cords for AC and DC, a packet of adaptors for anywhere in the world. The kind of thing only Jim could afford. A slow day at work, so Rhoda sat at her desk and read the instructions, plugged in the phone to get it charging. She had already bought two golf cart batteries, so her mom would be able to recharge using the DC plug.

At five p.m., she packed up and drove home. A full wedding planning kit from the resort on Kauai had also arrived today, so she was looking forward to opening that. She and Jim would sit on the couch and look through everything.

But when she arrived, Jim was already working out, running on the orbital.

Hiya, he said between huffs. He talked differently now, perky speech. Hiya and you betcha. She didn't know what was going on. He had a new receptionist, and she spoke like that, so maybe it was rubbing off.

Rhoda put the Pelican case on the bar, and the wedding planning packet. She might as well start fixing dinner. His workouts were getting longer and longer. He'd be at it for at least an hour and a half, every day now, and then he'd have to take a shower. Then dinner and early to bed. They were right here in the same room together, but he didn't like to talk when he worked out, and he had his iPod going anyway.

Rhoda opened the fridge, and she wondered how much of Jim she was marrying. What percentage. Ten percent of his attention, some larger percentage of his affection, ninety percent of his daily needs and errands, some percentage of his body, a small percentage of his history. She wondered what she was signing up for. Half of his money. She didn't like to think of it that way. They were supposed to be joining their lives together. They were supposed to be sitting together on the couch right now, looking at the sunset and the brochures.

Salmon, halibut, caribou, chicken. None of it appealed. She didn't feel like cooking. So she closed the fridge and walked over to Jim. She waited until he pulled out his earphones. He looked like hell, sweaty and splotchy. I'm gonna grab a pizza, she said. I don't feel like cooking.

He was huffing hard. I don't know about pizza, he said. All that cheese. Not good for the muffin top.

He had started calling his gut a muffin top, and he was on a diet. No alcohol or desserts or dairy.

I feel like pizza, she said.

How about a big salad. Can you fix us a big salad, honey?

Quit calling me honey. What the fuck has happened to you? Who are you?

Rhoda. What's wrong? Maybe you need to work out more, too. Make it every day. You'll feel better.

Rhoda looked down at her stomach. She was still slim. She

ran three times a week, and that was fine. How did her running not count as a workout? I'm fine, she said. I don't need to work out more.

I'm not saying anything about your weight. I'm just saying you might feel better.

This is a dumb conversation, Rhoda said. I'm not having this. I want to talk about other things. The satellite phone arrived, so I have to get that out to my mom. And the wedding planning kit arrived, so we need to look at that this evening.

I don't know about this evening, honey. Maybe this weekend, when we have more time.

Rhoda felt so angry suddenly she didn't know what to say. She didn't want to say anything bad. This was supposed to be their happy time, planning their wedding and honeymoon. So she just nodded and walked away, back to the fridge. They had some lettuce and tomato, an unripe avocado, smoked salmon, of course, that she could throw in. Pine nuts. Enough for a salad. Some cucumber left over. So fine, they'd have a salad. No need to fix it now. He wouldn't be ready for another hour and a half at least.

Rhoda walked into the bedroom, ran the bath, and stripped. Lay down on the bed naked, waited for the tub to fill. Felt a little cold but didn't care. Looked up at the ceiling. None of this was working out the way she had planned, and she couldn't even really think about it, anyway, because she was thinking about her mother all the time. Her mother saying she wanted to do something worse than throw a bowl through the window. She meant it. Rhoda could tell. She wanted to destroy. And how had that happened?

Rhoda sighed and went to sit in the water, even though the tub wasn't full yet. Added bubble bath. Like one of the dogs at work, waiting to be scrubbed. She put her arms around her knees and laid her head against them. Tried to focus on her breath and stop thinking, the hot water rising up.

When it was full, she turned off the faucet and laid back, closed her eyes. Smelled pear and vanilla, the bubble bath, too strong. Her body long and slim and weightless. She thought about a water wedding, just for fun. Everyone wearing scuba gear and weight belts, held to the ocean floor. Light brown sand rippling in wave patterns, a white wedding arch anchored down. A wall of coral for backdrop as she held Jim's hands, looking at his face pinched in a mask, a regulator in his mouth, lips pale pink. The guests arrayed in the sand watching, the women's dresses creating great colored plumes in the current, far-off coral tufts and fish gliding by. A parrotfish, lime and turquoise, swimming past Rhoda's feet.

Rhoda smiled. If only a dream could be made instantly. No arrangements. She could decide this was the wedding she wanted, and poof, it would happen. She didn't like waiting.

Rhoda dozed off, woke with a start, not sure at first where she was. The shower running, Jim finished with his workout. The bath water no longer hot. She rose and dried off, dressed, walked into the kitchen. Felt sluggish as she fixed the salad, no interest in the food. Over a week since they'd had sex, a very long time for them. She wondered what was wrong.

Jim came out just as she had the salad and plates on the table.

Fabu, he said. Another of the perky new phrases.

Panacotta, she said.

What?

Just sounded like it went with fabu.

Hm, Jim said. Then he served himself some salad. Raised the tongs too high. Made an arc in the air with each serving. As if this were a performance.

I'm worried about my mom, she said.

Yeah.

I need to get that phone to her right away. I need to be able to talk with her.

Jim munched on a big mouthful of lettuce. Looking outside, at the deck lit by floodlights, not at Rhoda. He finished chewing, then gulped half a glass of water. Thirsty, he said. After working out.

I'm really worried about her.

Jim stabbed another bunch of lettuce on his fork but then paused and gave her a quick look. Next time they're in, he said. You can run it out to the house.

No. I need to talk with her now.

Jim stuffed the lettuce in his mouth. Stared at his plate while he chewed. Then gulped the rest of his water. Can I have some more water? he asked.

Rhoda grabbed his glass and filled it at the fridge. Walked back to the table and was careful not to set it down hard.

Look, he said. I know you're worried, and you care about them. But I'm sure they're fine. And maybe it's good to have a bit more separation from your mother. Maybe you'll rely on her less.

This isn't a normal time, Rhoda said. There's something wrong with her. I'm scared.

Nothing's going to happen to them out there. Jim pushed some of the lettuce around on his plate, flipped a leaf over and flipped it again. Man, he said. This is just not that satisfying. I miss the pancakes and peaches. But pancakes aren't good for the muffin top.

I think she might kill him.

What?

Rhoda stood up and walked into the bedroom. She lay face-down on the bed, closed her eyes, could feel her pulse beating fast. She was afraid her mother might kill her father or hurt him in some way. Or she might kill herself. Rhoda didn't want to think this. She wanted to stop her thoughts.

A long delay, far too long, before Jim came to the bedroom. He sat beside her and put a hand on her lower back. They'll be fine, he said.

No they won't, she said, and she knew this was true. She didn't know how she knew, and she couldn't explain it to Jim. He wouldn't believe her. She sat up and wiped her eyes. Jim wasn't holding her. He was worthless to her. No help at all. Why was she with him? For the first time, she thought of not marrying him. Maybe she would be fine without him. It was only an engagement. I need to call Mark, she said. I need to get out there tomorrow.

Rhoda, Jim said.

Can you please just be quiet? She was holding her hands to her face, her eyes closed. She waited and he finally left. She scooted closer to the phone and dialed Mark.

Karen answered, but Rhoda didn't feel like chatting. She waited for Mark.

A call from the higher-ups, Mark said. How goes the fiefdom?

Rhoda knew she had to be careful. Mark, she said. I know this will sound unreasonable, and I know I'm asking a lot, but I really am begging. This is very important.

Wow, Mark said. I can't wait to hear. You've decided to live in a tent, like the rents, and you want me to take Jim's house?

I bought a satellite phone for Mom, and I need to take it out to her tomorrow.

That's cool. Can you get one for me? I've needed one for like, I don't know, five years now, for the boat. How the fuck did you afford a satellite phone? Just a rhetorical question. I know the answer, of course. Jim the minor saint.

Please.

I don't know, Mark said. I know Mom's a freak and you're worried, but they really are coming in soon for supplies, and it's cold out here now. The shore is icing up. It would suck to launch a boat.

It's thin ice, though, right? You can break through it?

Yeah, but they'll be in, probably just a few days.

Please, Rhoda said.

There was a long pause. Rhoda afraid to say anything more.

All right, Mark finally said. Don't say I never did anything for you. But I can't do it tomorrow. It'll have to be Sunday.

Thank you, she said. Thank you. But can we do it tomorrow? I'm really worried. I need to talk with her.

Sorry. Karen's family. We have a get-together tomorrow.

Okay, she said. Okay. Thank you. Rhoda knew this was as far as she could push. She would just have to wait. But she didn't know how she would get through two days. Her mom holding her at the kitchen sink, telling her she was alone. Telling Rhoda that she would be alone, too. But what was really frightening was how calm her mother had been. You can't say things like that and feel calm and not have something wrong.

The door frame didn't fit. Gary held it against the gap in the back wall. White-painted pine over rough bark, an unlikely marriage of materials. He had cut the gap narrow so he could adjust later, a decision made when he had imagined more time, believed in more time. Now he needed to cut away almost two inches of cabin wall.

He looked around, a quick glance behind, as if Irene might appear. He hadn't seen her yet today. She'd left early, before he woke.

Gary centered the frame so that it overlapped both sides. A door set on the outside of the wall, projecting four inches. And why not? He wasn't building this cabin for anyone else.

So Gary grabbed his hammer and nails, aligned the frame, and propped it with two-by-four cutoffs. If Irene were here, she could hold it in place, much faster, but she wasn't going to help now.

And the truth was, he did feel bad. He felt guilty. Wanted to apologize, even, and if she'd been here when he awoke, he would have tried. He shouldn't have called her a mean old bitch. He didn't like to think of it. Didn't like to think he had said that. But he knew he had. He had said it twice.

Gary sighed. His breath fogging. A good day again for working, cold and overcast, but he didn't feel any motivation at all. He hated not getting along with Irene. He wanted everything to be clear between them.

He braced his shoulder against the frame and set a nail at an angle, tapped it carefully. Then a harder hit, but it bent and he felt the frame move, no longer aligned.

Gary closed his eyes then, slumped against the frame, and tried to calm. He wasn't good at anything. He knew that now. The cabin a failure, the most recent in a series of failures. So fine. He still needed to get this frame attached. He'd spent the night in the cabin, and it had been cold, desperately cold. Not a way they could live through the winter.

Gary set the frame in place again, leaned against it, and tried another nail. Got it in most the way and then cracked the frame. So he stepped back about ten feet and threw his hammer into the wall. A slight echo from the trees and hill behind, then a muffled thud from the ground.

Gary stepped forward and picked up the hammer, tried again to align and fix a nail. It sank but felt light, and when he examined the back, he saw he had caught only a small bit of the cabin wall. No firm purchase because of the angle. Maybe a quarter inch of meat. Nothing that would hold. And the point was sticking out now.

Gary walked over to Irene's tent for a granola bar. On his knees, reaching in, his face close enough to her pillow he could smell her. So he lay down a moment, head on her pillow, and rested. Curled his knees so they were inside the tent. He would tell her he was sorry. The early cold weather a setback, but they were close to having the cabin ready, and maybe spending the winter together would help them return to who they had been.

But he didn't want her to find him like this. He would seem weak. So he got up, ate the granola bar while he looked at the door and frame.

To hell with it, he finally said. He hammered a dozen nails around the edges, all shallow, many of them bent or opening up cracks, but together they might hold. Sharp points projecting out the back. Then he grabbed the door, simple white pine, and placed it in the frame. Not sure how to line up the hinges, especially without anyone helping.

The part he didn't understand was how he had felt excited. She'd helped him all day—no food, in the cold, the pain in her head—and he'd been impatient, too, and she'd put up with that, and they had accomplished a lot, more than any other day. They put the roof on, the entire roof. But then she wouldn't do the last little bit, just tacking the window on. It might have taken fifteen minutes. And suddenly he was saying everything he'd wanted to say for weeks, for years. And enjoying it. A thrill. A physical thrill, a pleasure, even though she was crying. And how could that be? How could he enjoy that?

Gary propped the door on shims and nailed the hinges. He could feel the frame shift with the blows, rickety. He'd have to buy brackets in town, but hopefully it would hold for now. You have to think you're a good person. That was the thing. And how was he a good person if he enjoyed making her cry? Something wrong with him, something that needed looking at. Their marriage somehow had brought out the worst in him.

The window was next. He didn't feel like waiting for Irene. The frame thin, and aluminum, so it wouldn't crack and he wouldn't have to nail at an angle. They really could have done this last night in ten or fifteen minutes.

Alone building the cabin. That was the truth. Marriage only another form of being alone. He set the stool in place, held the window up, leaned against it, pinning it to the wall, and hammered a nail. Held the other nails in his teeth. Pounded one on each side and then could let go. Pounded in the rest, all the way around. That's not going anywhere, he said.

Gary stepped back and looked at his cabin. The outward shape of a man's mind, he had thought before. A reflection. But he could see now that was not true. You could find an outward shape only if you entered the right field, the right profession, if you followed your calling. If you took the wrong path, all you could shape was monstrosity. This was without doubt the ugliest cabin he had ever seen, a thing misunderstood and badly constructed from beginning to end. The outward shape of how he had lived his life, but not the outward shape of who he could have been. That truer form had been lost, had never happened, but he didn't feel sad any longer, or angry, really. He understood now that it just was.

Gary walked around back. He had meant for the door to open outward, but it opened inward. So he pushed in and propped it with a rock, the first time entering his finished cabin, a cabin with a roof, window, and door, and he set a stool in front of the window. This was not what he had imagined. In his visions and daydreams, the inside of the cabin had been warm, and he'd sat in a comfortable chair, smoking a pipe. There'd been a wood stove, the hides of bear and mountain goat, Dall sheep and moose, wolf. He hadn't seen what the floor looked like, but it had not been unfinished ply. And the walls had not let in air. The cabin of his visions had been small but had extended outward infinitely in that dreamtime of belonging. Its walls traveled outward into wilderness. This lake and the mountains became him. No voids, no distance. And there was no Irene. In all the times he had dreamed of the cabin, he had never seen Irene. He hadn't realized that until now. She was not sitting in a chair beside him, not standing at the wood stove. No place for her in Gary's dream. He was smoking his pipe, sitting here by the window, looking out at the water, and he was alone in the wilderness. That was what he wanted. That was what he had always wanted.

This island was not right for Irene. The trees too close, too crowded. Trunks no more than a foot wide, spaced three or four feet apart, every space closed by the lower dead branches, thin curved half-hoops aiming at the ground, brittle and fracturing as she pushed through. Never an open space, never a place to run or look out over ridges and valleys. If she found a moose, she would be close enough to touch its hide with her hand. Her bow would be unnecessary. Tangled constantly in the branches. She kept having to yank it free. She was moving fast, a walk that was just short of running. And this was who she was meant to be, walking fast or running through snow and forest. A more open landscape, perhaps, but the same cold and snow. The uncountable generations before her.

She held the bow close, tried to keep it from snagging. Felt exhilarated. Looking for movement, listening to the forest, listening beyond her own footsteps and scrapings. Her blood running thick and beating outward to echo in the forest, a kind of sonar. Nothing could hide from her.

She stopped dead, planted her feet, brought the bow up and notched an arrow. Pulled back hard against the pulleys, felt them turn and break free into the easier part of the pull, held the arrow tight against her cheek and sighted down the razored tip to a cottonwood trunk fifty feet away. Let the arrow fly, the whip of the release, and the arrow buried deep into the trunk. The flight so fast it was instant memory, not something that could be experienced, only known afterward. Irene ran to the cottonwood, examined the arrow buried into the flesh of the tree, four slits lighter against the bark, almost invisible, radiating out from the post, and if she peered into these slits she could just see the back edges of the blades. No way to retrieve this arrow, so she held the bow close again and ran on.

Exhaustion. That was what she wanted. She wanted to run until she could run no more. But she was fueled by some other source now, something beyond muscle and blood. She never tired. She crossed all the way to the shore on the other side of the island, broke free into tufts of grass and rocky beach and saw Frying Pan Island, its graceful curve, notched an arrow, aimed high, and sent it soaring into another forest. Stepped along the water's edge and hunted larger stones and shadows of reflection and ice, notched another arrow and ripped into the surface. Vanished then, hidden by ripples, and she thought she'd heard blades hit rock but didn't know whether she'd only imagined it.

Two arrows left, and she would save those. She needed trees again, hurried back into cover, hunted patches of moss, from one to the next, up hills and down into swales, over ridges. Everything closed in, the trees too tight. She was freed against gravity, lofted over hills, scraped and crashing through. She'd been awake for more hours than could be counted, and somehow this brought a new power, her footsteps light in the snow, the air something that could pull her forward. And it felt as if the entire island were rolling, slowly turning over, capsizing. She had to keep her feet moving fast to stay upright. The island born long ago at lake bottom, rising to the surface on some kind of stalk, and now that stalk had been severed and the island was top-heavy, the hills of rock, the trees, and it would roll over until its slick flat underside was facing upward, wet and dark and known for thousands of years only to the lake, new to the sky. What would happen then? But Irene would no longer be here.

Origins. That was the problem. If we didn't know where we had started, we couldn't know where we should end, or how. Lost all along the way. Pulled into Gary's life, the wrong life.

What Irene knew for certain was that this was not the beginning. She would not be made new again. And she would take Gary with her. That had been her mother's mistake, taking only herself. It was not right that Irene's father had lived on in some other life, a life without his wife or daughter, a life severed from its origins, a life that could not connect in any way to Irene. That life should not have happened, should not have been allowed.

Irene had lain awake all night again, and in those first hours she wept, raged against Gary and unfairness, injustice, wanted to punish but really wanted to come closer to him. Wanted to continue with him, as wrong as that was. Tried to find a path back, but finally she had calmed and known there was no path back. He didn't love her, and he had never loved her, but he had used her life anyway. This was truth. Nothing she could do could make that change. It was beyond her power. She had felt her mind a vacuum, windblown space inside her, lain there empty for hours, waited for daylight, and finally this exhilaration, a gift, a final gift. It felt almost as if the pain might leave, still crowding her, still pressurizing, but promising to leave.

Snapping through branches, running downhill now, everything passing too fast to recognize. She had known this forest, and if she slowed, she might find signs, might recognize monkshood, its purple flower, the weight of that flower bending, but she was moving too fast, running, a full run, no stopping now, and she didn't bother to shield with her arms. Let the branches scrape at her face.

Footfalls in snow and moss, the burn of skin on her hands and face and neck, the cold overcast sky above, and her body could weave on its own between trees. Irene, anything that could be called Irene, removed, quiet. Coming closer to the cabin, her legs slowed, a walk and then slower still, hunting as she had once hunted with Gary, making no sound, avoiding branches now, pushing at them carefully, bending to the side, not breaking. Emerging between the tents, directly behind the cabin. Standing still, listening for any movement, any sound, hearing nothing but a light breeze and small waves at the shore. Water and air, and blood, beating faster now. He wouldn't be in the tents. He'd be in the cabin or at the shore. So Irene pulled an arrow free, set it and notched it, black bow, black arrow against white snow, walked silently toward the cabin door.

The door frame new and mounted on the outside, white and out of place against the logs. Trash bags and flats of canned goods piled all around. Closer until she was nearly at the threshold, and still she heard nothing. The cabin seemed larger now, the back wall high. Rough bark, gaps, some logs projecting out farther than others. She hadn't noticed before how uneven the surface, valleys and ridges, a landscape set up on end. She waited at the threshold, let her eyes adjust, darker inside the cabin, but enough light coming from the window and gaps to see the plywood floor. The window itself not yet in view, set off farther to the right, blocked by the door. A dim space and no sign of Gary.

Irene stepped in, bow held close and ready.

Irene? Gary asked. He was sitting five feet from her, on a stool by the window. Lit in relief, the lines on his face. Old. What are you doing, Irene?

She stepped back. More difficult now that she was here and he was talking to her. He stood up, hands opening toward her, fingers in relief in this light. Irene, he said again.

She pulled back the arrow tight against her cheek.

I love you, Irene, he said, and suddenly it was easy again. She let the arrow fly, saw it disappear into his chest. Only the black feathers sticking out past his jacket. He was spun around to the side, looking down at his chest, and fell to the floor, facedown. The arrowhead and shaft sticking up into the air.

Gary crying. Or screaming. Some sound over the blood in Irene's head. She walked closer and notched her last arrow. His legs and arms moving, pulling himself across the floor toward the wall. And what would he find at the wall? She pulled the arrow back to her cheek, aimed down at his back, and let another arrow fly. Another cry from Gary, the arrow too fast to see. Just suddenly there, sticking up high. But it had nailed him to the floor. He couldn't crawl forward now. Arms and legs still moving, but not getting anywhere. Still not dead, and she had no more arrows. His screaming lower, a thing that did not sound human. Irene dropped the bow and didn't know what to do. She stood there waiting for him to die, but he wouldn't die. An awful, animal sound, the last sound a living thing makes. Her husband. Gary.

Irene walked outside, walked down to the shore. The lake a magnification of sky, white and overcast, cold. Irene felt hot, like she could sear through water and sky and snow, even rock. She was a giantess, powerful, able to crush mountains and scoop out lakes with her hands. Walked down the shoreline and this was her shore. Didn't feel the wind. Had the need to run, so she ran again, ran faster than she ever had before, the uneven stones and pools and ruffs nothing. She was sure-footed. The world had never been real. There was no gravity, nothing to slow her or hold her down. She ran as her mind willed, the world an extension of her. The waves, the grasses, the snow, all of it created in unison.

But then she had to slow, began to tire somehow. Walked on all the way to the far point, close to Frying Pan Island, looked across at its shore. Felt the urge to swim there, to cross the water, leave this island, but something held her back. She had more to do. She wasn't finished yet. So she turned around, walked back toward the cabin.

The exhilaration would leave her, she knew. It was a gift, but only a temporary one. She could feel it thinning, dissipating. Ran again, trying to recapture it. Her feet sloppy on the stones, ankles twisting. Making contact now, hard and unyielding, no longer floating above, no longer sure-footed. She slowed to a walk.

The tops of the mountains hidden from view, the summits, the wide bowls. Only the flanks below the cloud line. She wanted to cross to the mountains. The lake should have been frozen, like in her vision. She would cross and climb the mountain. That was how it was supposed to be. What she had done was supposed to happen later, in midwinter. But how could she have waited until then?

Panes of ice all along the edge, broken by waves. Small pools gone opaque. Dark rocks damp from mist or spray. This thin band, margin between water and earth. This time she had now, this brief time when anything might be possible, perhaps, when her life might be anything, but she knew there was only one possibility.

When she reached the boat, she untied the line. Thick cord, strong, thirty feet, more than enough. She walked up toward the cabin, and she went slowly now. Something in her didn't want to go.

Alder branches brushing against her, last time on what had nearly become a path, the growth beaten down by their passings. A place never meant to be their home, a place intended from the very first to be their end. And she had gone along with that, even though she knew. Had Gary known?

When she stood over him again, he was silent, no longer moving. No more of whatever that sound had been. Something she didn't want to hear. But now it was peaceful. He was quiet, resting facedown.

Irene set the stool at the other end of the cabin, a few feet from the side wall. Reached up and pushed the rope over a joist. The aluminum sheeting tight, but she could force it through, pulled enough to make a noose. Not sure how to tie the knot. Hadn't looked at what her mother tied. In movies, it was a big knot with many wrappings, so she wrapped and tied half-hitches, like Gary had shown her for the boat. It didn't look right, but it would have to do.

Irene hammered a nail on either side of the joist, forward of the rope, so it wouldn't slide, stacked cutoffs of two-by-eights on top of the stool so she could stand higher and have farther to drop. She stood on that pile, very precarious, and put the noose around her neck and cinched it tight, then realized the rope had to be loose for the snap. So she stepped down carefully, measured while she stood on the lowest step, and pulled the rope tight. Rough on her neck, damp. She needed to tie the free end somewhere secure.

Irene looked all around and couldn't find anything. No anchor point or post strong enough. But then she looked at Gary and thought of something beautiful. She tied the end around his upper body. Had to lift his head and one shoulder and then the other. She could smell him, his bowels voided when he died. Smell of blood, too. All of this increasing the pressure in her head somehow. That had promised to leave but hadn't. A splitting pain, and it made her work more urgent. She cinched the rope tight around him, tied it off. The arrows would keep it from slipping.

And then she had to step outside again. The smells too much, the pain in her head. She didn't know if she could go through with this. It was too much, really. Leading herself to slaughter like an animal. She didn't know how her mother had done it. And so much less trapped. Hadn't committed murder. For Irene, there was no choice, but for her mother, there had still been a choice. How had she done that?

Irene walked into the trees. Close cover a comfort now, hidden. Walked aimlessly among the trunks, followed patches of moss poking out through snow, the snow thin and light, in some places no more than a dusting, blocked by branches above. She lay down in a large patch of moss, curled on her side. Up close, like a tiny forest, each finger of moss as large and grand as any spruce and more perfectly formed. Not bent or misshapen, but symmetrical, with layers of branches exactly like a tree, and a defiance of gravity at this smaller scale, the ends of the branches unbowed. Hundreds of miniature trees reaching upward. She reached out and touched one of them, pushed it to the side and it sprang back. She snapped it off at its base, snapped off its neighbors, felled a forest.

Rose again and walked farther into the trees but didn't know where she was going or what she was doing. Circled back toward the cabin, and when she broke from the trees, stopped and looked at the tents and the cabin, the stove set up between. Their camp. Her husband dead. A murderer. That's how she would be known forever. Daughter, preschool teacher, wife, mother, murderer, suicide. The earlier ones would be forgotten. Only the last two remembered. She walked to the cabin door, stepped inside, and held her breath. Walked over to the stool and noose, placed her neck in the noose and pulled down with her chin, pointed a toe at the floor, checking to see whether she'd hit. There had to be air underneath still. It was no good if she hit.

She reached up with both hands to hold the rope, hung down on it and pointed her toes and still didn't touch. Swung in the open air and had trouble getting back on the stool, panicked for a moment she would be stuck like this, not properly hanged. But she caught the stool, freed her neck, then placed the pieces of two-by-eight on the top step, three layers, enough to create a good fall.

Holding the noose, she stepped carefully onto the two-by-eights. Stood there balancing, placed the noose around her neck. Afraid she'd use her hands, though. How do you not grab the rope with your hands, even during the fall? Impossible to stop that instinct.

So Irene removed the noose again, stepped carefully down, and walked outside to Gary's tent with the tools, found a folding knife. Returned to the cabin and stood over Gary, found the loose end after the tie around his chest, cut off a few feet, dropped the knife and tied one end around her wrist.

It shouldn't be this difficult. No dignity in life, ever. Even one's own death interrupted by crass things, small concerns. It wasn't right. And the pain had not left. It had promised to go but had not. You'd think enough had happened to clear it away. Irene was angry now as she stepped onto the stool, put the noose around her neck again, climbed onto the loose blocks of wood, precarious and about to fall, and she very carefully led the line from her wrist between her legs and tied it to the other wrist. Hard to make much of a knot, but she tried to make it tight.

No way out now. Hands tied, balancing on the blocks, noose around her neck. Breathing fast and hard, panicked, her heart clenching. Blood and fear. Not the calm she had imagined. No sense of peace. She didn't want to do this. Every part of her said this was wrong. But she kicked out then, launched herself into air, yelled from deep in her lungs, a yell of defiance, and then the noose caught and at first it didn't feel so hard but then it caught with a terrible weight, all her muscles pulled, a sharp pain, her breath gone, her throat crushed, and she swung in that cold, empty place. Her hands struggling upward, held back, and she would never forgive herself.

Rhoda would be the one to walk in the door and find this. Irene knew that now. She didn't know why she hadn't seen this before. She felt tricked. She was doing to Rhoda exactly what had been done to her. A cold day, overcast, just like this, her mother hanging from a rafter, wearing her Sunday best, beige and cream with lace, a dress come all the way from Vancouver, Irene remembered it now, white stockings, brown shoes. But her mother's face, the lines in her face, the sadness, her neck grotesquely stretched. All that could never be said. Irene knew now that it would not have been quick, that her mother would have known what she had done. Enough time to know what she had done to her daughter.

Rhoda stood on the shore as Mark tossed handfuls of rock salt onto the ramp. Like rice at a wedding. The urgency she felt left her almost breathless. She wanted to yell at Mark to hurry, but knew she couldn't, so she stood at the edge and looked at the water, waited for time to pass. She could almost make out the island against the far shore. The water and air oddly calm, only very small waves, overcast with low clouds but the clouds seemed unmoving, moored in place in the sky. Shouldering into one another, bulky and dark.

We'll just wait a few minutes for that to melt, Mark said, and then we should be good.

Rhoda couldn't respond or even turn around. She knew she would sound impatient, and that would start a fight with Mark.

Right-o then, he said. I'll be in the truck.

Rhoda angry at her mother, for saying that someday she would be alone too, her life spent and nothing to show for it. What kind of thing was that to say? And especially right after she had told her mother she was getting married. An early wedding gift.

But her mom was like that. Rough and not very careful with anyone's feelings. Or at least not lately.

Rhoda had the satellite phone and batteries, but she wanted more than that now. She was going to ask her parents to come in, to leave the island. The cabin and island were not good for them. The whole thing a mistake. They needed to live in their house, and they needed other people. Rhoda would come see them every day.

Rhoda stepped closer to the edge. A small ruff of ice, broken and piled by waves. The beginning of larger cracks and crevasses that would build all through winter along the shore, but there wasn't much now. Patches of clear water all the way to the dark rocks of the beach, the ice uneven. The lake and ice always moving. A few submerged pieces, miniature icebergs bobbing.

Next week, all of this would melt. Warmer weather coming, for a short time at least, and then the real cold would hit, an early winter. She had to make sure they came in before then.

Mark already had the truck running for the heater, but Rhoda could hear him shift into reverse, then hear his tires as he eased the boat back onto the ramp. She watched as the boat and trailer entered the water, slipped into cold, the tires crunching ice.

Then she held the rope while he parked, and watched him walk down from the lot. He was wearing that stupid pink Hello Kitty jacket, borrowed from Jason. And his Russian hat with the earflaps. Every day a joke for Mark, his life a fucking joke. And she was having to be nice to him because she needed his help.

What? he said when he got close. Why are you looking at me like that?

Sorry, she said. It's nothing. I'm just worried about Mom.

Right, he said. He pulled the boat close and waved an arm for her to board. Your chariot, my love.

Thanks, she said, and climbed aboard.

Cold as they crossed the lake. Rhoda pulled the hood tight on her coat, looked to the side to avoid the wind. No one else out here, of course. And how many other lakes in Alaska even less inhabited? How many lakes scattered across endless valleys and mountain ranges that no human ever visited? Skilak could feel like wilderness. It was easy to forget that this was one of the few toeholds in a narrow path of settlements, and that all around was the real wilderness, extending unimaginable distances. What happened there, no one knew. Something tempting about wilderness, something inviting and easy, and yet the truth was that the spaces became much larger once you entered them. Hard and cold and unforgiving. Even Caribou Island was too far away.

The lake grew as they crossed. Expanded as it always did, and made islands from its far shore, broke off bits of land and shaped them. The whimsical curve of Frying Pan, then the more solid chunk of Caribou. The mainland shore beyond lower and swampier, moose country with stunted black spruce and dead stands killed by beetles. Hundreds of gray-brown trunks bare to the sky, outlined now in white. Gliding past them in the calmer water of the back side, curving around toward the exposed coast where her parents were building their cabin. Rhoda would end this, bring them home. And then she could focus on what she needed to be doing, planning her wedding. A green, sunny bluff over blue ocean, far away from here. Steep mountains and waterfalls across Hanalei Bay, the beginning of the Na Pali Coast. It would be magnificent. And they would all be there, would all walk down into soft warm sand after the ceremony. Walking the beach in her wedding dress, holding Jim's arm, her parents and Mark following behind, kicking off her shoes and letting her feet feel the warm water, letting her dress trail behind her, not caring if the edges were wet. A place carefree, a day she had dreamed of all her life, the beginning, finally.

ACKNOWLEDGMENTS

I feel lucky. My editor, Gail Winston, is brilliant. My agents—Kim Witherspoon, David Forrer, Lyndsey Blessing, and Patricia Burke at Inkwell—have apparently infinite patience. John L'Heureux has been my mentor forever. And the University of San Francisco, where I teach, has given me the flexibility to keep writing. Then there's my wife, Nancy Flores, who was cheerful even when there was no book, no job, no money, and I wore the same sweater every day for a year.

Quite a few folks in Alaska have really helped me out, too. Especially Mike Dunham at the *Anchorage Daily News* but also Andromeda Romano-Lax and Deb Vanasse at 49 Writers, Rich King, who took me out on his fishing boat, the funny and generous Rob Ernst, who helped me on numerous occasions, and my good friend Steve Toutonghi, who was the first reader of the manuscript.

I also want to thank Tom Bissell, whose review of *Legend of a Suicide* in the *New York Times* is why *Caribou Island* will appear in at least eight languages and fifty countries, and Lorrie Moore, who selected *Legend of a Suicide* for the *New Yorker* Book Club. These are moments of generosity that change a life, and I'm grateful.

About the author

2 Meet David Vann

About the book

4 Genesis

Read on

6 Have You Read?
More by David Vann

Insights,
Interviews
& More . . .

Meet David Vann

Diana Matar

DAVID VANN was born in the Aleutian Islands and spent his childhood in Ketchikan, Alaska. For twelve years, no agent would send out his first book, *Legend of a Suicide*, so he went to sea and became a captain and boatbuilder. *Legend of a Suicide* has now won ten prizes, including the Prix Médicis for best foreign novel in France, the Premi Llibreter for best foreign novel in Spain, the Grace Paley Prize, a California Book Award, and the *L'Express* readers' prize (France). Translated into sixteen languages, *Legend of a Suicide* is an international bestseller and has appeared on forty Best Books of the Year lists worldwide, been selected by the *New Yorker* Book

Club and the *Times* Book Club, read in full on North German radio, been a national bestseller in France, and will be made into a film. David has also been listed for the *Sunday Times* Short Story Award, the Story Prize, and others. His novel *Caribou Island* was an international bestseller, read for two weeks on the BBC, short-listed for the Center for Fiction's Flaherty-Dunnan First Novel Prize as well as the Prix du Roman Fnac in France, and selected by the Danish Book Club. His new novel, *Dirt*, will be published by HarperCollins in June 2012. He is the author of the bestselling memoir *A Mile Down: The True Story of a Disastrous Career at Sea* and *Last Day on Earth: A Portrait of the NIU School Shooter*, winner of the AWP Nonfiction Prize. He has appeared in documentaries with the BBC, *NOVA*, *National Geographic*, CNN, and E! Entertainment, and has written for *The Atlantic*, *Esquire*, *Outside*, *Men's Health*, *Men's Journal*, *The Sunday Times*, *The Observer*, *The Guardian*, *The Sunday Telegraph*, *Elle UK*, *Esquire UK*, *Esquire Russia*, *National Geographic Adventure*, *Writer's Digest*, and other magazines. A Guggenheim Fellow and former Wallace Stegner Fellow and NEA Fellow, he has taught at Stanford, Cornell, and FSU, and is currently a professor at the University of San Francisco.

www.DavidVann.com

Genesis

Originally published on Powells.com

Two years ago, in late January 2009, I was walking on Skilak Lake, from the shore toward Caribou Island. It was early afternoon but looked like evening, the sun low. I didn't know how thick the ice was, or how safe to walk upon. The snow in drifts, like dunes of sand. No other human, and no bird or other animal or even wind. Just silence. The air so clear it seemed I should be able to touch things that were far away, the mountains above the lake.

I kept walking, but I was very afraid of falling through. I had no experience here. I'd visited this lake only in summer, when it was windy and blue-green from glacial silt, sometimes almost milky. I knew that if I fell through, there'd be no one to help and I'd simply freeze. But I wanted to walk out to Caribou Island. It had held a fascination for me for years. I'd begun writing a novel twelve years earlier. It was set here, but I'd never been able to write past the first fifty pages. I couldn't see the longer arc. I didn't know whose story it was or where to focus. And I felt that walking out to the island I might find how to tell the story.

I saw a long crack in the ice, indicated by the snow that had fallen on it differently. I knelt and swept away the snow with my glove and saw black. I'd wanted to see how deep the ice was, how thick, but the lake beneath was so dark the clear ice became essentially opaque. I was peering into nothing. The ice could have been two inches thick or ten feet thick. And something about gazing at the lake up close and not being able to see it or know it suggested something. I could imagine Irene walking out on this lake and trying to find her marriage and peering down and seeing nothing. I understood that it was her story, that I had to focus on her in this landscape, and that the rest of the novel would come from there.

And so this walk on the frozen lake became Irene's winter vision late in my new novel, *Caribou Island*, and I wonder whether other books are like that, with one scene or moment which was the genesis. The most important quality about this moment is its certainty, a certainty that it will not mislead. As I wrote *Caribou Island*, working on it every morning, I kept returning to describing the place, and the characters and story came from the landscape and the transformations of the landscape. At one point, Irene is running in the forest on Caribou Island and feels the earth tilting beneath her and knows the entire island is rolling over, top-heavy, and this is Irene being written in place, this is discovery of Irene in the landscape, and this is why I write.

Have You Read?
More by David Vann

LEGEND OF A SUICIDE

Winner of 10 prizes, including the Prix Médicis in France and Premi Llibreter in Spain

Appeared on 40 Best Books of the Year lists worldwide

Translated into 16 languages

International bestseller

In semiautobiographical stories set largely in David Vann's native Alaska, *Legend of a Suicide* follows Roy Fenn from his birth on an island at the edge of the Bering Sea to his return thirty years later to confront the turbulent emotions and complex legacy of his father's suicide.

"A son is a lot for a thing to be; so is an artist. With *Legend of a Suicide*, David Vann proves himself to be a fine example of both." —*New York Times Book Review*

"The writing in these stories, informed by both the empirical and the lyrical, is heart-wrenching and gorgeous."
—Lorrie Moore

"Brilliant. . . . Vann's prose follows the sinews of Cormac McCarthy and Hemingway, yet has its own nimble flex."
—*The Times* (London)

"Headlong narrative pacing, a memorable train-wreck father who gives Richard Russo's characters a run for their money, and a sure, sharp, inviting voice. So hard to put down that I am thinking of suing David Vann for several hours of lost sleep." —Lionel Shriver, author of *The New Republic*, *So Much for That*, and *We Need to Talk About Kevin*

LAST DAY ON EARTH:
A PORTRAIT OF THE NIU SCHOOL SHOOTER

Winner of the AWP Nonfiction Prize

On Valentine's Day 2008, Steve Kazmierczak killed five and wounded eighteen at Northern Illinois University, then killed himself. But he was an A student, a Deans' Award winner. How could this happen?

CNN could not get the story. The *Chicago Tribune*, *Washington Post*, and all others came up empty because Steve's friends and professors knew very little. He had reinvented himself in his final five years. But David Vann, investigating for *Esquire*, went back to Steve's high school and junior high friends, found a life perfectly shaped for mass murder, and gained full access to the entire 1,500 pages of the police files. The result: the most complete portrait we have of any school shooter. But Vann doesn't stop there. He recounts his own history with guns, contemplating a school shooting. This book is terrifying and true, a story you'll never forget.

"A carefully crafted account of a descent into fatal madness." —*Kirkus Reviews*

Have You Read? ***(continued)***

"I hated reading *Last Day on Earth*, but I kept coming back to it. Each chapter was taut, mysterious, and compelling. And when I did stop reading—I devoured it in three sittings—I was haunted by Steve, a mass murderer, and his slow, steady transformation from Deans' Award winner to shooter. What makes this book especially appealing is the parallel narrative—the writer living a screwed-up childhood, who, like Steve, finds himself in the possession of many guns and the urge to use them and potentially do harm. What the writer discovers is that the line between self-destruction and survival and success is frighteningly easy to cross. *Last Day on Earth* is written with a cold staccato passion—with intensive attention to intimacy of detail. It is riveting reading."

—Lee Gutkind, founding editor, *Creative Nonfiction*

A MILE DOWN: THE TRUE STORY OF A DISASTROUS CAREER AT SEA

National Bestseller
#4 *Washington Post* list
#7 *Los Angeles Times* list

A Mile Down: The True Story of a Disastrous Career at Sea is a harrowing—and heartbreaking—true story of one ordinary man's misadventures at sea. David Vann builds a ninety-foot charter yacht in Turkey, the ship of his dreams. But the war in Kosovo destroys his upcoming charter season, the Turkish builder takes advantage, and the boat begins falling apart as soon as it's launched. Vann faces an unrelenting crush of disasters, bad luck, and ill will, yet remains in good spirits and picks himself up repeatedly to carry on. A storm near Casablanca tears his rudder off, a German freighter captain endangers the crew to go for a salvage claim, and finally a freak storm in the Caribbean sinks the boat a mile down. As the author's debts escalate and his troubles multiply, he begins to wonder if he is merely repeating his father's dreams and failures at sea. *A Mile Down* is an unforgettable true story of struggle and redemption by a writer at the top of his form.

"Damn exciting." —Stewart O'Nan

"Pure adrenaline."
—Melanie Thernstrom

Have You Read? *(continued)*

"As if one of the heroes of *The Perfect Storm* had lived to write his memoirs."
—Julie Hilden

"At once memoir, confession, travel book, and thriller, David Vann's *A Mile Down* is so vivid and intense you will dread to see it end. . . . The book is a testimony of passion and courage in deadly storms and scarier calms, of a man wrestling with his ghosts and gifts in the very shadow of paradise."
—Robert Morgan

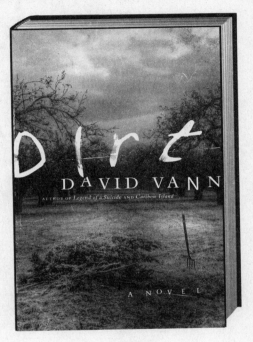